PENGUIN BOOKS

SI

Christopher Miller was born in New York City. He now lives in Vermont and teaches at Bennington College. This is his first novel.

# Simon Silber

## *Works for Solo Piano*

CHRISTOPHER MILLER

PENGUIN BOOKS

# ACKNOWLEDGEMENTS

The author wishes to thank Michael Dahlie, Eamon Dolan,
Deborah Eisenberg, Jayne Yaffe Kemp, Charles Newman, Carl Phillips
Lynne Sharon Schwartz, Eric Simonoff, and especially Sarah Pogell.

PENGUIN BOOKS

Published by the Penguin Group
Penguin Books Ltd, 80 Strand, London WC2R 0RL, England
Penguin Putnam Inc., 375 Hudson Street, New York, New York 10014, USA
Penguin Books Australia Ltd, 250 Camberwell Road,
Camberwell, Victoria 3124, Australia
Penguin Books Canada Ltd, 10 Alcorn Avenue, Toronto, Ontario, Canada M4V 3B2
Penguin Books India (P) Ltd, 11 Community Centre,
Panchsheel Park, New Delhi – 110 017, India
Penguin Books (NZ) Ltd, Cnr Rosedale and Airborne Roads,
Albany, Auckland, New Zealand
Penguin Books (South Africa) (Pty) Ltd, 24 Sturdee Avenue,
Rosebank 2196, South Africa

Penguin Books Ltd, Registered Offices: 80 Strand, London WC2R 0RL, England

www.penguin.com

First published in the United States of America by Houghton Mifflin Company 2002
First published in Great Britain by Hamish Hamilton 2002
First published in Penguin Books 2003
1

Printed in England by Clays Ltd, St Ives plc

*For my parents*

# Simon Silber (1958–1999)

## Disc One

## Disc Two

## Disc Three

## Disc Four

# Introduction

This set presents the only authorized recordings of every piece that Simon Silber honored with an opus number. If we discount the daylong sonata left unfinished at his death and the chord-a-day diary begun when he was two, the four-CD set includes almost the whole of Silber's oeuvre. At the start of his second career, the precociously retired virtuoso vowed to compose nothing but solo piano music because he didn't trust anyone else to interpret his works. His last will and testament includes a clause forbidding pianists from recording his music or performing it in public, and another clause outlawing transcriptions and orchestrations. He didn't even want to be whistled. As his adviser, I tried to dissuade him from these misguided provisos: to record a "definitive" version was, I argued, to embalm a living organism. But Silber wouldn't listen. All performances, then, are by the composer.

Like every complete set, the one you've just bought is uneven. I resist the urge to specify outright the pieces worthy of attentive listening, but attentive readers won't have too much trouble guessing. That, by the way, is one reason to read these liner notes *before* you "face the music"; an even better reason is that the notes do something I've been unable to make Silber's oeuvre do, rearrange it as I may: compose a lifelike portrait, in mosaic, of a picturesque composer as he showed himself to his last best friend and handpicked biographer, me.

If the designer of this booklet has obeyed my instructions, the buyer is probably wondering about the photo on the front, or will wonder when informed that the handsome bearded man staring calmly at the camera is not Silber but the writer of these notes. Silber is the other guy, the hazy one appearing in three-quarters profile with his head tilted back and at least one of his eyes shut, holding in his raised right hand what might be but isn't a conductor's baton (or a sorcerer's wand — the tip is just above my head, as if I were the sudden outcome of some reckless incantation) and standing a good yard farther back from the camera, at the fraying edge of its focal range, so that he appears both smaller and blurrier than his biographer. I chose this particular snapshot (snapped by the composer's hated elder sister, though not, I think — as he insisted at the time — as evidence for a commitment hearing) because it comes closer than any other photograph to capturing the man I remember.

Simon Silber was a complicated person, a perverse chameleon forever changing colors the better to clash with his surroundings. When I try, though, like one of the blind men feeling the elephant, to fasten on a single image, I always see him as I saw him one summer morning a week before his death: coming up the sidewalk with his eyes shut and his head thrown back, raptly conducting an imaginary orchestra with the thermometer he carried everywhere. (He had been morbidly afraid of overheating ever since the fever, the previous winter, that had cost him nine IQ points — almost the first thing he ever said to me was, "Believe it or not, I used to be even smarter" — and at the height of which he had forgotten overnight how to tie his shoes.) Silber lived in Forest City all his life and knew the town so well by the time I met him that — he claimed — he could "see" his surroundings even with his eyes shut. Sometimes he had to feel for his eyelids with his fingertips to make sure those eyes were open. He couldn't just wave a hand in front of his face, he said, because if his eyes *were* shut, he'd involuntarily visualize that hand. He had once walked a block and a half down Tree Street, turning his head this way and that to admire the scenery, seeing houses, neighbors, cars, trees, flower beds, etc., that perfectly fit the sounds he heard, the smells he smelled, and the feel of the sidewalk underfoot, as well as everything he remembered of the road he was on . . . until some glitch in the circuitry had caused him to veer and collide with a telephone pole, and his eyes had opened as wide as he'd been assuming they already were.

Or maybe he was making all that up, but he really did manage somehow to navigate with eyes shut. Maybe by sonar: as much as other people's noises bothered him, he was forever emitting some kind of music. He was the most — maybe the only — musical person I have ever known. His cleaning lady, Edna, who claimed to be able to read minds, claimed that when she tuned in Silber's, on the rare occasions when he let her within mindshot, music was all she could ever pick up — "a beautiful Beethoven symphony." (Silber hated Beethoven and would not have allowed a bar of that composer's oeuvre to run through his mind without shaking his head to skip to another groove.) One winter morning I stationed myself in his path as he strode up High Street singing "The March of the Davidsbündler Against the Philistines." As always on those early-morning walks, his eyes were shut, but at the last possible moment, and without breaking his stride, Silber deftly sidestepped his biographer and continued on his way; and afterward he had no memory of the encounter. During the year I knew him, I took advantage of Silber's abstraction to bootleg a few of his sunrise recitals for posterity — following him around at a less-than-respectful distance with a hand-held tape recorder — just in case posterity ever came to value Silber as highly as did Silber himself, who lately had taken to saving his Food Town receipts: "They'll want to know what I ate."

Posterity has yet to return a verdict. Silber lived and worked in obscurity; the bizarre and tabloid-selling circumstances of his death have provoked more interest in his life than in his work. It was decided that a boxed edition would do better if the box included a fat booklet of "liner" notes heavy on the anecdotes and light on technical discussion of the works in question. I have done my best to oblige. Silber's sister and — alas — executor, a woman I've never seen reading anything other than stock quotations, wanted editorial control of these notes, but there I stood my ground, and got my way for once: when I send my manuscript off to the printer this afternoon, no one but I will have laid eyes on the text. The picture of a high-minded but clay-footed composer that emerges, pixel by pixel, in the words that follow, is one unretouched by his possibly well-meaning but uncomprehending sibling. There may even be one or two warts the subject himself would have wanted painted out, since in the treacherous course of our acquaintance — a long and increasingly lightheaded climb with as many switchbacks as the path up Mount Parnassus — I couldn't help seeing sides of my employer which he never meant to show posterity; but his days of always getting what he wanted are no more.

That Silber and I were no longer friends at the time of his death — that the news of his demise was neither unexpected, when it reached me, nor entirely unwelcome — might seem to raise a doubt as to my fitness for the job of commentator, but (as anyone who really knew him will attest) never to have hated Silber would mean never to have known him.

— Norman Fayrewether, Jr.

*February 28, 2000*

# *Disc One*

1. *Variations in a Minor*          15:55

| Little League | 2:01 | BB Gun | 0:55 |
|---|---|---|---|
| Monopoly | 2:39 | Piano Lesson | 3:06 |
| The New Puppy | 1:58 | Fun with Firecrackers | 1:43 |
| Popping Wheelies | 2:20 | Theme | 1:13 |

This charming suite of miniatures composed in '97* is Silber's witty answer to Schumann's *Kinderscenen.* The range of moods and textures encompassed by the work is all the more impressive given that all seven variations are set, for the sake of a pun, in the same key as the theme (performed for no good reason at the end). The piece is a perfect gallery of inspired tone paintings — the puppy variation with its scampering-feet figure punctuated by yapping staccato chords, the sudden *sforzando* detonations of the BB gun, the little fugue (in "Little League") on "Take Me out to the Ball Game." My favorite variation, though, is "Piano Lesson," technically the most demanding of the seven, though it depicts a very rudimentary musician. Silber — himself a prodigiously gifted pianist —

---

* It will be noted that, in sequencing the pieces in this set, I have eschewed the tedium of chronological order in favor of a subtler, more intuitive approach.

liked the idea of forcing virtuosi to bring all their skills to bear on the task of sounding comically inept. (*Variations in a Minor* was, significantly, the last work composed before the change in Silber's will forbidding the recording of his music.)

The only possible objection to the *Variations* is an extra-musical one: the all-American boyhood evoked by the subtitles is a lie. Our composer lived in the same house all his life. After his death I helped his sister break into his sealed boyhood bedroom (one of several rooms that over the decades, for various reasons, Silber had "retired"), and among the dusty clutter we did in fact discover a red and white Little League uniform and an ancient Monopoly set with wooden houses and hotels; so presumably these objects played a part in Silber's boyhood, unless he'd bought them later on at flea markets in order to bamboozle his biographer, or in order to compose music about them, as a photographer might buy such things to take their pictures. Well and good, but he had always hated firecrackers ("even in the womb"), and of course there was never a puppy. Silber's life was a losing crusade against all noises but his own, and he never thought of dogs as anything but an especially noxious source of noise pollution. And then there is the matter of all the ugly secrets buried — like beloved pets in a suburban yard — in Silber's real boyhood, secrets deleted from the idealized past he set to music, secrets that I will exhume in due course. For the point of this note is not to decry the disparity here between life and art, but just to emphasize the necessity of my annotations to anyone even pretending to listen intelligently to Silber's profound but also profoundly personal oeuvre. Listening to his music *without* first reading my notes would be like trying to watch a pay-per-view movie on cable without first agreeing to pay for the privilege: any titillating glimpses of the truth you may obtain despite the badly scrambled signal will be few and far between.

This piece, composed on Silber's eighteenth birthday (October 17, 1976), was in his opinion his first adult composition, and the only one he ever played in public, as an unrequested encore to an all-Schumann recital mounted by Silber's father as a birthday present. The recording on the disc is a live one made on that occasion by the elder Silber with a portable battery-powered RadioShack recorder.

Though all but the last of his recitals were held in Forest City, Silber's playing had made him a regional celebrity by the time of his sudden retirement in 1979. To judge from the old clippings in his sister's scrapbook, he'd been famed for his light touch, his unorthodox tempi, and his habit of wearing bulky red earmuffs while performing. Twenty years later, his towns-people — those who didn't call him "the spaz" or "the psycho" — still referred to him as "the pianist" or "the ex-pianist," never "the composer." The few I met who'd even heard of his composing seemed to feel he was trading illegitimately on his hard-won prestige in another profession, like a star athlete who ventures a second career as an actor or singer.

A similar sense of Silber's presumption — subjecting his audience to his own music when they'd paid for Schumann — may have contributed to the poor reception of *"Chopsticks" Variations* at its premiere. The work is a set of eleven variations on that most rudimentary of piano pieces, "Chopsticks," and, like most Opus no. 1s, amounts to little more than protracted throat-clearing in preparation for the greater statements to come. The only notable feature is the endless eleventh "variation," actually a note-perfect reprise of the moronic original theme, but taken at such a slow tempo that there are rests of as much as seven seconds between successive notes, stretches of scratchy amplified silence during which, despite the low-fidelity recording, one can distinctly hear nervous laughter, bursts of eager but premature and reluctantly aborted applause, a medley of voices saying things like "Pssh!" and "Je-sus!" and, increasingly, the sound of chairs scraping and foot-steps retreating. After the final sonorous chord, there is a hush, and then we hear, very close to the microphone, the deafening ovation of a single pair of hands, either because everyone but Silber's father had already left the auditorium by that point, or because any other, more precipitate *claqueurs* still in atten-dance believed themselves to have applauded enough already in the course of the work now finally concluded. Or maybe they were still waiting, when Mr. Silber turned off his tape re-corder, to make sure that this time the work was really over, and not about to lunge back to life once again like a horror-movie monster.

Twenty-two years later, Silber played the piece for me, one dark and desolate November afternoon, at a bright and lively coffeehouse so near my modest Forest City lodgings that I'd come to think of it as my living room, complete with a fire-place, a sofa, and a bad upright piano. Spurning the bench, Silber stood at the piano (out of tune, of course, and in even worse condition than the rental horses at a public riding stable) and played so softly that, although I stood beside him, I could hear him only during brief and random intermissions in the crowded house's din. This time at least no one walked out in disgust: people went on slurping coffee, rustling papers, talk-ing politics, and otherwise ignoring Silber.

### 3. *"Babbage" Permutations*                    1:47

I learned of Silber's existence by way of an old LP (though not so old it should have felt entitled to proclaim its stereophony as a selling point) that I found in '94 in a Tacoma thrift store oth-erwise boasting in its record bin only the usual picked-over thrift-store assortment: Johnny Mathis, Ferrante and Teicher, Herb Alpert and the Tijuana Brass. The disc was a recording, from 1979, of Schumann's *"Abegg" Variations,* a set of changes rung on a theme ingeniously derived from the letters of a surname — that of a certain Fräulein Abegg — treated as musical notes. The label, Argent, was one I'd never seen before. I had never heard of the performer, Simon Silber (nor for that matter of "the prestigious Erlenmeyer Competition" at which he had won a silver medal in 1979), much less heard him perform during what the liner notes described as a "brilliant, tragically brief public career." I wondered what the tragedy had been — nothing as simple as death, evidently, since the notes (signed only "SS") shifted unexpectedly into the present tense at the end to announce that, "a composer in his own right, Mr. Silber lives in Forest City, Oregon." Moreover, a sidebar mentioned Silber's ambitious plan of recording Schumann's complete output for solo piano. I wondered if he had planned to do so in alphabetical order, or maybe numerical order, since the *"Abegg"* *Variations* — billed as Silber's "astounding debut recording" — was Schumann's Opus 1, just as if *he* had planned his oeuvre in alphabetical order. I also wondered how the pianist had managed to fill both sides of an LP with a piece of music that as ordinarily performed lasts no longer than eight minutes. I bought the album only because its cellophane wrapper was still intact, at a moment in recording history when virgin vinyl was coming to seem collectible as such, regardless of what noises had been chiseled into its grooves.

Charles Babbage was a nineteenth-century English inventor with as much of a claim as anyone to be called the Father of the Computer. The *"Babbage" Permutations,* composed in 1980 and patently inspired by the Schumann work, is simply an exhaustive computer-generated set of permutations on the sequence "B-A-B-B-A-G-E," played here in the evenhanded manner of Glenn Gould — whom my friend admired and resented to the end — with a studied lack of dynamics intended perhaps to give the impression that we are hearing music not only composed but performed by a machine. Because the permutations are exhausted in alphabetical order and the piece — like Silber's homage to another Schumann work — is in the key of A minor, *Babbage* begins with a run of rising phrases (AABBBEG, AABBBGE . . .), ends with a run of falling ones, and so has a clear overall shape, more than can be said for some of the composer's later, more painstakingly constructed compositions. Silber claimed that it had taken him "all of two minutes" to get his computer (a 64K Tandy) to permute those letters, and that he had never again collaborated with a CPU. Thus, the piece can be seen as representing in real time the rise and fall of Silber's interest in computer-generated beauty.

### 4. *The Music Room*                                    8:20–∞

The music room was a sound-tight basement room to which, throughout the first eight years of our composer's life, all music in his house was confined. From day one, Mr. Silber took a morbid interest in his son's development, devoting much of his own life to the project of rearing a famous pianist. Wanting absolute control over the impressionable young musician's influences — and wanting also to inspire Simon with a lifelong sense of music as a special thing, a sacrament, and not just a part of the environment as unavoidable as salt in processed foods, and as much to be taken for granted — Mr. Silber had prohibited all music, live or otherwise, except in that one room, throwing out the TV set, the radios, the stereo, and keeping all the other rooms with pianos in them locked. Silber used to call himself the only great pianist to have learned piano underground (somehow or other his father had gotten a baby-grand Steinway down there). The composer was eight before he heard a note of music elsewhere in the house, and thanks to the short leash on which his father kept him, he'd heard precious few outside the house either.

In addition to confining music to the music room, Mr. Silber had ordained that in that room Beethoven's late quartets should *always* play, continuously (he'd made a special tape loop), night and day, even when no one was down there, even when no one was home, even when Simon was trying to practice (though his father did turn down the volume then, but never all the way, and less and less as years went by),* so that music came to seem an *attribute* of the room, like the musty smell of the adjacent laundry room or the cool of a walk-in cooler.

More than once I tried to get Silber to talk about how it had felt, all those years, knowing that those deaf-man's quartets were playing down there all the time, over and over and over, even when he was asleep. I wanted to hear about the dreams in which that room had figured, wanted to know how such a room would *function* in dreams. I wanted a guided tour of Silber's windowless basement (it had been sunk at least a yard deeper than ordinary basements, so that none of it stuck above the surface). Silber, though, would not unlock the door at the top of the basement stairs, and didn't like to talk about the space beyond that door. He did tell me once that the music room was no longer there: soon after his father's death in 1980, Silber had not only pulled the plug on Beethoven, but had had the basement remodeled, knocking out all the interior walls to abolish the music room and disperse the eeriness that had accumulated in there over the years. I could tell that the room had traumatic associations for Silber even before I learned from his sister that their father had often compelled him to spend the night down there — all alone in the dark — as a small child.

Silber was only three when his mother was killed by a hit-and-run driver. Any grief his father may have felt at the time was not enough to stop him from enacting — the day of her death, according to Silber — several policies his spouse had

* According to Silber, the Beethoven had gotten louder every year, and was "almost deafening" by the time our composer turned eight. A curious sentence from Mr. Silber's journal may explain the purpose of that slow crescendo (assuming the crescendo wasn't an illusion due to young Simon's increasingly sensitive hearing): "The sooner he learns to hold his own artistically, to MAKE HIMSELF HEARD in a world already resounding with music, the better." (7/14/66)

opposed while she lived. Mrs. Silber had, for instance, vetoed the plan to keep Simon in the basement night and day — in the soundproof room, a sort of isolation chamber, that Mr. Silber had furtively readied down there while his wife was in the maternity ward. She'd even threatened to leave and take the children with her, and their father had reluctantly backed down, knowing he'd never win a custody battle.* Once his wife was out of the way, though, Mr. Silber was free to manipulate Simon's experience as he saw fit. Luckily for Simon, Mr. Silber had by that point decided that it wasn't necessary after all for the young pianist to spend his whole childhood locked in the basement (a decision Mr. Silber would later regret, out loud and at length). But our composer's father did take to sending him down to the music room any time the child was exposed to a loud noise: Mr. Silber — who believed that most musicians in our noisy era are "too habituated to the hubbub of the hum-drum" to hear the music of the great composers as *they* heard it† — also seemed to think that those quartets would somehow purge the sonic toxins. At an age when other children are taught to fear stray dogs, busy intersections, poisonous berries, strangers with candy, Simon was taught to fear the noises of the outside world — and not just taught but traumatized. Any

---

* It was to such instances of "maternal interference" in the first three years that his father later was often to attribute Simon's failure to develop as expected into the greatest pianist of his day. Mr. Silber blamed his wife so bitterly, in-deed, as to make one wonder whether he'd been at the wheel of the car that killed her. A not-atypical entry from his journal: "Just woke up from another dream about his mother, so furious I wanted to desecrate her grave. She 'meant well,' no doubt — has a mother ever not? — but her meddling cost me my ONE OPPORTUNITY to give the method a fair trial. More convinced than ever now that if not for the BRAINLESS interference of that inane — but no, *de mortuis nil nisi bonum*." (3/23/80) For an account of Mr. Silber's "method," see *Our Father*.

† For Mr. Silber, judging by his journal, the world of sound consisted of music and noise; the more noise Simon was exposed to, the less musical he'd be — and Mr. Silber deemed most sounds (deemed, indeed, most so-called music) noise. "Is it a coincidence that the greatest works of music known to man — the late quartets — were composed when Beethoven's son was stone-deaf? A coincidence that as the world grows louder and louder, what passes for music grows more and more ugly? A child is a keyboard on which the world plays

time a loud noise was anticipated — every summer afternoon as the ice-cream truck approached, all day long on Independence Day — he was sent upstairs to his soundproof bedroom; and any time he was exposed in spite of such precautions, he was sent down to the basement, sometimes overnight, whether or not the exposure was his fault. If it ever occurred to Mr. Silber that overnight confinement to the basement might just terrify a three-year-old, he probably considered that a plus: next time Simon would try twice as hard to avoid forbidden noises.

Most of this I learned from sources other than Silber himself. *He* would talk about the music room only as a model for *Day* (the daylong sonata he'd been composing for almost two decades): a space you'd feel free to leave and enter as you pleased, like the ocean to a bather, but that while you were in it would inspire you with awe, when heard at the only appropriate volume, loud. It comes as a surprise, then, that the medley with which Silber chose in 1981 to commemorate this room (if not to atone for *erasing* a room — smashing a vessel brimming with memories) should be so ethereal, less an ocean than a mist. Soon after I met him, Silber gave me a cassette he had modified to play the piece over and over, *ad infinitum* — a frail avatar of his father's magnificent tape loop. (Your disc has been encoded likewise to repeat the track till told to move along.) I dutifully went home and tried to listen to the tape, but the music — despite its quotations from Beethoven's greatest quartets — was so insubstantial, so easily tuned out, that almost at once I forgot it was on. After a minute I found myself thinking, I know what I'll do now, I'll listen to a record, and got as far as selecting *Carmina Burana,* tipping it out of its sleeve, and

---

nonstop, never letting up on the sustaining pedal. No wonder most people can't really HEAR ANYTHING by the time they're adults, what with such a RUCKUS resounding in their heads." (10/15/78)

Note that Silber's father refers to the famous composer — his favorite — as Beethoven's *son.* As a rule, when Mr. Silber's journal mentions "Beethoven," it doesn't mean Ludwig but Ludwig's father, Johann, one of Mr. Silber's role models.

walking over to my turntable before I remembered, on seeing a cassette playing in the tape deck, that I was *already* listening to music, and with the volume up so loud, per the composer's instructions, that a moment later Billy, my retarded next-door neighbor, started pounding on the wall.

Shortly before Silber's sudden bloody death, I saw the manuscript of *The Music Room* and discovered that its title had once been *The Waiting Room:* evidently our composer had set out to write the kind of music heard in elevators, waiting rooms, and shopping malls. His homage to the music room had been an afterthought, like a gift you buy for X but wind up giving to Z instead. Gazing at the shamelessly repackaged piece, I laughed and then reflected that I would never have met Silber if I hadn't come across a little ad, one summer day in 1997, as I sat in a dermatologist's waiting room paging through a magazine called *Author,* hoping I wasn't catching anything from the last patient to sit in my chair, and wondering whether the outlandish loudness of the should-be-background music was a cause or an effect of the receptionist's deafness.

> BIOGRAPHER WANTED
> Exp'd author needed to write biography
> of Famous living composer. Contact
> P.O. Box 321, Forest City, OR

The ad (rubbing shoulders with others beginning "Top $$$" and "Poems Needed" and "Self-Publish") intrigued me: I had been thinking of writing my memoirs — convinced at thirty-seven that my life was over — but wondering if it wouldn't be wiser to practice on someone else's life first. There was something teasingly familiar, too, about that "Forest City, OR," and as I waited to show Dr. Fleisch a mysterious traveling blotch, about the size of a transdermal patch, that had orbited my torso twice in the year since I'd started to monitor its progress, I recognized the town as home to "a composer in his own right, Mr. Silber." Could it be? I waited till no one was looking and furtively tore out the page with the ad.

At that point I'd been working for almost fifteen years as a lowly aide in a Tacoma public library and had almost forgotten why I had opted for such a career. Before I forget altogether: back in 1982 when I headed out into the real world with a B.A. in philosophy, I'd been sure that I was better than any job I could hope for, and that the best way to prevent myself and others from identifying me with some occupation — with whatever I wound up doing to pay the bills — would be to choose a job so far beneath me that no one could possibly make that mistake. But others had made the mistake from the start, and lately I'd been making it myself. Part of the appeal of the Forest City job was that it sounded — *sounded* — a little less demeaning than what I had been doing, and lately I was less and less convinced that I was better than my job gave others any reason for supposing.

The day after my visit to the dermatologist, I replied to the composer's ad, possibly exaggerating my credentials as an author. (I was basically an unsuccessful thinker — or rather, though my thoughts themselves were well worth thinking, I had not succeeded in placing many printouts in the hands of people who might want to think along. All I had to show for myself, in fact, were several thousand unpublished aperçus, a long unpublished poem about epistemology, and a privately printed collection of assorted aphorisms entitled *So I Gather* — a book the reviewers I sent it to had greeted with the sort of sullen silence a city slicker might encounter entering a small-town diner. Since its publication, I'd stopped writing altogether, though I flattered myself that *my* silence spoke volumes — slender, exquisite volumes befitting the successful minor poet I might easily have been, if I hadn't acquired early on the ruinous habit of clarity.) I also mentioned my fervent if recent enthusiasm for such "underrated masterworks and undiscovered gems" (so I put it in my letter) as Paul Dupin's *The Death of Uncle Gottfried* and Jan Ladislav Dussek's four-handed piano sonata. Two or three months earlier, as a means of coming to terms with my own increasingly manifest destiny as a nonentity, I had stopped listening to anyone better remembered than Dussek (the fattest composer on record, in later years bedridden by obesity and apathy), and since then had been working my way in alphabetical order through the not-so-great composers, the more-or-less deservedly more-or-less forgotten, telling myself: *You tried the best, now try the rest.*

5. *Crows*                                                     0:04

Silber wrote this piece the day I met him. I witnessed its composition, and since by that point his methods were highly unorthodox (though not yet as deranged as they were destined to become), an anecdote is in order.

In August 1998 — a full year after answering that little ad, or long enough to have forgotten all about it — I was startled one hot night at around three A.M. by a phone call from someone who identified himself as Simon Silber.

Now, I trust it won't detract from the "credibility" of these liner notes if their author — an aficionado of coincidences — admits that at the moment of that fateful phone call, he was standing in pajamas at the window of his tiny, stuffy, hideous, no-longer-bearable third-floor apartment, wanting to jump to his death but afraid that a fall from that height to the pricker bushes below might only cripple him for life instead. (To mollify those readers who hate coincidences, I'll add that it wasn't the first time that summer I'd stood at the window and wanted to jump.) After all, biographers are people too, and our frailties are what enable us to discern the same defects in the great and would-be great. My reasons, that night, for wanting to die — aside from the sorrows already alluded to — needn't concern anyone: these notes are not about me.

While I tried to remember where I'd heard his name before, Silber told me all about the book he had in mind. The idea seemed to be to make him famous by writing about him as if he already *were* famous: his fame, when it came, would — like all fame, according to Silber — be an illusion; in this case, one akin to a back-formation like *burgle,* later mistaken for the root of the word it really derives from.

I asked why he'd taken so long to call and Silber explained that back when he received my letter, he'd already hired a biographer — who, however, hadn't worked out.

"What was the matter with him?"

"Too nosy," Silber said meaningfully, after a meaningful pause.

He went on to give me a little quiz about classical music. I remember only one of his questions — "Why is Dussek a better composer than, oh, Beethoven, for instance?" — to which I aptly retorted, "Why indeed?"; by that point I'd tired of nonentities like Dussek, and gone back to listening to entities again. (It occurs to me that if I'd persisted in listening to also-rans at the rate I'd been doing, I would've been just about up to the S's at the time of Silber's phone call.) In any case, I must have passed the test. Before hanging up, we agreed that I would drive to Forest City first thing in the morning. Silber had said he was looking for an author untainted by the "educated" musical prejudices of the day, and that I sounded like just the man for the job.* He'd also said I'd be expected to relocate, but that was fine by me — all I'd be leaving behind in Tacoma was a studio apartment I rented month to month, an apartment that wanted me dead.

After hanging up, I got in bed but couldn't sleep. At last I got up and found my thrift-store copy of Silber's *Abegg* record,† which I had added to my collection without ever listening to the disk inside, since that would have meant broaching its cellophane wrapper. Now, reluctantly, I did just that: the time had

---

* Later, when our friendship was well enough established to allow a little harmless persiflage, Silber liked to say that it was precisely my "profound ignorance of music, past and present, theory and practice," that had induced him to hire me.

† I have since learned that over the years he donated dozens of copies of the record to secondhand stores throughout the state, after painstakingly distress-

come to satisfy my curiosity (so infinitesimal at first that it had been able to grow for years before becoming a nuisance) as to how the pianist had made an eight-minute piece fill an LP. I shook the glossy virgin disk out of its paper inner sleeve and placed it on my turntable, then turned off the light and lay back down. By the end of the first measure, some thirty seconds later, I had an answer to my question. Half awake, I lay there in the dark with another well-chosen note arriving every five or ten seconds, or *almost* long enough for me to drift off in the meantime — a sort of Oriental torture, but a fun one; I remember thinking that the theme, as played by Silber, was too beautiful to bear. At some point I fell asleep — and awakened with a scream. I got up, turned on the light, and warily got back in bed. The music had ceased, but according to my clock I hadn't been asleep for long; probably what had jarred me awake had been the click of the tone arm returning automatically to its cradle. Back when I owned a cat I'd noticed that that incidental click, metaphysically so different from the music that preceded it, never failed to turn her head, though she seemed not even to hear the music itself, no matter how loud it got. As for my scream: in light of later revelations, I am tempted to claim that already I sensed something sinister about Silber's mind; and maybe I did. For me, though, there was *always* something uneasy, if not outright unhealthy, about listening to music as I drifted off to sleep: the music had a way of taking over my brain and driving me out, so that later when I came back to myself with a start I would find I wasn't home. And yet the recording left me wanting to know more about this stranger who, by lending me his ears, had enabled me to hear the *"Abegg" Variations* — which till then I'd written off as so much peppy juvenilia — as the thing of beauty that *any* piece of music, even the tritest of singing commercials, turns out to have been all along when heard with the ears of a genius.

---

ing each LP so that it would seem already to have been much loved and listened to — unlike the mint-condition specimen I owned, which, although I came across it in Tacoma, I suspect to be the very one he had given his sister.

I fell asleep again looking forward to our appointment.

Forest City was farther away than it had looked on the map, and though I set out right after lunch, evening was approaching when at last I located Silber's red-brick house, half-hidden from the road by a stand of Douglas firs, in what looked to be the oldest and most moneyed part of town, where the streets took their time in getting where they were going and the vast front lawns kept shabby invaders like me at a distance. As I pulled up in front, an ice-cream truck approached from the opposite direction and stopped parallel to my car to feed an appallingly fat little girl who'd just lumbered out of the big half-timbered house across the street. I hadn't eaten in six hours and, late as I was, I paused to buy an ice-cream sandwich from the ice-cream man, or ice-cream adolescent — an acned crack-voiced kid who looked too young to drive.

Silber had told me to go to the back door — not (as I thought at the time) to teach me my place, but because a decade ago, interrupted once too often in the heat of composition, he had disconnected his doorbell and plastered over his front door from inside. I started up the long and needlessly non-Euclidean driveway; as I stepped out of the waning daylight into the sudden dusk beneath the firs, a black crow came walking briskly toward me. The bird swerved in passing to give me a wider berth and continued down the gravel drive: I was reminded of a man trying to run with his hands in his pockets. Other birds were crowing raucously, and when I rounded the corner of the house I saw several dozen on the telephone lines that ran along the back of Silber's property. A tall skinny man in a pale blue tuxedo stood in the yard with his back to me and a rifle in his hands, not far from a derelict swing set so rusty there was no telling what color it had been. Other composers might shake their fists at the heavens, as Beethoven did on his deathbed, but Silber had a horror of mere empty gestures: he pointed the gun skyward, took aim, and pulled the trigger. It was a BB gun and not a real rifle, but real enough for the crow in Silber's sights. The bird fell backward off its perch (as the luckier flew off in a rush of wingbeats) and dropped with a thump to the spotty yellow lawn that looked like what might live above a leaky toxic landfill. Nothing else grew in the yard, though there were half a dozen tree stumps.

In the sudden silence, I must have done something audible to Silber, if not to me. He looked over, frowned, and said, "If you're here to read the meter —"

"I'm here to write the memoir."

"Oh!" He glanced at the gun, then at the crow I'd seen him kill, and, turning his attention to the gun again, he reddened. He puckered his face for a moment, as if trying hard to place a half-familiar melody. And then he took a tiny spiral notebook out of his hip pocket.

"I spoke to you last night," I said. "I'm Norm."

"Simon Silber," Silber said proudly, and recoiled with a start from my attempt to shake his hand. (Later he would tell me that he never shook with anyone — a phobia left over from his virtuoso days — but in the year I knew him I saw him shake hands several times. What with my powerful build — I used to wrestle, back in junior high, and am still quite mesomorphic for an introvert — I must have looked like one of those he-men who like to squeeze.) He did accept a plastic ballpoint pen a moment later, when his silver fountain pen failed to write, and after clicking the button in its base to extrude, retract, and then extrude its tip again, as if till now he'd never encountered such a gadget, used it to make some marks in his notebook. Then he handed back the pen and explained that he'd decided to transcribe those crows as music, the wires as musical staves, but that first he'd needed to "erase" just one wrong note. He claimed that his transcription corresponded to the crows' arrangement on the wires in the fraction of a second between his erasure of the one and the departure of the others. The same odd sense of right and wrong that had allowed him to kill the superfluous bird had also forbidden him simply to omit it from his transcription: in order not to transcribe it, he had had no choice but to exterminate it first.

"What are you going to do with it?" I asked, nudging the non-noteworthy crow with my shoe.

Silber thought again, then said: "Guess I'll throw him away." He picked up the dead bird by its tail and carried it as nonchalantly as if it were a dishrag over to a trash can recessed in the cement by his back door so that only the lid was visible. Stepping on the lever that made the lid pop up, he dropped the carcass into the secret garbage can and let the top crash down again.

"And what are all those green spots?"

To its credit, Silber's sickly yellow lawn was mottled with frisbee-sized patches of a much lusher, livelier green, patches that looked so much better fertilized than the surrounding grass that I was asking about them. Silber shrugged and said that maybe they marked the spots where a mole had died in its burrow.

## 6. *My House*                               2:38

This ingenious piece lasts two minutes and thirty-eight seconds because that is how long it took Silber, one rainy day in 1988 when he had nothing better to do, to race through his house from attic to basement, entering each room, touching the far wall, running back out into the hallway and on to the next room and the next, all the while panting the particulars of his progress into a tiny tape recorder. The year before he'd painted every room a different color, and this project seems to have given him a conceptual grasp of his house that he hadn't formerly enjoyed: though he'd lived there all his life, till then there'd still been rooms he didn't know the names of, and that he tended for that reason to avoid, almost as if the power were out in those rooms, as if they were too dark to use. Now, though, he could call them by their colors, as he did the day of his '88 stunt. The following day, he composed a musical tour of his house corresponding moment by moment to that panted transcript, finding the perfect chord for each color and sustaining it just as long as he had spent in the corresponding room, composing a "hallway" theme almost criminally reminiscent of the "Promenade" from *Pictures at an Exhibition,* and using for the stairways a descending whole-tone scale. Though the uncanny accuracy of his musical portraits, the magic by which he evokes not just the color but the whole mood of each room, can of course be gauged only by those of us who have been inside the house in question, those who haven't can still form surprisingly high-resolution images by listening to the music and letting it conjure up that dwelling room by room.

I want to say that Silber's house and Silber's music were so inextricable that he could discuss the former *only* by means of the latter, but that would be untrue: our composer was all too able to put his thoughts into words. "Well," he'd said, after disposing of that crow, "I guess if you're going to write my biography you'll want to see inside my house." He sighed. "I guess I could give you a quick tour."

The house was big, but not as big as readers will assume on hearing that the tour lasted three hours: Silber always liked to mess with the tempo, and the day I met him, as if to atone for the disrespectful speed of his '88 sprint, he must've decided to see how slowly he could show someone his house without once ceasing to babble about whatever happened to have happened in whatever room we stood in. I regret to say I didn't listen to his monologue. Indeed, it took me two hours to understand that we would be on our feet for the rest of the evening, that the tour wasn't just an inane, insanely protracted, about-to-be-concluded formality before the real business of the evening, our sitting down to talk. In the year I knew him I never did see Silber sitting down except in his car. There wasn't a single chair in his house — or for that matter a piano bench, though I saw three pianos. I didn't get to hear him play that evening, but I got to watch: one of the first stops on our tour was a yellow room enshrining a magnificent piano, a Bösendorfer ninety-seven-key Imperial. Standing at the keyboard, Silber raised his powerful hands overhead like birds of prey about to swoop, then launched into a tempestuous performance of what he afterward identified as a Scriabin etude, but even if I'd known the piece, I wouldn't have recognized Silber's rendition, which was absolutely silent, like a televised recital with the sound turned off. I did hear the clicking of his fingernails on the keys and the muted thumping of the hammers on some nonreverberating surface, but not a single note. When he finished, Silber explained that he suffered from periodic "episodes" of greater-than-usual ("even for *me*, I mean") sensitivity to noise, and that back in '94, at the height of one such episode, he'd replaced the Bösendorfer's strings with rubber pads. Otherwise, he said, the action was intact, and better than that of his other pianos: this was still his favorite (not counting the Steinway in his recording studio), and the one he practiced on, though once a month he'd play some scales on the concert grand — still strung — in the blue piano room, just to remind himself, he said, of "what pianos *sound* like."

As for Silber's policy of never sitting down, it was central to his whole aesthetic. He liked to classify the arts according to the position in which they are characteristically enjoyed — Sedentary (concerts, movies), Recumbent (novels), Erect (paintings) — and he hated the ones intended for sedentary consumption. That in fact was his official reason for having abandoned the concert stage: he believed that people should listen to music lying down (which was how he claimed to eat his meals, on a specially built sofa) or better yet walking around, since there were Ambulatory arts (sculpture, architecture) too, and these, according to Silber, were the best of all. He disapproved even more vigorously of the sedentary *production* of art, his official reason for composing on walks and urging me, too, to compose on walks, with the microcassette recorder he gave me the day we met (since he wanted my book about him to be itself a work of art). Even in bad weather he spent several hours a day out walking around, and continued to walk around even after he went back indoors. Especially at times of inner turmoil, he would pace all night — along the hallways, up and down the stairways — so that by dawn he'd often covered the entire house. Back in '89, he'd even had his house remodeled to create a special *pacing lane,* lengthening the long third-story hallway by encroaching on the red guest bedroom at its west end. He claimed that several years ago, at the height of some unspecified "crisis," he'd worn a pedometer for a week and found that he was walking an average of eleven miles a night *inside* his house.

But back to the quick tour. Because, as I say, I didn't understand at first that it *was* the business of the evening and that I'd already been given the job and that therefore (or furthermore, or nonetheless) I would not set foot in his house again so long as he lived, I was too impatient, waiting for my "interview," really to pay attention to Silber's patter, which sounded rehearsed if not till now recited. Halfway up the stairway to the third floor, Silber noticed my distraction, wheeled around, and demanded: "You getting all this?" Though I nodded that I was, I so manifestly wasn't that he said, "Wait here," ran back down to the first floor, and returned with a cassette recorder no bigger than a bar of soap. "Here," he said. "You can even keep it — I just bought a better one. All you have to do now is walk around behind me." And I did as I was told. (Later, I'm ashamed to say, I taped over Silber's chat without replaying or transcribing it.)

So my recollections of the tour are few and vague. I do recall that the vaultlike door at the top of the basement stairs was locked and that my guide didn't offer to unlock it (just as well: another level would have meant another hour); that every room was a different color, and generally the loudest available shade of the color in question; and that the light fixtures all had rheostats: whenever Silber turned on a light, he would dial the dimmer switch up to its brightest setting with a slight but unmistakable *gradualness* that seemed to reflect some private theory, no doubt evolutionary, about the maximum rate at which the human iris should be asked to constrict. I also remember thinking that as many rooms as Silber showed me, and as big as some of them were, there weren't enough rooms to account for all the space occupied by the house, or indeed for the long doorless stretches along certain hallways. Finally I asked my guide where all the rooms had gone, and he explained that over the years he had "retired" the rooms where something bad had happened by plastering over their doorways and painting or papering over the plaster so that a visitor walking down the hallway would never guess a room had once been there.* In one case — what had been his practice room — he'd gone even further, not only plastering over its doors (with yet another grand piano still inside), but removing the windows and bricking up their sockets so meticulously that no trace of the room was visible from *outside* the house either. Silber said that there were other rooms he stayed out of due to bad associations, but that he no longer resorted to plaster because lately he'd been having so many nightmares about the rooms he'd erased: by sealing them off, he'd succeeded only in making his house even eerier.

"But I *am* tempted to seal off this one sometimes," he said as he led me into a Day-Glo orange room on the third floor. In the center of the room, an old-fashioned safe — the boxy kind that still falls out of windows in cartoons — sat on the floor below a ceiling-mounted smoke detector. Silber said the safe contained the manuscript of *Day,* and that the room — otherwise bare except for a little red fire extinguisher just inside the door — was called the dayroom.

It was almost midnight when the tour ended, and *my* house was at least five hours away. Silber would have turned me out anyhow, no doubt, if he hadn't just made the mistake of identifying the last room on our tour as "one of the guest bedrooms." I slept surprisingly well — till six A.M., when I was awakened by piano music. I found my host downstairs, standing with his

---

* These rooms — five in all — are omitted from *My House,* though Silber adds a special unspeakably spooky shudder to the "hallway" theme each time we pass one.

back to me in a purple dressing gown at the concert grand in the blue piano room. He ignored my greeting and, a little later, my goodbye, utterly engrossed in transcribing with his left hand the rapid nervous tune he was performing with his right. When we got around to talking terms by telephone that evening, Silber repeated that I would have to move to Forest City. And since, according to him, the housing market was tight, he thoughtfully offered to find me a suitable place. What he found, and committed me to for a year (September 1998 through August 1999) by forging my signature on the lease, was a furnished room in a shabby clapboard house belonging to his sister and zoned (as far as I could tell) for single men, a much smaller house than Silber's, though it had to shelter half a dozen hapless bachelors and not just a solitary genius too selfish to spare a few square yards for his biographer. Admittedly, my room was big and sunny and even came with a kitchenette; it might almost have counted as a studio apartment, except that due to some fluke in the local plumbing code, there was no bathroom; I had to use the communal one at the far end of the hallway, assuming it wasn't already occupied by one of the other lodgers. The man in the room above mine also liked classical music, or at least he liked, and played *ad nauseam,* the only classical recording he appeared to own: three favorite Beethoven piano sonatas — the *Moonlight,* the *Pathétique,* and the *Appassionata.*

On September 1, 1998, I loaded my few belongings into my car and moved to Forest City. (It took only one trip: just as certain anorexics make a point of staying slim enough to squeeze into a favorite pair of pants, I made a point of owning no more stuff than I could stuff into my car.) From then on, Silber and I met only outdoors or — when he wanted to play a new piece for me — at the Bean, the busy coffeehouse with the bad piano: my employer, who hated his sister, refused to set foot in my dwelling (even though he'd deemed it good enough for me) and never again invited me into his.

This is one of several Silber compositions that could be called "road music." Like the other specimens (*Route 111, Rainy Night*), it communicates a special urgency heard nowhere else in Silber's oeuvre, for nothing else excited him as much as motoring. I'd venture to say he knew more about cars than the average composer. His mother's father had been a mechanic, and for a while Silber himself had wanted to be one, as a nightingale might want to be a crow. At sixteen, he'd even gotten a job at the Main Street Garage, though he'd stormed out after half a day of fetching wrenches, mopping floors, and making coffee. Over the next few years, he bought, repaired, and resold a succession of old cars in his own garage — the closest he ever came to gainful employment. One day when I called to ask about that chapter of his past, he told me to come over — not to his house but to his garage. It was a big one, built of the same red brick as the house, with a carriage house upstairs — complete with a kitchen and bath — where Silber had lived as a disgruntled adolescent, during his mechanic phase, and where *I* should have lived during my year as Silber's hireling. (What better place for a salaried biographer than in the servant's quarters?) Downstairs there was room enough for at least four cars, though Silber owned just one, a sporty red convertible he had received for his twenty-first birthday. Opening its hood, he told me everything I'd never wanted to know about reciprocating engines, pointing here and there with a dipstick as he talked. I tried to follow, but my eyes kept wandering to other parts of the garage, which for all I knew I'd never see again. In one corner, an old bicycle — a boy's green three-speed with red plastic streamers hanging from the molded plastic handles — rested on its steadfast kickstand; in another corner stood a tank of banned insecticide.

But I took in some of Silber's explanation. I remember my amazement at how patly the four piston strokes — intake, compression, power, and exhaust — corresponded (at least for this creator) to the stages of creation, if one thinks of publication as exhaust. Silber told me that the engine was itself a work of art — as worthy of aesthetic contemplation, he insisted, as any sonata — and that sometimes he went out to the garage and raised the hood just to gaze. He didn't seem to care about the body, though; at least, he never washed it, and had never done anything about a big dent dating from the night in 1988 when he "accidentally" hit a "deer." (The reason for those quotation marks will become clear in the course of these notes.)

Given his lifelong obsession with cars, it's no surprise that the composer did his best work on the open road. Roughly once a week, at midnight, he'd head to a favorite convenience store for a cup of coffee and a packaged pastry, then drive around for a couple of hours, slowing down and speeding up according to the interest of the landscape, or to the rhythm of his own thoughts, and intermittently humming or singing into a hand-held tape recorder as the caffeine kicked in and his head teemed with music.

During the year I knew him, Silber let me ride along about a dozen times. The first night, the week I moved to Forest City, was warm enough to leave the top down — the first time in my thirty-eight years that I had ever ridden in an open car, the wind in my hair, the bugs in my face. I'd had a bookish, under-privileged adolescence, and the reader can imagine my exhilarated sense, as we sped through the dark, of making up for lost time. All I needed was a beer and the blare of rock-and-roll, instead of decaf and the clamor of Silber singing snatches of potential compositions (most of them atonal) to his tape recorder. He was so inspired that first night that he ran out of tape, but afterward I had a hunch that the whole session had been staged for my sake, or the sake of the biography, like a TV dramatization of a real event — that Silber hadn't actually composed a single note that night, just trotted out something he'd already written. Probably *he'd* been drinking decaf too, knowing that with me along real composition would be impossible, and real — caffeinated — inspiration thus unwelcome.

Soon he came to see me, though, as a benign distraction, a nuisance to tune out the better to tune in his music, on nights when utter solitude wasn't what he wanted. Roughly once a month he'd phone at eleven P.M. and say to meet him at the stroke of midnight in front of the KwikStop on Main Street, three blocks from my rooming house. Then we'd drive around for two hours — to the minute, boasted Silber, as if proud of his compulsion,* though I never bothered to verify the claim by clocking one of our excursions. He spent the better part of each drive crisscrossing Forest City in every direction, sometimes leaving town but never going more than a mile or two before turning back, as if fastened to his birthplace by an elastic cord. Sometimes, like a tour guide to his own past, he would point out sights of biographical interest: "We went fishing there one time"; "That's where my dad took us to get the swing set." After a few rides, I noticed that his weekly drives all followed a fixed route, the same one every time, though I never bothered to ask why. I'd decided the day I met him that Silber was a bundle of meaningless neuroses, and I had pretty much left it at that.† In any case, my rooming house wasn't on the route — that was why he always made me meet him in front of the KwikStop and dropped me off there afterward.

Silber didn't always compose on these drives. Sometimes we talked, or rode along in silence. One night when I came aboard, his radio was playing the first movement of Schubert's "Unfinished" Symphony, a work that "wouldn't be half bad," said Silber grudgingly, if not for its sudden changes in volume — now murmuring, now bellowing, "like a bore who notices

---

* In 1986 he'd invoked this compulsion in court while pleading guilty of reckless driving but innocent of purposely running over a neighbor's Airedale. Back in his performing days, he'd prided himself on playing certain works in exactly the same time — to the second — every time.

† Perhaps I was too hasty in throwing up my hands, not even trying to make sense of eccentricities that would have yielded to the least reflection. Even a dimwit like Silber's *first* biographer had (I later learned) succeeded in illuminating some quirks I dismissed, and still tend to dismiss, as not worth the effort.

that you aren't listening to him," said Silber, "so he grabs you by the shoulders and yells, 'Hey! I'm *talking* to you! I'm talking to *you!*'" Rather than changing the station, though, Silber amused us both by forestalling every dip or rise in volume with a quick, precisely compensating clock- or counterclockwise twist of the volume knob, so transforming Schubert's breathtaking mountain range into a prairie.

He was, indeed, a consummate knob-twister. One rainy day in '82, he'd spent several hours out in his garage modifying his windshield wipers. At first he had planned only to retrofit his car with the hiccuppy intermittent option he'd begun to notice on more recent models, but then he'd seen a way (adjustable gearing) of giving his wipers ten different speeds, from lightning-fast to once-a-minute, so assuring him, he said, "the perfect rate for any rain." Not till my last ride, two nights before his death (see *Rainy Night*), did I see the wipers in action: though as far as I could tell the rain was falling steadily, Silber adjusted them half a dozen times in as many miles.

The final movement of these late-night drives was interesting. After more than an hour of sticking as close to his hometown as a timid child to his father, Silber would head north on Main Street, sometimes pausing at the KwikStop long enough to run in for another cup of coffee, if he felt himself on the verge of inspiration ("the same way *you* might feel on the verge of sneezing," he explained once, as if *I* could hope to understand true inspiration only by analogy to some bodily function). He'd cross First Avenue and continue north on Route 28, as Main Street was called outside of city limits. After a mile he'd turn off 28 onto 111. At that point there was always a marked change in his mood — marked, for one thing, by his falling silent, and for another by a sort of straining excitement, as if he'd waited all his life to go where he was going. He headed east on 111 for about a dozen miles, to Forest City's larger neighbor Lumber, where there was a junior college, a general hospital, a classical radio station that refused to broadcast Silber's compositions, and a big building called Erlenmeyer Hall. We always came to a stop by a pay phone in back of Erlenmeyer Hall, at the edge of a vast parking lot deserted at that hour but lit as bright as day by halogen lamps. We'd sit there for a minute, in a sober silence I knew better than to interrupt. Sometimes my employer would get out and use the pay phone to call KDOA (as he referred to the radio station because of its stale playlist) and, disguising his voice with an absurd Teutonic accent, ask for one of his own works. (Once he told me that for years he had called from his home phone, until one announcer finally granted a request but only after announcing on the air that he had traced the call to the composer of the piece in question.) And then we'd turn around and head back the way we came.

Gradually I realized that what made these late-night drives so exciting for Silber was the illusion, each time he found himself eastbound on Route 111, that *this* time he might just keep going, might abscond, abandoning his house and all that it contained, most notably his past. He kept a fat red duffel bag on the passenger seat, a bag whose purpose the composer refused to explain ("Never mind the stupid bag"), although I had to hold it in my lap every time I rode with him, since it was too big to stuff behind the seats (and Silber said the trunk was filthy). When, on my third or fourth ride, he went into the ever-open KwikStop for a second cup of coffee, I seized the opportunity to rummage through the bag. I found a compact road atlas, a toothbrush, a rolled-up tuxedo, a change of underwear, a portable alarm clock, a dozen different pill bottles (including both amphetamines and barbiturates), a water bottle, a travel iron, a packet of trail mix that had expired more than a decade ago, and an apparently random assortment of tourist brochures with titles like "Romantic Cincinnati" and "The Busy Visitor's Guide to the Twin Cities." During our next few drives, I noted a certain predictability in Silber's moods (outward-bound excitement; homeward-bound dejection) and a certain pattern to his stray remarks ("One of these nights you might just have to hitchhike back into town";

"What if I kept heading east instead of turning back? I'd never have to see those stupid trees again"). At some point I understood that Silber had a fantasy as stale as that trail mix, a fantasy of abandoning Forest City forever, abandoning music, and starting over somewhere else, as something else, something other than a great composer. The bag was his travel kit, ready to go. By the time I met him, his freewheeling fantasy (all the more poignant — or, if you prefer, idiotic — in light of the phobia I'll discuss later) was so habitual that not even the presence of a passenger with no such plans and no such kit — no toothbrush — could stop Silber from pretending.

No doubt the composer never quite forgot that his fantasy was just that — a fantasy — and his sense of possibility a mirage, a highway psychosis, but it revived as often as he hit the open road, and inspired a special excitement that sometimes resulted, not in a change of address to be sure, much less a change of vocation, but in an artistic breakthrough.

It was on one of his drives, for example — a solo jaunt one luminous September night not long after I moved to Forest City — that it first occurred to him that the limitations of "old-fashioned" (i.e., written) musical notation were responsible for his failure to realize some of his more newfangled ideas. There'd been a full moon that night, and Silber, on a whim, had pulled off the road just to gaze at his engine by moonlight. After a minute of gazing, he gasped: he'd just "understood" (his word) that the engine of his car was not just a work of art but a piece of music. Not the hubbub of the engine running — *that* was just an unfortunate static he had to tune out on these drives to hear the melodies in his head — but "the engine itself." And not just music "of a sort" or "in a sense," but music pure and simple. (*He* seemed to know what he meant.) He'd found a pen and drawn some hasty staves on the back of an old speeding ticket, then attempted to transcribe the music in question, but was unable. He'd also tried to hum the music to his tape recorder, but again he was unable. And yet as he gaped at his engine in awe, he "literally heard" the music it embodied — at least until a car of rowdy teenagers roared by and shouted drunkenly at Silber, drawing his attention for one crucial instant, since when he looked at the engine again, he could no longer hear what he had heard. He spent the whole next day and half the night in his garage, glaring at the engine in an effort to remember the soundtrack of his big roadside epiphany.

Although he never managed to decode his engine's musical notation, the whole experience left him convinced that music *could* be represented or embodied by a three-dimensional object, and indeed that there were musical ideas too manifold to map in *two* dimensions. The following night he went for another drive and, on returning, composed an unusual fugue. He called the next morning to say he'd just ticked off another opus on his little opus counter, and that he wanted me to be the first to hear it.

I'm afraid I proved unworthy of the honor when he played the fugue for me that afternoon — not at the Bean, but in a skylit room above his garage. Just about the last thing Silber's father did, before dying of a broken heart (or so Helen, Silber's sister, diagnosed his coronary), was to help his son set up a recording studio in the carriage house. The studio was little bigger than its piano, a Steinway concert grand my friend had made his father buy him at the time, since none of the six pianos they already owned was worthy of the world-class recording artist he still dreamed of being, though by that point he no longer played in public. Needless to say, the dream had not come true: when his Schumann record (pressed just days after his father's death) failed to astound the music world, Silber had lost all interest in other composers; and when, in 1985, another vanity-pressed record, this time of Silber's own music, fared no better than the first (no better than my aphorisms!), he'd decided — what he still contended — that the world simply wasn't ready for him yet. By that point, in any case, he was betting everything on *Day:* once he finished it, he'd be a household name, and his two LPs collector's items, and all the idiots who hadn't bought them when they'd a chance — well, *they'd* all be sorry.

So I got to hear the fugue on Silber's best piano, in the silence of his soundproof studio. (There was a double-glazed skylight, but the other windows had all been bricked up, either to keep out neighborhood noises or to keep in Silber's music, as if each chord were a sort of trade secret.) But fugues are not for everyone. Silber was so fond of them, he'd listen to two at once, or to two identical recordings of the same one staggered to produce a metafugue. He was proud of being so good at rubbing his belly and patting his head. He once claimed that he could read two unrelated stories in adjacent columns of the *Forest City Ranger* simultaneously — a boast that struck me as at once implausible and unimpressive. He spoke of buying nine identical TV sets, stacking them in a three-by-three array, tuning them to nine different stations, and watching them all at once, like a bingo addict playing on nine cards — not as much of a feat, to be sure, as playing blindfold chess on nine boards at once, but symptomatic of the same unhealthy craving, the need to have more going on at the same time than most of our pleasures (even complicated ones like fugue appreciation and chess) are designed to offer. I myself was spared that morbid craving; if anything, I tended to feel that there was more than enough to keep track of in even the simplest pastimes, and always looked for ways to simplify them further. Lately I'd been stocking up on Music Minus One LPs — performances of famous works with one important part left out, for the music student to supply on his own instrument. (One can play along with *any* record, I suppose, but when one adds oneself to Music Minus One, one feels integral and not superfluous.) But I wasn't a student musician and didn't play along or even hum along: I liked to listen to those understaffed performances just as they were, in order to relax. Even an ordinary trio, with all three musicians toiling away at once, could seem too *busy* for me to enjoy, too much of a three-ring circus.

So it may say as much about me as about the composer's new fugue if I admit that, after the initial statement of the theme (reminiscent of "Route 66"), all I heard was an excited mob of random notes. Afterward, when I politely asked to see the score, Silber led me back downstairs to the dark garage and over to a workbench with a large dark object on it. When he hit a switch, a spotlight revealed what looked like a precocious second-grader's prizewinning science-fair model of an especially big and complicated molecule.

"Are those Tinkertoys?"

"Yep," said Silber proudly. "The thing I just played is called *Tinkertoy Fugue*." He said that "in exactly the same way" the engine of his car stood for a piece of music (whatever way *that* might have been), this Tinkertoy construction stood for one too, for the one I'd just heard. The music was too various and subtle, he insisted, to transcribe on paper the old-fashioned way.

It wasn't the last time our composer found conventional written notation insufficient for his purposes, even if it had been good enough for Bach, Beethoven, and Brahms. For about a month after his Tinkertoy epiphany, he continued to tinker with Tinkertoys, and Lincoln Logs, and Legos. He even fashioned, and spoke of patenting, a line of hybrid connectors that enabled him to use those disparate building elements within a single structure. He assembled a series of objects (each dismantled within a day or so to free up parts for the next) that stood for works of music he had heard in his mind's ear, though the music was so rare and strange (he claimed) that he couldn't reproduce it at the keyboard. *Tinkertoy Fugue* is unique among his 3-D "compositions" in having a recorded performance to show for itself. Silber insisted, though, that the fugue on your disc is no more than a rough translation, a crude approximation, of the ineffably delicate music he had heard one night on Route 111. That may explain why, when I later played a tape of the multifarious fugue for a music teacher (Cletus Pitchford — see Disc Three) at Lumber Junior College, he described the piece as "a beginner's effort — really just a canon on the lines of 'Row, Row, Row Your Boat.'"

### 8. From *Day:* 4:55–5:00 P.M.                    5:00

This is a small fraction of a composition at which Silber labored for almost twenty years: a daylong piano sonata. (He insisted on calling it a "sonata," though only two of the seventeen movements he completed were in sonata form.) To be exact, your excerpt represents $1/288$ of *Day's* projected length. The work was still unfinished at the time of Silber's death, and no wonder: he'd set out to score a real day — from midnight to midnight — in real time; the finished product, when performed at the only possible tempo ("that of reality itself," insisted Silber), was going to last exactly twenty-four hours; but when I met him, Silber had been stuck for years at five P.M.

The frenetic five-minute excerpt on your disc is the end of a rather obsessive (not to say repetitive) hourlong crescendo of excitement — one that will remind some of Ravel's *Boléro* — culminating in an earsplitting blast from a real factory whistle. After trying in vain to get his piano to whistle, Silber decided to cheat and supplement his instrument with a real whistle, at this one point in the composition, so much importance did he attach to the corresponding time of day.

Silber had gotten the idea for a daylong sonata on June 21, 1980. In what sounded almost like a mystical experience, he had "realized" something so obvious as to be vacuous: that the *day* is the basic unit of human consciousness, the standard building block — the Lego — of which lifetimes are compounded. It followed that there could be no loftier subject for a magnum opus, and Silber had just decided that the time had come for him to embark on his. Indeed, he'd been so eager to get started that he'd chosen that same day as the one to set to music, a choice whose hasty nature he'd have time to regret later. He said his main reason for choosing a specific day was so he could "do" sunrise and sunset, phenomena as irresistible to our composer as to any landscape painter. He'd even consulted a *Farmer's Almanac* to establish to the minute the sun's whereabouts (relative to Forest City) on June 21, 1980.

Otherwise, he said, *Day* was a day in the abstract: there was no minute-to-minute correspondence between the daylong sonata and the real day it represented (most of whose minutes, anyhow, Silber had long ago forgotten). He wanted his sonata to have universal relevance — to say something timeless about ten A.M. in general, not just to set one certain ten A.M. to music. And ten A.M. had been a snap; but for years now, as I say, my friend had been mired at five, maybe because he thought of the nine-to-five workday as a fundamental fact of the human condition, albeit one from which his wealth exempted him. More than once I recommended that he get a job himself, for a week or two at least, but Silber only snorted and told me that the job of the true artist was to contemplate life from afar, sitting out as much of it as possible — to paint the sweaty peasants from a respectful distance (ideally upwind) and a picturesque perspective, not to help them sow and reap. Well, as the young say nowadays, "whatever." Maybe Silber was afraid that hands-on experience with the workday would force him to go back and rewrite the whole sonata, undoing two decades of work. Or maybe he just couldn't face the prospect of a job even for the sake of his magnum opus.*

I was never sure if Silber's awe of five P.M. was a cause or an effect of his composer's block, but he always spoke of that indifferent hour with a wide-eyed earnestness that seemed almost religious. I'd learned not to bother him between four and six P.M.: every afternoon he spent an hour thinking himself into a phenomenological frenzy, trying frantically to focus all his faculties on the time of day — on "time itself," he said — in hopes of catching whatever it was that happens at five. And then he

---

* In 1997, he had in fact taken a job at the car-parts store on Main Street, but once again had quit the day he started, and well before quitting time.

spent another hour fuming at his failure. He knew there had to be a whistle, but for the life of him he couldn't think what to put next.

"Tell me how it feels, Norm," he implored me more than once in the year I knew him, "tell me how it feels when the whistle blows at quitting time." And I did my best to tell him, though I wasn't sure that even factories still used whistles, and in any case I'd never had a factory job. In fact, I'd never had a nine-to-five of any kind. As I say, I'd majored in philosophy in college, and still called myself a Philosopher, though the U.S. Department of Labor's great *Dictionary of Occupational Titles* — an otherwise exhaustive list that recognizes such improbable professions as "Sock Examiner," "Animal Impersonator," "Worm Sorter," "Bedspread Folder," and "Mirror Inspector" — jumps unaccountably from "Philologist" to "Phlebotomist." No wonder, then, that I'd never succeeded in getting the world at large to acknowledge my vocation, much less to remunerate me for it.

It didn't help that I'd decided in my early twenties to walk away from academia — that haven for the elsewhere unemployable — despite a fast start as a scholar. My father was an eminent professor of aesthetics, and for a while there I planned to follow in his footsteps. But then I suddenly grew up (a trauma I'll recount in another note), and after twenty-two years of wanting to be just like him, I wanted more than anything *not* to be like him, even if that meant forgoing all the good things he had beaten me to: an adoring wife and son, an academic sinecure, and — as far as the arts were concerned — a complacent taste for the tried-and-true.

So I'd stormed out of the classroom and into the workforce. During the next year, I held a dozen different part-time jobs, from telephone solicitor to busboy in an all-night pancake house to stockboy in a house-and-garden store. None of the jobs lasted more than a month. Though as I say I made a point of seeking work that was beneath me, I was unable to hide my contempt for my duties, my coworkers, my employers, or the public. I'd probably have ended up sleeping under bridges and eating out of dumpsters if not for nepotism: in 1983, eager for a change of scene, I moved to Tacoma to work as an aide in a suburban public library run by my aunt Lucy, who took me on — and kept me on, year after year, even when patrons complained about me — as a favor to her favorite sister. I worked at that library, part-time, for fifteen years, first at the circulation desk, then at the reference desk, and finally (when I was deemed too "abrasive" to deal with callers too stupid or lazy to look up the capital of Portugal themselves) behind a door marked AUTHORIZED PERSONNEL ONLY, sorting just-returned bestsellers prior to reshelving, flipping through picture books looking for crayon marks, rewinding videos whose viewers hadn't bothered to. Though the money wasn't much, I managed to scrape by. For years I told myself I was only biding my time until my ship came in. Not that I ever hoped to get rich with my aphorisms, but I really had believed, year after year, that it wouldn't be long before the world at large recognized me as a thinker to reckon with, one who also happened to sort books for a living, as Spinoza happened to grind lenses. In December '96, I borrowed money from my mother to subsidize the publication of a book of aphorisms, since it hadn't interested the other kind of publishers, the kind that pay *you*. Naive, I'd expected deafening applause. The silence that ensued instead was still resounding in my ears when, in August '97, I read Silber's ad while waiting for my dermatologist. By that point, I had lost my conviction of imminent glory, the delusion that had allowed me to live for so long on so little.

In December '97, my aunt died and was replaced by a hardliner named Martha. In April '98, Martha fired me for being "arrogant, contemptuous, grumpy, haughty, pompous, rude, self-deluded, surly, touchy, unreliable, and vain" (as she put it in her parting comments). I started reading want ads instead of aphorisms — though for all their brevity the ads had more in common with a fortune-teller's auguries: "Successful candidate will be hardworking go-getter with three years experience in re-tail . . ." But I am not a go-getter, and was still unemployed when Silber called a few months later. He entered my life at a juncture when I badly needed *something*, and though he wasn't really what I needed, my need itself was so urgent that — like a starving child eating dirt — I seized on him.

But enough about me. I mention my own sorrows only because Silber, at the time I met him, was undergoing something similar, or as similar as a rich man could. (*Part* of my sorrow was the stigma of my poverty, the scorn of philistines who'd never deluded themselves that they were destined to do more than get and spend, and who'd always hated me for thinking *I* was. If all the gold I'd thought I was amassing in my notebooks was only fool's gold, then all the dolts who'd spent their youths amassing real gold instead — and who now of course had much more gold than I did — were only right to consider me a fool.) When I started working for him, Silber hadn't added a second to *Day* in four years. In general, those had been barren years for him: aside from the daily chord in his chord-a-day diary, he'd managed only *Variations in a Minor.* For a while there he'd been convinced he'd lost his talent and would never write another note, but his dry spell ended the very day we met (see *Crows*), and ended with a vengeance: it was my good luck to know him during the last and most prolific year of his life, though maybe it wasn't just luck. Or maybe I was *his* good luck, since I can't help thinking that I was to thank for that creative burst, if only as a sort of talent scout from a posterity whose interest the composer had perhaps begun to doubt.

### 9. *My Face* 10:09

This piece was composed as the soundtrack to a remarkable short film begun by Silber's father and completed by the composer. I wanted very much to include the film itself in your boxed set, on a disc of its own, now that such things are possible, but Silber's sister vetoed that proposal and indeed asked me not to mention the movie at all in my notes, so I'll content myself with describing it at length. Silber himself considered the film so important that he sought me out to give me a copy — the first time he ever came looking for *me*.

Silber's birthday, though I didn't know it at the time, was October 17. I spent the morning of the eighteenth at the Bean, working on the "Eccentricities" section of Silber's biography, while outside it rained relentlessly. My employer, for whom the number twelve and its multiples were magic, had told me to divide the book into twelve chapters ("*You* can decide how to organize my life, just so long as it divides by twelve") and to finish one a month, since I had a one-year lease; but to his dismay I proved unable to adhere to such a schedule. He didn't mind that I'd chosen to arrange the book by topic and not by epoch, but he hated my way of working on all twelve at once, jumping around as my mood dictated (as Prokofiev is said to have done with the twelve movements of his three "War Sonatas," though admittedly *I* didn't have the excuse of a war for my scatterbrained approach) rather than finishing each before proceeding to the next. He was understandably anxious to see regular installments of the book he was paying me to write, but the first few months all I was able to give him, when the end of the month rolled around, were a dozen rubber-banded stacks of index cards — three-by-five-inch cards of the kind I also used to enter sweepstakes without purchasing the sponsor's product — representing my scribbled additions to each of the subtopics into which I'd divided my subject. Nonetheless he paid me once a month, on the last day of the month, or just in time to cover my rent, which was due on the first. Meeting him at the Bean, I'd hand over a manila envelope and he'd hand me a check whose signature, he once predicted, would one day be worth more than what I'd get by cashing it. The next time I saw him, he'd return the index cards, now in *thirteen* bundles, of which the fattest was always the stack of cards he'd crossed out in red — facts about himself I was forbidden to use. He was after a certain chiaroscuro; he knew exactly which parts of his past he wanted spotlit, and which relegated to darkness. To his credit, he had sense enough to defer to me on matters of syntax and grammar, and never queried specific word choices (unless with a view to reducing an already flattering half-truth to some even more flattering fraction). The contempt implicit in this policy did not escape me: my employer let me take care of the words the way he let his cleaning lady decide which furniture polish to buy; he didn't stoop to know about such things himself.

That morning, anyhow, I felt like writing about Silber's eccentricities, insofar as I felt like writing about him at all. At noon I bought a piece of cheesecake as incentive to continue and then, seeing that the rain had stopped, moved outdoors, to one of the white plastic tables on the sidewalk. After wiping off my chair and table with brown paper napkins, I sat down and took a bite of cheesecake, then reluctantly set down my fork, picked up my pen, and, labeling a fresh card "ECCENTRICITIES," wrote: "Like so many geniuses, Silber —" I put down the pen and picked up the fork again, not ambidextrous enough to write and eat at the same time. *Was* he a genius, or just a nut? Even as I asked myself, I saw him coming up the street, carefully choosing his steps according to some private rule that made it look as if he were crossing a minefield. As always, he wore a tuxedo; today's — it looked like one left over from his stint as a concert pianist — was gray. In one hand he carried the battered violin case he liked to use on long walks as a lunchbox. (Some of my employer's eccentricities were plainly affectations, though I wasn't ever sure about their motive. By that point I no longer assumed that he was just behaving the way he thought a genius should; now I suspected that the idea was to embarrass his sister — of whom, alas, more soon. Later I would realize that Silber's harmless quirks were actually a smoke screen to conceal aberrations of a more sinister kind, the way a serial rapist might affect good-natured gruffness.)

In his other hand, he held a red umbrella, still open, though the rain had stopped. He must not have noticed, unless he was using the umbrella as a parasol. Spotting me, he cocked it to one side in greeting and — from a distance of maybe thirty feet — shouted, "Happy birthday!"

"Thanks," I said, when he was close enough to hear me. It wasn't my birthday or even my birth month, but by that point I'd understood that Silber was not only a "surrealist composer" — as he liked to call himself — but a surrealist talker.

"*My* birthday," he explained a moment later.

"*Your* birthday? When?"

"Yesterday, *biographer.*"

I felt myself blushing as I apologized. I had of course determined Silber's date of birth the day I started his biography, but since at the time I hadn't foreseen that we'd become friends, I hadn't forwarded a carbon copy of the date to the part of my brain responsible for remembering red-letter days. And anyhow —

"Don't worry about it," said Silber, with a dismissive wave of his umbrella. "Here — I got you something." Turning his back, he set his violin case on the sidewalk, opened it, and rummaged around. (His paternal grandfather had been a talented amateur violinist and — though this came out only posthumously — all four members of the reclusive Silber Quartet, an ensemble that in the mid-fifties had acquired, by means of its recordings and despite its refusal to give live performances, a small but ardent following drawn by what one critic termed the group's "uncanny unity of tone and purpose." Insanity would seem to run in Silber's family — just as it is said to run in mine, though I trust that *I've* been spared.) Finally he straightened up and turned to me with a package wrapped in Sunday funnies from the *Forest City Ranger.* "Happy birthday," he repeated, and went on to explain, before letting go of the package, that people should *give* presents on their birthdays, to thank their friends and families for putting up with them for another year. (Silber, of course, believed nothing of the sort.)

"Thanks," I said again, unwrapping what I glumly took to be another book, as if I didn't have enough of those already.

But no, it was a videocassette in a book-shaped plastic case, with a typewritten label on the spine: *My Face: The First Forty Years*. "Huh," I said. "What is it?"

"You'll find out."

That autumn, like most autumns, was a lonely time for me, and to fill the evenings I had bought a big TV set with a built-in VCR. Silber, who knew next to nothing else about me, knew about my VCR: he'd bumped into me one day as I emerged with a pair of new releases from a nearby shop with an embarrassing name — T&A Video — though it stocked a small selection of nonpornographic titles too. As a matter of fact I'd been planning to visit T&A that afternoon, and Silber's gift was not enough to change my plans: to judge by the narrow band of black videotape visible through the clear plastic window, the birthday cartridge would be good for only ten or fifteen minutes' worth of entertainment.

That evening, after viewing, re-viewing, and rewinding my rental, I stuck Silber's tape in the player. When I hit PLAY, I heard a piano and saw the face of a baby I identified at once as my employer. At first glance I assumed the baby was a newborn, though the longer the camera dwelled on his face, the less certain I became. After maybe twenty seconds of waiting for something to happen, I was about to fast-forward when I realized that something *was* happening: the baby was growing visibly older as I watched. Within a minute, he was no longer a baby at all, but a preschooler. A couple of minutes later he was an adolescent, though by that point he'd undergone an even more traumatic transformation, suddenly changing (at around the age of ten) from black and white to color. I watched the young composer experimenting briefly with a ridiculous toothbrush mustache, noted a new grimness as he hit adulthood, watched his eyes grow more and more inscrutable as he passed through his twenties and into his thirties, and at the end saw the Silber I knew; before giving way to static, the last few frames even displayed (I reviewed them frame by frame) the pustule then in full bloom just outside his right nostril.

It wasn't a dream: it was nothing less than a time-lapse film of Silber's face and its vicissitudes over the course of a lifetime. He explained the logistics to me the following evening when I intercepted his after-dinner walk. Once a day, every day, from the day my friend was born, his father had sat his son in front of the same baby blue backdrop, humored or browbeaten him into the same neutral expression, adjusted his head like a barber to the same forthright angle (the one favored in graduation portraits to suggest that the graduate is facing boldly his or her future), and squeezed the bulb. Skillful editing had done the rest.

Silber, who'd continued the ritual himself for almost twenty years after his father's death, had finally abandoned the film — or decided it was finished — the day he turned forty: that, he said, had been his birthday present to *himself* (one of the forbearing people, after all, who'd put up with him for another year). He said he was tired of the daily photo shoot, and also that he didn't like what was happening to his face. ("I'm not talking about aging, either.")*

---

* Mr. Silber hadn't intended the movie to span forty years: it was meant to end the day of Simon's historic debut at Carnegie Hall, which in his father's vivid vision of the future was scheduled to occur early in 1979, when the pianist was twenty and fresh from an attention-getting victory in the Erlenmeyer Competition. A comically elaborate cinematic "treatment" in Mr. Silber's journal, complete with storyboarding, reveals that he had planned to film parts of the certain-to-be-legendary concert and to graft the footage onto the end of *My Face,* framing his first concert shot — a close-up headshot — so that it would segue seamlessly from the last image of the time-lapse film. The camera would slowly pull back and *My Face* would metamorphose "as if by magic" into real-time footage of Simon approaching the end of the endless slow movement of the *Hammerklavier* Sonata (which movement would've played, though at a lower volume, barely audible, throughout the time-lapse sequence). The camera would dwell for a minute on a midrange view of Simon at the Steinway, zoom in on his hands, then cut to a reaction shot of the enraptured audience. Next would come a jump cut to the thundering finale, followed by a thunderous standing ovation — and then a cut to Mr. Silber, also standing (in a white lab coat, as likely as not), in front of their house in Forest City (but

In the background of each shot, in the upper left-hand corner, is a legible tear-away calendar. At twenty-four frames per second, the calendar's date advances too fast to be more than a blur (like time itself, when you scan the past too quickly), but by viewing the movie frame by frame, it is possible, for anybody with nothing better to do, to find the image corresponding to a given day — to find Silber, for example, as he looked (relieved) on the day his father died, or to ascertain (to the week* if not the day) the point where he grew up, if "growing up" is understood to mean setting your jaw, once and for all, and resolving to endure a life you no longer expect to enjoy.

Viewed at twenty-four frames per second, the film is just over ten minutes long. As for the soundtrack on your disc, the piece contains no chords, only individual notes, one for each day in Silber's life up to age forty, or 14,610 in all, minus about a dozen days on which, for one reason or another, he didn't sit for a photograph. Those days are represented by rests, but extremely brief ones, since in order to keep pace with the images, Silber had to perform a phenomenal twenty-four notes per second.

Judging from old clippings in a scrapbook Helen showed me, her brother had started out as a slow-tempo pianist. After one particular concert given when Silber was seventeen — an hourlong performance of Chopin's "Minute" waltz — a critic for the *Forest City Ranger* had suggested that the performer lacked the technique to play any faster, and even went so far as to call him "the pianistic equivalent of a hunt-and-peck typist."

---

with "applause still audible, indeed redoubled"), expounding his theories (see *Our Father*) and taking credit for his son's achievement. Just as the Suzuki method was first introduced to music teachers in America by means of an amazing movie (see, again, *Our Father*), so too would the Silber method be.

And why had our composer continued sitting daily for his father's film, once his father was no longer alive to compel him? Evidently Silber had sense enough to know just what a special document it was. More than once, in fact — and rather tactlessly, I thought — he called the film his "*true* biography." His ultimate abandonment, less than a year before his death, of that biography (or rather physiography) seems ominous in retrospect.

* January 14–January 22, 1979; see "Selections from *My Life*" (Disc Two).

Such insinuations must have incensed our composer, to judge by a no-less-bewildered review of his *next* recital, at which he raced through Beethoven's last five sonatas — more than two hours of music at the hands of most pianists — in *less* than an hour. At subsequent recitals, he set speed records that still stand for Bach's *French Suites* and Liszt's *Sonata in B Minor*.

Even so, Silber admitted that not even he could have performed *My Face* live at soundtrack speed — the speed at which it is heard on your disc, thanks to the magic of the recording studio. Although the piece may sound like just another frantic perpetuum mobile, a crowd-pleasing series of scales and runs, the composer claimed (and is borne out by the score) that the distance between successive notes was determined not — as usual in virtuoso pieces — by considerations of fingering, but solely by the emotional distance traversed by Silber between the days in question, as measured by the corresponding photographs. And not even Silber could move his hands up and down the keyboard fast enough to plot his change of moods, from one day to the next, at a rate of twenty-four per second. What matter are the intervals between the notes, however, and not the notes themselves, so we must discount Silber's claim that the time-lapse film, with its moment-for-moment correlation between image and sound, would serve future musicologists as a Rosetta stone to his music. For such a key to the composer's private language — a key that, if it doesn't open the door, at any rate fits in the lock — one must consult his musical diary, as in due time we will.

10. *Ode to the West Wind*          11:11

I first heard this piece, one windy night, in circumstances worth recounting here. On November 21, 1998, I went to bed, as always, at 11:59 P.M., but found myself awake again a little after 1:00, listening to faint piano music. I glared at the ceiling: sometimes I suspected my upstairs neighbor — a certain Mr.

Stickney, according to his mailbox — of playing his Beethoven solely to annoy me. If I returned from the library, say, entering our rooming house on tiptoe and closing doors as stealthily as possible, I might hear, from above, when I got to my room, the thousand strings of the Longines Symphonette, but as soon as I unwittingly alerted Mr. Stickney to my presence by coughing or turning on my TV set or programming my microwave to heat a frozen dinner, he'd promptly switch to the *Moonlight* Sonata, sometimes turning up the volume too, for an effect more solar than lunar. I had complained to our landlady — Silber's sister, Helen — but she wasn't sympathetic: as long as Mr. Stickney didn't play his music late at night, she said, I had no right to silence him. Who was I, she wondered, to act as an arbiter of musical taste? Most people, she reminded me, happen to *like* the *Moonlight* Sonata. I hung up with the sense that she was friends, or friendly, anyhow, with Mr. Stickney, who'd probably lived there forever. For a while I fantasized about beating him up: I'd seen him at the mailboxes once or twice, and he was shorter than I am.

Although I could put a name and a face to the music, I'd yet to speak to their owner. So far the only fellow lodger I had been unable to evade a conversation with was my next-door neighbor Billy, who lived on pop and snack cakes, laughed aloud at sitcoms, and sported a bicycle helmet indoors and out, though as far as I could tell he didn't own a bike. According to him, Mr. Stickney was a substitute teacher at the local junior high, though they must not have used him much, since even in the daytime he was almost always home and listening to music.

I, too, played my music whenever I was home, but that was mainly to mask other noises, especially Mr. Stickney's. Deep down I knew that silence would've been better to work by, if only I could afford it. Sometimes I'd notice a sudden surge in my writing when a record ended, like the surge in water pressure at the bathroom sink when the toilet tank finishes refilling, as if the music — even if I'd ceased to hear it — had been diverting a substantial fraction of my attention. As if my neighbor (and his predecessors in half a dozen other thin-walled rooming houses and barely partitioned apartments) were the real reason for my failure.

Several times in recent weeks I'd been on the point of going upstairs to complain about the Beethoven, but so far I hadn't, for the same reason that so many people hesitate to confront a noisy neighbor: I was afraid to personalize the nuisance, since if the person behind it proved to be rude or unreasonable, the noise I'd somehow borne till now would thenceforth be unbearable. Till now, though, my neighbor had always called it a night by eleven P.M. This time he had crossed the line. The music wasn't loud — it was barely audible — but that I could hear it at all, at this hour, meant it was too loud to tolerate. And I was about to stomp upstairs, pound on the door, and complain — to insist on my right, at that hour ("It's 1:17!"), to absolute silence, when, at 1:17 by my clock radio, I realized that it was my own radio I was hearing: hours ago I'd turned the volume down during a talk break, and then forgotten that the thing was on. Happy to have been, for once, my own worst enemy, I turned off the radio, then turned it back on and back up, wondering how I could have mistaken this series of random notes (all falling within the same octave, C to c′) in sudden clumsy fits, or fitful clumps, for Beethoven at his best-loved.

A minute later the music stopped and the suave announcer identified the work as "our own Simon Silber's answer to the famous Shelley poem 'Ode to the West Wind.'" According to legend (continued the announcer), Silber had composed *his* ode, on five successive nights in November '91, by transcribing his next-door neighbor's wind chimes. The announcer added that exactly seven years ago, days after the piece was completed, its composer had been convicted of stealing the chimes in question "so that he wouldn't have to listen to them anymore."

I'd heard that rumor before but had always dismissed it,

though Silber made no secret of hating wind chimes. More than once in the course of our walks I'd seen him wince and glare at some neighbor's tinkling porch. Back in '91, it seems, the discount store on Main Street had sold these chimes — chrome-plated tubes cut to eight different lengths — for 97 cents a set, and for a while there every other house in town had sported them, to Silber's dismay: according to him, the tubes were each a sixteenth of an inch too long, and in consequence all the notes were flat. (The recording of *Ode* on your disc was performed on a carefully de-tuned, or re-tuned, piano.\*) That, insisted Silber, was "obviously" why the 97-Cent Store had sold the chimes so cheap, though in fact only someone with perfect pitch, like Silber himself, could have heard the defect without a pitch pipe. Though he was usually able, on walks, to tune out the ill-tempered chimes together with everything else, sometimes on windy nights he found the noise so nerve-racking that he had to stay indoors.

I mentioned the broadcast to Silber the next day when I ran into him on Main Street on my way to the supermarket — an errand I didn't complete because Silber happened to be headed in the opposite direction. (Some days I got rerouted like that more than once, since Forest City was a small town and Silber the town's most visible pedestrian. Unable to think except on the move, he spent more time walking around than anyone else I'd ever met; he taught me everything I know about walking, aside from the rudiments of course. Well, I wouldn't have been

---

\* Silber told me once that he always had his pianos tuned sharp, for the same reason that he got his hair cut short: so he could hold off longer before doing it again. Only the piano in the little studio above his garage, where he recorded his music for posterity, was tuned right. Silber didn't really mind noise per se, no matter how discordant, so much as *other people's* noises. I never got to hear the out-of-tune pianos, but they must've been much sharper than those chimes were flat, since even Silber's tin-eared, business-minded sister heard the sharpness. Soon after he hired me, he called her from the Bean to discuss the posthumous arrangements (just in case he died abruptly, as he lived in fear of doing) for the biography and a boxed set of his works. At one point I heard him reassuring her: "Don't worry — this one [the piano in his studio, presumably] isn't as sharp."

writing a book about him in the first place if I hadn't been a tagalong at heart.) Did he know he'd been on the radio last night? Silber sighed and said that for twenty years now he'd submitted a tape of each new work to KDOA, but that except for his *Ode,* which they played every year, and *Crows,* which they had recently given its broadcast premiere, they refused to air his music. (It will be noted that Silber's method in *Ode* and in *Crows* is identical; in both cases, the artistic results are of less interest to this listener than the psychological compulsion that led the composer again and again to take as his raw material the very noises that annoyed him — have I mentioned that he hated birdsong even more than wind chimes? — to the point of madness.)

When I asked Silber why KDOA played *Ode* — why that one work — he shrugged. I mentioned the rumor the station was propagating.

"I don't want to talk about that."

"But —"

But he had started humming something from *Kreisleriana.* One of the more exasperating aspects of my job was that, though only too happy to talk about himself, Silber decided which parts of that self and its past were discussed. As soon as word got out that I was writing his biography, his townspeople began to bombard me with rumors — in the silent-study room at the public library, in the checkout line at Food Town — but Silber would not comment on those rumors. When asked a question that he hadn't wanted to be asked, he would fall silent, or rather stop talking and start humming. *Had* he been arrested, years ago, for stealing wind chimes? Had he once been in a mental institution? Had he been — was he still? — under suspicion of arson? Why did the kids on his block all fear and mythologize him, and what kernel of truth had inspired their wild mistruths, assuming he *didn't* eat cats and dogs, say, or hoard his own feces in mason jars, labeled and dated, down in the basement? The closer I felt myself drawing to any interesting truth about Silber, the less he talked and the louder he hummed, and far from illuminating some dark secret, I had to content myself, time after time, with inferring its existence the same way astronomers infer a black hole from the misbehavior of light in its vicinity.

The next morning, anyhow, I headed over to the library, where I'd been doing most of my writing, and where I'd discovered that back issues of the *Forest City Ranger* were preserved on microfilm. I found the reel for the week of November 17 to November 24, 1991, and threaded it into the viewer. Sure enough, the top story for November 23 was headlined "Local 'Composer' Convicted of Theft." The defendant, pronounced guilty of stealing wind chimes from his next-door neighbor's porch and from the front porches of seven other houses along the route of his after-dinner walk, had been ordered to return and rehang the stolen goods. He'd also been sentenced to a semester of community service: teaching an ear-training class at the elementary school.

Armed with a white-on-black photocopy of the article, I ambushed my employer that evening at 8:07 at the corner of Thirteenth and Tree. He'd forbidden me the day he hired me to set foot on his property (lest I disrupt him at a crucial moment, like the acquaintance who dropped in on Coleridge as the poet was composing "Kubla Khan,"), and since he'd also rigged his answering machine to intercept incoming calls in silence — and since he'd then forget for days on end to check his messages — the best way to reach him, when I really needed to, was to intercept his nightly walk, which like his weekly drive had a fixed route.* Since he also followed a rigid schedule, a block-by-block timetable, I always knew exactly where to find him, rain or shine, at 8:07, 8:18, or 8:54 P.M.

---

* Silber's first biographer conjectured that the route of our composer's after-dinner walk had an autobiographical significance, that it was no more or less than a nightly review of the walker's childhood and its key locations — the library, the candy store, the houses of ex-friends, etc. I remain unpersuaded. When you live in a town all your life, every inch of every block must come to have *some* personal association.

Silber scanned the flimsy photocopy, scowled, and abruptly crumpled it into a ball.

"But I'm your biographer!"

"The only reason you're working for me," he said slowly, as if talking to a retarded person, "is that my *first* biographer kept sniffing around like that." He nodded back over his shoulder, where he'd tossed the wadded sheet.

"I'm sorry." On agreeing to write a book about him three months earlier, I'd asked Silber about Tom, the first biographer, but Silber said, "Never mind him." I'd asked to see Tom's manuscript (since that manuscript, like mine, was presumably its subject's property), but Silber had refused, not wanting me to build on Tom's foundation but to start again from scratch, excavating my own hole without unearthing too much dirt. But it wasn't always easy to predict which parts of his past he would object to my unearthing. He often made fun of his sister's obsession with respectability, and once said he didn't mind appearing — to his townspeople and to posterity — as a mad genius à la Schumann, but that he didn't want to look like "just another two-bit lunatic." I'm still not certain I get the distinction, but my sense was that in the case of the wind-chime episode, he was less ashamed of the crime itself than of the punishment he'd acquiesced to. The news item I'd shown him was in three columns, and it wasn't till he'd reached the top of the third, where it described his humiliating "sentence," that Silber had gotten upset.

"So no more microfilm," he concluded.

I apologized again but secretly resolved thenceforth to keep two books, like a dishonest businessman: sure, I'd write the insipid hagiography I was being paid to write, but I'd also find out the truth about Silber, and tell it in a thoroughly *un*authorized biography. I had been saving the censored index cards, and that night I sorted them back into their original twelve topics and filed them in a shoebox I labeled "The Thirteenth Stack" — my working title for the unauthorized biography.

From then on, any censored cards went in that box, so I can say that Silber himself selected the contents of the shadow biography: everything he cut from the official version, and *only* what he cut (or would've cut, in the case of cards I knew better than to show him in the first place), was guaranteed a place in the unofficial by virtue of his very desire to suppress it. The second, secret portrait would be a sort of photographic negative of the official publicity shot, reversing the distribution of light and shadow. It didn't take a genius to guess which one would sell better.

# Disc Two

### 1. *The Not-So-Identical Twins*            6:56

By December it was cold enough that I could always tell, on returning to the rooming house, which of my fellow bachelors were home by consulting the row of green enameled gas meters out front, since each of us had his own separately metered gas-fueled heater, and to save on utility costs, each of us turned off his heat when he headed out. Sometimes I pretended that each meter measured the passage of time* itself in the corresponding apartment, sometimes the presence and progress of life. If, at any rate, the second meter from the right registered a flow of gas, I knew that my upstairs neighbor was home, ready to torment me with favorite Beethoven sonatas, and rather than enter the building, I would cross the street and kill an hour at the Bean before returning to reread the meter. It was at the Bean, one cold October day, that I first heard *The Not-So-Identical Twins.*

That morning I'd sat up abruptly from a dream in which my employer took off his shoes and demonstrated his ability to play piano with his toes; he was about to perform a four-handed sonata all by himself when I woke to the sound of the

---

* We were also billed for electricity, and I made a point of unplugging my clock as well, when I left the building for any length of time, though that meant that when I returned I not only had to plug it back in but to reset it.

*Moonlight* Sonata. I'd been having all kinds of musical night-mares since moving to Forest City, and often I discovered on awakening that I hadn't escaped the music as simply as that. Rather than try to eat breakfast by moonlight, I got dressed and went over to the Bean.

The coffeehouse was always busy at that hour, and that day the only open table was the wobbly one by the upright piano. I bought a mug of coffee and a sticky bun and sat down with my back to the piano: no one ever played it, but I was beginning to hate all pianos on sight. By wedging several packets of artificial sweetener beneath the shortest of my table's legs, I was almost able to eliminate the wobble, almost. Finally I straightened up, took a sip of coffee, and was lifting the bun to my mouth when I heard a sudden clamor from the piano.

I spun around in fury and was surprised to see my employer standing, not six feet away, at the keyboard with his back to me. I was even more surprised to see that he was wearing a black leather jacket with BADASS emblazoned in red on its back, and most surprised of all to see a pair of drumsticks protruding from the left hip pocket of his grimy jeans: Silber always claimed to hate percussion instruments, though technically, of course, the piano is just that, as no one could help but be reminded, that morning at the Bean, by the violence of Silber's playing. He seemed determined to inflict pain with every note — though the piece, I realized, was a dreamy and delicate Schumann miniature (*Traumerei*, in fact) amplified out of all recognition. As he played, Silber bobbed and wove his head ecstatically in a sort of cross between nodding "yes" and shaking "no" — an equivocation as tricky as drawing good diagonals with an Etch-A-Sketch. Twice a second I was treated to a glimpse of his face in profile (left, right, left, right), and it looked like he was enjoying the noise.

When he finished with Schumann, he paused for a moment, as if for applause (customers were either scowling or ignoring him), then embarked on a piece I had never heard before. I took it for some kind of call and response, with the right hand trying but failing painfully to repeat, on the tinkly top octave of the keyboard, the left hand's progressively more complicated utterances. Maybe Silber was upset, but that alone couldn't account for the right hand's missteps, since it had had no trouble with the Schumann, and his *left* hand was as nimble as ever.

When he finished, seven endless minutes later, I said, "Silber?"

"Yeah?" Slowly, insolently, he turned around and stared at me with even more contempt than I had come to expect from my employer. He hadn't shaven recently, and I was wondering if it was alcohol I smelled when he demanded: "Who the hell are *you*?"

"Oh." I'd heard rumors of an identical twin, though the first time I had asked my employer if there were any brothers, he'd said: "Sorry, the subject's off-limits." So I'd changed the subject and resigned myself to writing the biography of a man who refused to talk about his siblings. And yet here was one now, a brother who must know all kinds of secrets about the composer, and who might not be as close-mouthed as their sister was proving to be.

"Thought I was Simon, huh? Don't worry — not even Helen can tell us apart half the time. So how do you know my rich asshole of a brother?"

I explained that I was writing that asshole's biography.

"Oh — you're the one I'm not supposed to talk to. Look, we gotta talk. I can tell you everything you need to know about him: he's my fucking *brother*. Gotta run, though — can you meet me at the Warthog in an hour?"

The Warthog was a bar at the corner of Tenth and Main. Walking there an hour later, I was still marveling at the resemblance between Simon and his brother, who claimed his name was Scooter. Granted, they had identical genes, but from the rumors concerning Silber's evil twin, I had pictured a muscle-bound thug.

As always, there were several motorcycles parked outside the Warthog — one reason I had never set foot inside till now. As I entered, the jukebox was blaring a song about a barmaid with a bad crush on a sailor. I sat in the booth farthest from the music, ordered a diet cola, and tried, as I waited for Scooter, to ignore the stares (less hostile than incredulous) of the other patrons. I sat through a song that compared the singer's lust to a 103-degree fever; a song about a fugitive from justice, on the lam because of some unspecified crime; and a song whose singer said goodbye to his woman because, as much as he still loved her, his freewheeling nature just wouldn't let him stay put, and the time had come for him to move on. In the middle of a song about a telepathic trucker, Scooter slid into the seat across from me with a brimming pitcher of urine-colored liquid and two filthy glasses. (My cola still hadn't arrived.) He got out his drumsticks and played a paradiddle on the puddled tabletop.* Then he poured our pints and said, "By the way — you're buying, Professor." He'd already settled on a nickname for me. (As for his — almost as old as he was — it alluded to his favorite mode of locomotion as a boy; his real name was Peter.)

Once I got over the initial shock of Scooter's rudeness, I found him outright affable — so affable, in fact, that he was hard to talk to because his drinking buddies were forever interrupting. He seemed to be everybody's friend, and half a dozen times he put our interview on hold to greet some hulking felon as enthusiastically as if they'd known each other all their lives, though most of them, he later said, he'd met only the day before. Scooter was as social as his twin was anti-, so maybe sociability has more to do with alcohol than with heredity. On hearing that I lived in the same dismal rooming house — the same room, in fact — as the first biographer (who'd befriended Scooter too), he brought down his initial asking price ("a buck a fact") for information about Simon: all he wanted in exchange was beer. He didn't even want *good* beer. I gathered

---

* Silber later told me that his brother loved a hullabaloo of any kind and had a diabolical ability to fashion a noisemaker from whatever was at hand, on one occasion exceeding a hundred decibels with nothing more than a ball of yarn, a box of Q-Tips, and a bag of marshmallows.

that he was living off an allowance from his sister, blackmailing her with the threat of further tarnishing the family image, if that was possible. In exchange for his subsidy, Scooter was expected to stay out of Forest City altogether, and not to do anything elsewhere that would find its way into the *Forest City Ranger*. He officially resided in Missoula, in a trailer park, but it sounded like he spent most of his time on the road — drinking, chasing women, breaking laws, and raising hell.

Scooter provided me with all kinds of tales of his twin's more recent antics — tales I've included, where appropriate, in these liner notes — but he seemed even more reluctant than Silber himself to talk about their childhood, cheerfully resisting my attempts to steer the conversation in that direction. My initial sense was that he'd put the past behind him, and that that was why he struck me as the sanest and the sweetest of the Silbers. Not that he wouldn't have strangled his own grandmother if he thought he stood to profit from her death, but except for selfish motives he wouldn't hurt a fly. (Speaking of grandparents, Scooter revealed (as Simon refused to) the secret of the Silber family fortune: back in the forties their father's father had patented a revolutionary sewage-treatment process, and though he'd later sold that process to a German firm, the proceeds had been enough to buy a life of cultured ease for his son and then for our composer.)

I, who never drank at all, wound up getting "loaded" before lunch. I was still a little drunk when I met Silber at the Bean that afternoon to talk about the book. When I told him what I'd done that morning, he slammed his fist down on the wobbly table hard enough to spill my coffee and to turn the heads of other patrons. At first I assumed that Silber, like Helen, was simply ashamed of their brother, and that his hatred was really self-hatred, as if Scooter were the shadow of futility that Silber had spent his life fleeing. After all, it must be hard to keep telling yourself you're a genius when your identical twin so clearly isn't. Silber even forbade me to mention in the book that the two *were* identical twins. He would've preferred that I not mention Scooter at all. As a rule, he refused to talk about his brother, and hadn't communicated with him in years unless one counted a recent hate letter he'd absentmindedly sent to Scooter instead of to Helen, its intended target.*

But that doesn't explain why my employer threatened to fire me if ever *I* communicated with Scooter again. No, even before I learned the history of their enmity, I sensed that it was rooted in the distant past — that the animosities that made them bare their teeth were older than those teeth themselves. All three siblings hated one another, for that matter, but where Simon and Helen had hammered out a surly peace agreement early on — of necessity, since they'd both decided to remain in Forest City — Simon and Scooter were sworn enemies for life.

And insofar as Silber's hatred of his brother wasn't just a nursing of old grudges, its main cause wasn't shame (I soon realized) but *envy:* Scooter was the son who had gotten away, the one who'd escaped Forest City. Like a jaded prince idealizing paupers, our composer sometimes yearned, and more and more as years went by, to swap lives with Scooter — to give up his big house and bigger ambitions in exchange for his brother's freedom and lack of ambition. Silber's twin — small-time thief and low-grade alcoholic — aroused all kinds of pitiable insecurities in my employer, as if Silber were afraid I'd quit my job and (in exchange for a stolen Mercedes?) write about Scooter instead. With the anxious scorn of a jealous lover denouncing a rival, Silber warned me about Scooter's criminality, though I later saw his rap sheet and discovered that most of his crimes (if we discount a penchant for car theft) were of the endearingly victimless variety: public drunkenness, public urination, reckless endangerment, disorderly behavior. I hadn't seen his rap sheet in December '98, though, and of course his brother's warnings served only to increase my fascination with him, giving him an aura of danger that that silly leather jacket never could've generated all by itself. Scooter's recklessness was

---

* According to Silber, though, all of his letters were really addressed to posterity, in care of this or that irrelevant contemporary.

catching, and — notwithstanding Silber's threat — I met him again at the Warthog the following day.

Our second talk was unremarkable till Scooter said something about Simon being so busy playing piano as a kid that he'd never learned how to live.

"But *you* must've spent a lot of time at the piano too," I said, "to play as well as you do now."

I'd said the wrong thing: Scooter fell silent, stared at his hands, and didn't seem to hear me when I spoke to him ("Scooter? . . . Scooter, you okay?" — it was like calling down a mineshaft). For a minute there, he looked as tired and unhappy as anyone I'd ever seen. And then he snapped out of it, but not before I'd understood that his rowdy, gregarious, publicly pissing persona was not exactly an act, but an ideal — an ideal of goodness, perhaps — that took a constant effort to live up to, since if such behavior is first or second nature to some people, it could never be so to a Silber. As so often, it was seeing someone at his most unhappy that alerted me to unsuspected depths in the wading pool of his personality.

I got a clearer view of those depths a few minutes later. We'd resumed our conversation — which suddenly felt carefully, painstakingly lighthearted — and I was telling Scooter about my aphorisms when he interrupted:

"That thing you heard me playing yesterday, after the Schumann — you realize, Professor, that it's *supposed* to sound like that. That's how Simon wrote it." And he went on to tell me all about the odd piece he'd played at the Bean, and about the fifteen years of brotherly hate that had culminated in its composition.

According to Scooter (and as far as I can ascertain, he was telling the truth — lying was another crime he seldom stooped to except for selfish motives), he had been the victim, and Simon the victor, of an elaborate nature-versus-nurture experiment conducted by their father: by beating his brother out of the womb by a minute or two, Simon had not only won the fortune accruing to a firstborn son upon the death of a rich and old-fashioned father, but had also selected himself as the son whom Mr. Silber, while alive, would educate according to the "Preparation," an insanely rigorous pedagogical method of his own devising, and one that, if followed to the letter, was certain — so Mr. Silber believed — to produce a world-class musician. I'll say more about this method later (see *Our Father*); for now, it's enough to know that it dictated — and down to the last detail — every aspect of Silber's upbringing, from the layout of his bedroom to his leisure options when he wasn't making music.

Silber's grooming for greatness had begun when he was born, with actual piano lessons from his father ensuing two years later. Scooter, the control in this experiment, began conventional piano lessons the day he turned four — the youngest age at which the town's best teacher, Signor Pergolesi, would accept pupils. Scooter was required to practice two hours a day, but otherwise was left to do as he pleased. In most respects he had a much freer childhood than Simon.

But not a happier. Scooter claimed his life had clouded over once and for all with the death of his mother when the twins were three, but the darkest clouds seem to have blown in a year later, when it looked like Scooter might refute his father's theories by surpassing Simon at the keyboard. Though Simon had a two-year head start (four years if one counts the supposedly crucial groundwork of the pre-piano years), Scooter had caught up with him within a few months of starting lessons. At four, the twins were old enough to understand at once that they were in a deadly earnest rivalry, and that their father was rooting for Simon. This knowledge, which might have been expected to favor the favorite (and to such a degree as to belie any pretext of testing two educational models on a fair footing), seemed to help Scooter instead. The helpless desire to win his father over drove him to work at his music with an inhuman intensity that not even the Preparation could inspire in his golden twin. And Scooter had *almost* succeeded in usurping Simon by getting off to such a fast start that his father briefly considered switching everything around, using Scooter to show off the Preparation and making Simon the control, but by that point it was already too late to change his bet, or not unless he wanted to repudiate his theory as to the key importance of the early years. It was simpler to dismiss Scooter's rapid progress as beginner's luck. Mr. Silber may have had an inkling, too — though if so it didn't merit a mention in his journal — of the sibling dynamic at work, and may have feared that even if he did change horses in midstream, whichever one he saddled with his favor would always be the slower.

Within months, in any case, poor Scooter had understood that he wasn't *allowed* to win. His predestined role in life, the one his father had ordained and set his heart on, was to fail, to fall short of Simon. Mr. Silber wanted that as ardently for Scooter as he wanted Simon to succeed. The obvious solution would've been to quit, to give up on music altogether, even knowing that it was only as a musician that he could ever matter to his father. To give up on his father, then, and resign himself to orphanhood. But even that sad option was forbidden Scooter: the experiment needed a control, so Scooter was compelled, year after year, to continue taking lessons, practicing hard and doing his best — and yet somehow contriving to fall short of Simon, though they had the same genes and Simon was being trained by a lunatic.

Scooter probably would've gone insane himself if his father hadn't finally permitted — or rather commanded — him to quit the day he turned fifteen. A few weeks earlier, in a disastrous attempt to motivate Simon, Mr. Silber had pretended to change his mind after all, officially pronouncing Scooter the new favorite, the one who'd make his father famous. And Scooter had risen to the occasion, overtaking Simon almost overnight, but his father hadn't really meant it; Mr. Silber was only messing with Simon's head, as one says nowadays, and seemed not even to notice that he was thereby messing with Scooter's too. There could be no question, at that point, of changing favorites. Even if Scooter had gone on to be the greatest pianist of his day, there was no way his father could claim him as a product of the Preparation.

As for Simon, rather than outdoing himself in an effort to regain his father's favor, he had become severely depressed. Suddenly Scooter was so clearly the better pianist that not even his twin could delude himself on that score, and he responded by playing worse and worse from one day to the next, even after their father relented, reinstated Simon as the favorite, and made it clear to Scooter that he was once again forbidden to surpass his brother. Finally, in a frantic attempt to arrest Simon's tailspin, Mr. Silber had ordered Scooter to give up piano forever, whereupon Simon had in fact rallied, while Scooter had lapsed into the alcoholic torpor in which I found him twenty-five years later. The experiment no longer had a control, but that was a small price to pay, considering that Mr. Silber's ill-judged gambit had almost put an end to Simon's performing career even before it began, in addition to making our composer profoundly unhappy for a few weeks there.

But art is born of suffering — like babies, for that matter, according to their mothers — and the pain of seeming briefly to have lost his father's favor somehow prompted Simon to produce his first substantial composition, admittedly a rather mean-spirited one, *The Not-So-Identical Twins.* In this piece (of which I had heard Scooter's mirror-image transposition*

---

* Though they liked to use the left/right opposition as a handy emblem of their rivalry, Simon and Scooter themselves were both left-handed. Soon after they were born — as soon as it was determined that the twins were "lefties" — their father (a musician and left-hander in his own right) had commissioned a left-handed *piano,* a custom-built model with keyboard reversed, so that the high note was at the far left for a change. (Since the most difficult fingering, he'd reasoned, is mainly in the treble clef, left-handers are at a disadvantage with a standard piano — one more object built for, and taken for granted by, the right-handed majority.) By the time the piano finally arrived a year later, though, Mr. Silber had thought the better of training Simon on such an instrument: he didn't want his son to become famous as an oddity, a novelty. And he knew that Simon would be obliged to use right-handed pianos in the competitions that then as now were the springiest springboards to stardom for young pianists. In any case, the long-awaited instrument proved to be a disappointment: though it had cost more than a good "right-handed" model, its ac-

that morning at the Bean), the right hand plays a series of virtuoso figures, and after each the left attempts to play the same
tune, at a much slower tempo, in plodding whole notes on the
bottom octave of the keyboard (a depth intended to suggest
the thickness of a mental defective's voice?), purposely botch-
ing certain notes for comic effect. Though Silber was only
fourteen when he composed it, his brother would never forgive him. The composer himself would probably not have ap-
proved the inclusion of *Twins* in this boxed set, but in my
opinion the piece's historical interest more than makes up for
its utter lack of artistic merit.

After our second talk at the Warthog, Scooter and I made
plans to meet a third time the following day, but he never
showed up. Brandi the barmaid was pretty sure that he'd left
town the night before. A few nights later, though, I got a call as
I was changing into my pajamas: "Norm, it's Scooter. Listen,
I got some more dirt on my brother — really compromising
stuff."

"Oh, you're still in town. Weren't we supposed to meet again
the other day?"

A pause, and then, "Oh, sorry — I forgot. Anyhow, I got this
really confidential stuff about my brother. Maybe I shouldn't
even show it to you. I mean, it would really make him look *bad*
if you put it in your book."

"What is it?"

"Can't tell you over the phone — it's too sensitive. It could
even get him arrested. Actually, I better not tell you at all. Forget I mentioned it, okay?"

---

tion and acoustics were worse than mediocre, and it was soon banished to the
lumber room beyond the blue piano room, though for the next five or six
years, it was rolled out every so often to entertain guests with a stunt: the twins
would perform the same easy piece ("Me and My Shadow") at the same time,
side by side at two pianos (Scooter always at the lefty), creating the illusion of
a single Silber performing alongside his reflection in a mirror. Scooter added
that, throughout their childhood, Simon had been forbidden to lay a finger on
the backward piano, lest it superimpose an inverted and potentially distracting
— potentially disastrous — set of key-to-note associations on the set that must
be second nature to a pianist.

"No, no, wait! I'll pay you!"

Finally, in exchange for fifty dollars, he agreed to meet me — not at the Warthog this time, but at the convenience store on Main Street. I put my clothes back on and walked over to the KwikStop, pausing en route at a cash machine, since I'd promised to pay cash.

I found my informant out front, just beyond the jurisdiction of the sensor opening the automatic door, in a different leather jacket, even rattier than the other one. I handed him the money and he handed me a sealed envelope, disappointingly light for what it had cost.

"This better be worth it."

"Don't worry — it was." And he walked away across the parking lot, not even waiting for me to open the envelope.

When I did, I found a scrap of staff paper with a penciled message in my employer's handwriting: "I KNEW I COULDN'T TRUST YOU." I heard an engine gunning and looked up to see Silber calmly heading elsewhere in his red convertible.


## 2. *Norm's Norm*                                     3:01

Christmas was coming and I still hadn't spoken to Mr. Stickney. I knew who he was: a little man about my age, with a little potbelly, a bald spot, and a body odor so tenacious that his students couldn't very well be faulted for referring to him (and I understand they did) as Mr. Stinky. But we hadn't spoken. Once or twice, as we passed in the lobby, he'd looked like he wanted to strike up a conversation but was too intimidated by my scowl; and one evening at the Bean I caught him gazing at me, across the crowded room, with what I could've sworn was admiration, but I told myself I was seeing things (as I'd done, over the years, in the case of several evident admirers: more than once, what I'd taken for physical attraction, or intellectual

respect, or all-around approval, had proven anything but —
and of course no one had *ever* accorded me as much admiration as I felt I deserved).

We finally introduced ourselves, according to my diary, on
the evening of December 17. I'd come home from the library in
a bad mood — I'd been reprimanded in front of other patrons
for yawning aloud, if you please, in the Quiet Room — only to
find the *Moonlight* Sonata in full effect overhead. I couldn't
even yawn without a reprimand, yet was besieged on every side
by other people's noises. Clenching my jaw, I began to make
dinner, but as I tried to open a can of mushroom soup, my
dinky hand-powered can opener broke, one of its chrome-
plated handles snapping off as soon as I'd punctured the lid,
and in a sudden burst of fury at the life I'd settled for, I raced
upstairs resolved to stop the music — if need be, by force. It
took all my self-restraint to knock and not pound.

"Look," I said, when Mr. Stickney opened the door with a
book in one hand and a little canister of flavored coffee in the
other, "I'm an easygoing guy, but —" But at that point I broke
off, struck by the photograph on the back of his book. There
was something very familiar about the intelligent and unfor-
giving face that occupied the whole back cover, even the zone
where you tend to find blurbs. But of course: it was mine. The
face and the book. Mr. Stickney had been reading *So I Gather,*
my neglected book of aphorisms. I was face to face with an actual Reader.

"*Some people shudder to think, and some think in order to
shudder,*" he said, quoting me from memory. Behind him,
the *Moonlight* Sonata wove its spell. My discerning neighbor
looked at me expectantly, and reverently — I'd been right, for
once, about an evident admirer. "I'm Gordon," he said, ex-
tending his hand.

I shook it and said "Norm" and then, "Do you have a can
opener I could borrow?"

"You bet!" Gordon fetched his opener (an electric model, so

it might've made more sense for me to fetch my can and open it in his room), then said, "I was just making some gourmet hazelnut coffee — care for a cup?"

I hesitated, dreading some kind of grotesque advance: just that week I had learned to my alarm that a rumor was afoot, in our evil-minded town, romantically linking me and my employer. But I couldn't pass up my first-ever chance to talk to a reader.

Gordon's room was very sparse and tidy. Unless one counted three school-bus yellow boxes of baking soda stationed around the room, all open, and presumably meant (I never asked) to absorb odors that Gordon was too lazy to track to their sources, or of which he himself was the source, the only decoration was a faded poster from a long-ago exhibit of hazy impressionist paintings at some faraway museum. While my host made coffee (instant, but with old-world pretensions), I reviewed his music collection. It didn't take long: substitute teachers don't earn very much, and poor Gordon owned just eight recordings, all CDs, all but one in the easy listening genre. Nothing you'd find on the jukebox at the Warthog, and nothing I'd listen to either. As I'd already surmised, he had exactly one classical recording, the one he had been forcing me to listen to, the one now playing.

After a minute, Gordon proudly handed me a sweet and foamy potion in a mug with a PBS logo — it looked like what they'd give you for the smallest pledge to rate a gift at all. "So," he said, after taking a sip from his own mug (embellished with the name of the famous newsweekly to which I already knew he subscribed, since our mailman refused to put our magazines — even highly private ones — in our mailboxes, but left them on the little table in the lobby, for everyone to see), "I've always wanted to meet a real author."

We wound up talking for more than an hour, long enough for the Beethoven CD to run its course. When the music stopped, Gordon jumped up and restarted the disc — and I realized that all these months he'd been blaring the *Moonlight* So-

*nata* not to annoy but to *impress* me. He must've heard from Helen that I was a highbrow, an authority on music, and of course a published author. (It was Helen's copy of my book he had been reading — I had given it to her as a goodwill gesture, knowing she would never read it.)

In the next couple of months I would have many more conversations with Gordon, sometimes in my room and sometimes in his. Architecturally the two rooms were identical, except that his room seemed a little smaller, possibly because the walls were thicker. Unlike my employer, who had more rooms in his house than names for colors in his vocabulary, Gordon was compelled by poverty to enjoy his favorite colors serially. Every time I saw his room the walls had been repainted; there were large solidified drops of paint below the windowsills, preserving in cross section (I'd snapped one off) the multicolored history of these changes like geological strata. I pictured the room getting smaller with every coat.

Although I didn't like his room because it smelled like Gordon, and didn't want him spending too much time in mine for fear that it would start to smell like Gordon too, we seldom spoke outside the rooming house because I was embarrassed to be seen with him.* In retrospect, I don't know what I'm more ashamed of: to have been so false a friend, or to have stooped to such a friendship in the first place, with someone I might pity but could not respect to save my life, let alone his life. But then I never really considered it a friendship (though I'm afraid he did), and after one of our chats would either — depending on the weather — congratulate myself on a good deed well done, or berate myself for having sunk so low. More than once, on leaving his room after an hour of tepid flavored coffee and insipid conversation, I felt as dejected and disgusted with myself as if I were leaving an adult movie theater. But I was lonely, and

---

* Not that I saw initially just how ridiculous he was — I didn't; I refused to. He was my first fan, and vanity induced me to think as well of him as possible: poor Gordon was all I had to point to when I asked myself, What sort of people read and admire the aphorisms of Norman Fayrewether?

sometimes so lonely as to welcome Gordon's company, for want of any better. I was like a convict reduced to eating gruel, too hungry to refuse it but unable to delude himself that he's eating something good.

I avoided poor Gordon in public, but I couldn't very well forbid him to approach me at the Bean. Once, as he was standing by my table and recounting symbol by symbol some pretentiously meaningful film he'd just seen, I realized to my chagrin that my employer had come in and was watching us with amused contempt. Gordon followed my distracted gaze, saw Silber, and scowled — by that point he'd already confided his suspicion that the composer had murdered his first biographer, who'd occupied the room I did and who like me had befriended the substitute teacher upstairs.

I was still wondering how to handle the situation when Silber turned and left without a word, though presumably he'd come in to tell me something. After that brief face-off, he went home and (the same day, I think) composed *Norm's Norm,* an obnoxious *badinage* representing me with an offensively plodding and ponderous leitmotif of whole notes; as for Gordon (whom Silber afterward referred to as "your Norm," or sometimes even "your very own Norm"), he is represented by the "puppy dog" theme from *Variations in a Minor.*

### 3. Selections from *My Life*      0:19

| December 13, 1961 | 0:03 | September 27, 1973 | 0:03 |
|---|---|---|---|
| March 11, 1964 | 0:03 | January 14, 1979 | 0:03 |
| October 27, 1966 | 0:03 | January 22, 1979 | 0:03 |
| April 1, 1969 | 0:01 | | |

All of Silber's music is autobiographical, but never more obsessively than in *My Life,* the chord-a-day diary he began keeping on his first birthday — October 17, 1959 — at his father's prompting. Throughout the second year of his life, Silber was allowed near a piano only once a day, at bedtime, when his father led him down the stairway to the Steinway in the basement and let him play a single chord. Not only was that bedtime chord the only music baby Simon was allowed to make all day (more than once he'd been punished for humming); it was the only music, too, that he got to *hear* all day, apart from whatever snatch of Beethoven happened to be playing when they reached the basement, and he looked forward to it all day long.

The following year, Mr. Silber had permitted him more time at the piano, and later (though not till Simon was eight) had allowed him to practice upstairs, but even then — and even after Mr. Silber's death — our composer had continued, every night at bedtime, to go down and play a chord summing up the day just ending.* Even as a grown man, he continued, night after night, to feel some of the same excitement he had felt at age one, and some of the dread: all his life Silber was scared of the basement. And yet in 1988, when the bedroom where he'd slept ever since his father's death suddenly became unusable (see *Annex to "My House"*), Silber had dragged his mattress down there: either he'd decided finally to face his fears, like people do on television, or else the rest of the world, the part aboveground, had caught up and was now just as frightening to Silber as the basement, which at least was quiet and cool. He still spent his nights down there when I met him ten years later.

I have several reasons for omitting *My Life* from this otherwise exhaustive compilation. For starters, the work is too long,

---

* He kept this custom up for the same reason that he continued sitting daily for a photograph: not in deference to his father's memory, but because one of the few points on which they'd agreed was that Simon was destined for greatness, one way or another, and therefore worthy of all the autobiographical attention he could lavish on himself. It is a measure of Silber's near illiteracy that his navel-gazing never took the form of a *real* — verbal — diary.

consisting as it does of more than fourteen thousand chords, each of which Silber allotted three seconds to sound and subside. In addition, *My Life* was conceived not by our composer but by his father (who supplied the title too, as if the life were his),* and not as a work of art but as a way to track his son's developing harmonic sense — a sort of sonic counterpart to the daily photograph.† Finally, I omit the piece, if piece it is, because its composer didn't see fit to record it, possibly because it wasn't finished.

Listeners will have to settle, then, for a few sample chords, as played (on the piano in my current living quarters; see — not yet, though! — *Afterthoughts*) by this biographer, and corresponding to red-letter days in the composer's past. Taken together, they should provide a rough connect-the-dots sketch of Silber's childhood.

On the afternoon of December 13, 1961, when the twins were three, their mother — Elsie — was killed by a hit-and-run driver (never apprehended) while walking home from a dentist's appointment. Silber claimed not even to remember her. Scooter remembered. According to him, his mother had been a better pianist than his father, a much better cook, and a much much better parent. Scooter said that though she had never played favorites, neither had she ever mistaken one twin for the

---

* Clara Schumann's father — mentioned more than once, and always with approval, in Mr. Silber's journal — not only scheduled her day-to-day life almost minute by minute, dictating when and for how long she took walks, for instance, but *wrote her diary for her,* in Clara's voice, throughout her childhood, expressing the feelings she ought to be feeling and thinking what should be her thoughts.

† It is clear from Mr. Silber's journal that the ritual was furthermore intended to instill a sense of awe, to make the point, night after night, that a single chord can be as fraught with feeling — can pack as big a wallop — as an entire day. Our composer's later efforts to set a day to music in real time (see *Day*) suggest, though, that the lesson never "took."

Silber said once that his father had also made him play a special chord every year on his birthday summing up his *life* to date, but those chords appear to be lost (unless they're just the *My Life* chords — none of them especially striking — for October 17).

other — unlike their father, who had gotten them wrong more often than not. Scooter also claimed that Elsie had been a "real beauty," and to prove it gave me a photograph of his parents embracing. The black-and-white snapshot is dated "1/17/58," and the photographer at whom the two appear to be laughing may be Helen (seven at the time, and still an only child). Opinions might differ as to Mrs. Silber's "beauty"; less open to debate is Mr.'s resemblance, at thirty, to our composer at that age.

I asked Silber once if he ever wondered how he might have turned out if his mother hadn't died, but he got indignant: "I *like* how I turned out." The chord the three-year-old composer played the day she died is as striking as that evening's time-lapse photograph for its lack of grief. Several explanations suggest themselves to this explainer:

1. Silber had not yet been informed of his mother's death (easier to believe if he had gone on to display more emotion the *following* day, or the day after that).

2. Silber *had* been informed, but the event had not yet registered either on his face or in his music — both of them sensitive and finely calibrated seismographs to chart his inner tremors, but both prone to interpolate a delay (ranging in length from seconds to decades, depending on the event) between input and readout.

3. Silber's grief at the death of his mother was offset by exultation at his new position as the undisputed favorite among the Silber children, since (one assumes) the mother had loved all her children equally, whereas the father always favored Simon. And like complementary colors that when mixed together yield gray, Silber's mixed emotions on that evening canceled each other out to yield that unreadable expression, that neutral pewter chord.

4. By the time of his mother's death, Silber's deepest feelings were already expressing themselves in ways his fellow humans found inscrutable, and though this chord and that photograph are not the ones we'd expect in the circumstances, we can't therefore assume that they fail altogether to acknowledge

Mrs. Silber's passing; they might have been completely different if she hadn't died.

In the interests of completeness, we had better entertain one
other possibility:

5. Silber didn't care.

On the night of March 11, 1964, five-year-old Simon played
what would remain the most ambitious chord of his career.
Knowing it might result in a spanking, he had run down to
the music room ahead of his father, jumped up on the piano
bench, and fallen across the keys in such a way as to sound all
eighty-eight at once. Silber later liked to say that that one
chord or, rather, cluster — which had in fact earned him a
spanking — anticipated everything he was later to compose for
his favorite instrument. By the time it occurred to him, he had
been playing a chord every night for upwards of four years, and
transcribing them himself for two, but this seems to have been
the first time he ever approached the piano with a *concept*. Is it
too much to call that concept his first composition? Certainly
it set the tone — hostile reception and all — for those that followed.

The chord our composer performed on October 27, 1966,
won't be audible unless you turn the volume all the way up. On
the score, the chord is marked *pppp*, though as far as I know the
quietest notation in common use is *ppp* or *pianississimo*. I asked
Silber once about that extra *p* (after spotting one on another of
his scores), and he told me that it meant the faintest sound one
can inveigle from a piano and still be said to have played it at
all. Lacking his fabled lightness of touch, I wrapped my little
tape recorder in a sock and stuck it in my sock drawer to record
the chord.

By the day in question, eight-year-old Simon had long ago
internalized his father's fear of noise. Scooter told me, for ex-

ample, that one summer evening when the twins were six, they'd been playing in the back yard, on the swing set, when a neighbor's kitten came through the hedge and started meowing — and Simon had run inside crying in terror, hands over his ears. Not till they were eight, though, did their father realize that the Preparation had been *too* successful at inducing a noise phobia — that Simon had developed an incapacitating allergy to noise. At that point, on the day this muted chord commemorates, Mr. Silber had announced that Simon had to be exposed to *more* noise, from then on, in order to build up his tolerance. Our composer didn't know yet that within the next few days his father would install a small TV set in the living room, buy Helen the canary she'd been begging for, and even allow Scooter to start practicing at home (after years of paying a hard-of-hearing neighbor to let the boy practice at her house). That first day, though, Mr. Silber had already forced our composer to listen to a neighbor's power mower, to another neighbor's dog, and finally to the ice-cream truck, making him sit out on the front steps for each ordeal, and forbidding him to put his hands over his ears. The next day the venue switched to the back steps, where Simon was compelled to sit for Scooter's gleeful, father-sanctioned detonation of a string of firecrackers.

Luckily for our composer, this experiment — of exposing him to the loudest noises handy — lasted just a week (long enough, however, to exacerbate the problem it was meant to remedy). But the TV set was allowed to stay, Helen got to keep the canary, Scooter continued to practice at home, and Simon was forbidden to seek refuge in his room — was barred from his own bedroom, in the daytime, for the rest of his odd childhood. He was also banished from the basement at that point (except at bedtime, when he still went down to play his nightly chord): from then on he practiced upstairs, aboveground, as if Mr. Silber had concluded — rightly? — that the basement was to blame for Simon's strangeness. Beethoven continued to play down there night and day, though — till the day of Mr. Silber's death — as a reminder of how the world *ought* to sound.

Silber was ten years old when, on April 1, 1969, Helen's canary died in suspicious circumstances. That afternoon, the cleaning lady (not Edna, but a no-less-antiquated predecessor) noticed, or claimed to have noticed, one of the twins slipping into his sister's bedroom, and a little later noticed that Helen's pet canary had stopped singing, but thought no more about it until Helen got home from cheerleading practice, went into her room, and came out screaming, still holding in one hand a pink-and-white pompom; in the other hand she'd held a small canary yellow thing with its head twisted 180 degrees from its normal alignment. The twins had both denied entering their sister's room, but instead of pointing fingers at each other, had closed ranks for a change, blaming the cleaning lady for the very crime she claimed to have witnessed. It isn't clear whether they expected their father to believe them, or just hoped he'd be more reasonable than to punish both for a crime that only one had committed (even if he knew for a fact that one or the other was guilty). Either way, they'd been wrong: Mr. Silber made the twins buy their sister a replacement bird, docking their allowances for months.

Thirty years later, when I asked them separately about the incident (after hearing of it from Helen herself), each twin insisted that the other had done it. Neither blamed the maid. Who really killed the bird? Such an act might not seem out of character for Scooter, a future felon who at the time was already grounded (on the strength of Simon's testimony, to be sure, and notwithstanding Scooter's strident denials) for killing a stray cat. On the other hand, Silber does seem to be smirking in that evening's photo, though it is a smirk perceptible as such only in the context of the microtonal range of expressions allowed by his father's ambitious time-lapse project — which, in order to register larger changes in Silber's face and soul over the years, had to minimize daily fluctuations (unlike *My Life*, whose purpose was precisely to record such fluctuations).

I hope it won't be seen as a presumption of guilt if I pause here to discuss Silber's lifelong hatred of animals, and particularly pets. Silber hated everything that made a noise, and in 1994 had chopped down all the trees in his back yard because he was "tired of hearing" the wind in their leaves and the birds in their branches. (For the sake of appearance, or in observance of some local statute, he had spared the trees out front, but he thought of his back yard as a fiefdom where he ruled absolutely. The reason the yard was so sickly was that he drenched it every summer with a long-outlawed insecticide to kill off all the crickets.) He was capable of getting irate at the rain as it pattered on his roof. But — like all of us — he especially hated noises he could blame on other people. So a cherry bomb was worse, decibel for decibel, than a thunderclap. Dogs were his bêtes noires, though, because unnecessary noise seemed to be their *raison d'être* — and also, I suspect, because he'd never had one when he was growing up. So my friend had always thought of dogs as something strangers owned — as one more foreign custom that made his neighbors hateful, frightful, alien, and hard to coexist with. In 1988, his next-door neighbor, Mrs. Talbot — the same ancient dowager who later would accuse him of stealing her wind chimes — had accused him of strangling her yappy back-yard beagle. They hadn't spoken since, though like all his neighbors she continued to torment him on other wavelengths. Silber claimed she'd bought the chimes expressly to annoy him — the same reason she had bought the beagle, he insisted, while also insisting (though with less conviction) that he hadn't strangled it.

On the day of the canary's death, in any case, our composer didn't play an ordinary chord, but a suspiciously chipper arpeggio of sixteenth notes (or, in *my* rendition, quarter notes) evidently mimicking the song of a canary, and perhaps alluding as well to its sudden unnatural death, since he didn't sustain the notes as in most of the diary entries, but allowed them to die as soon as sounded.

The tormented chord performed on September 27, 1973, was played one-handed, like those for the week that followed. The other hand was in a sling. On the day in question, Mr. Silber had announced at breakfast that Simon, almost fifteen, had already had his chance to show what *he* could do on "the good piano," as they all called the Bösendorfer with the extra keys (the instrument that Silber later silenced by unstringing). It was Scooter's turn now, Mr. Silber said; from now on, Simon was to use the Bechstein in the blue piano room — the *second-best* piano.

This seems to have been the first time their father consciously exploited sibling rivalry to motivate Simon. Though both twins recalled their childhood as one long, exhausting, and soul-killing competition, their father — possibly because he'd been an only child, or maybe just because he was insane and didn't factor human nature into his equations — had never considered that his tidy little experiment might be affected by the fact that subject and control were brothers living under the same roof and more interested in their father's immediate approval than in some abstract vision of future glory.

As we've seen, the attempt to motivate Simon via sibling rivalry failed miserably. But that's not to say that his father's ukase didn't get a rise out of Simon. On the contrary, our composer got so worked up that he lunged at his exultant brother (whom he would later describe to me as "dancing around like they do on TV when they score a big touchdown") with a dinner fork, winding up with a bent fork and a sprained wrist — Scooter may not have been learning much else at Forest City Junior High, but he had learned to fight well enough to beat the stuffing out of his home-schooled twin.

Simon's playing, as I say, continued to get worse even after his wrist was better (and even after his father restored him to his throne at the Bösendorfer), and finally — on their fifteenth birthday — Mr. Silber had ordered Scooter to withdraw from the lifelong competition, now convinced that sibling rivalry was precisely what was wearing Simon down and holding Simon back. Maybe so: certainly that rivalry, and their father's constant morbid demand that Simon outdo Scooter, took its toll on Simon too. Our composer must've felt, all those years, like a boxer the mobsters keep betting a fortune on, and must've envied the palookas no one wants to win. At any rate, Simon showed a dramatic improvement as soon as Scooter was no longer a contender.

Years later, Mr. Silber would apologize to Simon for the whole episode, insisting that he'd never given Scooter any chance of surpassing him, but had feared that — what with puberty and all — Simon was losing interest in his destiny, practicing less fervently, etc. Worried that his favorite son would throw away all the talent and training that had been lavished on him by nature and nurture respectively, Mr. Silber had sunk to the expedient of exploiting Simon's insecurities, wrongly supposing that nothing would motivate the boy like the sound of his father praising Scooter.

As far as I know, Mr. Silber never did apologize to Scooter.

Our last two chords, dated January 14, 1979, and January 22, 1979, are notable for their contrast — the *Sturm und Drang* of the first versus the eerie, almost lobotomized calm of the second — but even more so for the gap between them. Seven days of silence (each one written in the score as a whole rest) intervene between the two dates in *My Life,* and seven frames of blackness in the film. I noticed the gap one frigid winter night when, with nothing better to do and nothing more entertaining to watch (it was too chilly to walk to the video store, and my car wouldn't start in the cold), I replayed the video of Silber's face. The gap — more than a quarter second of blackness — occurred almost exactly midway through the film (and thus the life it chronicled). By rewinding and advancing frame by frame across the gap, I was able to determine that there was indeed a week missing from the record: January 15 to January 21, 1979. When I asked Silber about the missing week, he not only refused to talk about it, but forbade me sharply ever to mention it again, convincing me that *something* must've happened in that interval of blackness. But what?

Finally I returned to the public library and investigated the mystery the same way I'd investigated the wind-chime incident: by viewing microfilms of the *Forest City Ranger*. Once I'd traveled back to 1979, it didn't take me long to find what I was looking for, which proved to be the front page of the January 15 edition:

### Local Pianist "Snaps" at Competition

Last night was a disgraceful one for Forest City when local legend Simon Silber assaulted a judge during the finals of the Erlenmeyer International Piano Competition, in Lumber's stately Erlenmeyer Hall. Around 10:30 p.m., the twenty-year-old pianist interrupted his own performance of Mozart's *Fantasy in C Minor* to jump down from the stage and lunge at Myra Handler, one of three judges seated in the front row. Still wearing the bright red earmuffs he wore throughout the preliminary round on Friday, the pianist grabbed Ms. Handler by the throat and had to be restrained by the other judges and by fellow contestants, including the winner of this year's competition, Young-Seong Oh. Silber claimed that Ms. Handler had provoked him by yawning aloud.

Ms. Handler, 83, was unharmed and says she doesn't plan to file charges. Silber was not arrested, despite his attempt to attack her again when he was forbidden to resume his performance of the Mozart *Fantasy*, which had already gone on for more than an hour when he tried to strangle the elderly judge. In comparison, Young-Seong Oh's performance of the same piece lasted only twenty minutes.

Silber's sensitivity to audience noise was no news to those who have seen the troubled pianist perform in Forest City over the years, or those who saw him in Friday's preliminaries. On Friday, Mr. Silber interrupted his performance several times to frown at the audience. "He looks just like a kindergarten teacher waiting for the class to settle down," another contestant was heard to remark.

Simon was the second Silber to cause a stir at Erlenmeyer Hall this weekend. At the beginning of Friday's preliminaries, his twin brother, Peter (not a contestant), jumped onto the stage in a red tuxedo, apparently intoxicated, and hit the piano with a shoe until he was ejected by security personnel. The piano had to be retuned before the competition could continue, causing a forty-minute delay. Peter Silber was not in attendance on Saturday.

Though reluctant to discuss any part of that disastrous weekend, Silber later did confirm the paper's account of Scooter's shenanigans. Silber said that Scooter had swiped the family car that Friday to keep Simon from reaching Erlenmeyer Hall, as he and his father finally had by taxi, arriving just as the houselights were dimming, or just in time to see Scooter run down a side aisle and leap onto the stage in Simon's tuxedo — the only one that Simon owned at that point, the bright red one his father had just bought for the occasion. Scooter had made off with it that afternoon while Simon was in the bathtub, forcing the contestant to perform in one of his father's (older, drabber, tighter) suits. After taking off one of Simon's glossy new black dress shoes, Scooter had faced the audience and said: "My name is Simon Silber and my interpretation of this first etude is sort of unorthodox." And then he'd started randomly whacking the keys with the heel of the shoe. His father had not only disowned (and evicted) the imposter on the spot, but had managed to get him arrested and held till the competition was over. Nonetheless — and even now — Silber blamed his breakdown in the finals on his brother's antics the evening before. He had never forgiven Scooter; more than once I heard him vow to kill his twin "some day" (just as Scooter had been vowing for years to kill him, and both had vowed at one time or another to kill Helen, who no doubt had vowed to kill them first, for they were a bloodthirsty clan). Silber was convinced that Scooter had disrupted the competition with no other purpose than to sabotage him, to ruin his chances by wrecking his nerves or even getting him disqualified. Knowing Scooter, though, I think it's just as likely that he had been planning (if he had a plan at all) to impersonate his twin in earnest, earnestly believing, with the aid of alcohol, that even though he hadn't touched a piano in years, he was still better than Simon — but then at the last moment had either caught sight of the real Simon Silber or else had been sobered by stage fright.

When I asked Scooter about it, he too refused to discuss the competition, or the mystery week that followed, though he did confirm my hunch that the seven-bar rest corresponded to a hospitalization of some kind. He wouldn't say *what* kind, or where (and I scanned the microfilm in vain for a follow-up to the Erlenmeyer story), but I understand that Lumber General Hospital has a whole locked ward devoted to psychiatry.

Scooter did say that Simon had "come back different," that they no longer knew him after his hospitalization, and that it was just as futile for me to hope I'd ever know the Simon he'd grown up with, Simon as he'd been *before* his breakdown. If so, the photos corresponding to our last two chords represent, respectively, the last image of the Simon whom Scooter had known, and the first image of the one I would later work for.

### 4. *Sudden Noises from Inanimate Objects*    14:33

Silber's father died of a heart attack in June 1980, when the twins were twenty-one. Scooter was in jail at the time for stealing a police car. (Later he regretted that he hadn't been at liberty, so that his failure to attend the funeral could be seen by those who did as voluntary.) In December, after an especially ugly incident (see *Helen*), Helen got her own apartment, and for the first time in his life, Silber was alone in the big house he'd grown up in. As ardently as he had wanted the house to himself, Silber became very jumpy that winter, in the wake of his sister's departure, and (maybe because he had started hearing voices, as he later hinted) morbidly sensitive to sudden noises from inanimate objects: a silently burning log suddenly popping in the fireplace, or collapsing and falling through the grate; ice cubes melting and shifting in a glass; melting snow slipping from the roof and landing with a plop; the house itself settling; a cookie sheet fresh from the oven, fitfully cooling and contracting; a precariously balanced can of oven cleaner striking the floor after falling off the edge of a countertop due to a draft or to vibrations from a passing truck or to a colliding midge, or for no better reason than that it *should* have fallen off already, without a nudge of any kind, and after unaccountably *not* falling for minutes or hours or days, was bound finally, suddenly, unaccountably, to fall.

*Sudden Noises from Inanimate Objects* is an evocation of all these sounds and others, interspersed with eerie stretches of silence or near silence whose function is to make the sudden noises more surprising. The piece was composed in January '81, on New Year's Day — the first New Year that our composer rang in by himself. I'm advising all but the most well adjusted listeners to skip the track, which probably comes closer than any other Silber work to communicating — like an illness — the derangement that can complicate excessive solitude, as a cough a cold. Knowing Silber's cruel sense of humor, that may be the reason he gave me a tape of *Sudden Noises* the day before Christmas, the day after I mentioned that I had no holiday plans, hoping that he would include me in his. Instead, I got a cheap cassette whose only virtue as a gift (if that's how he'd intended it) was that it didn't leave me feeling guilty for not having gotten *him* something. Nonetheless, I forced myself to sit through most of the interminable piece, but ejected it, just in the nick of time, when I felt myself succumbing to its eeriness — I'd begun to feel that the sun would never rise, and that I'd never be with friends or family again, never again be with people at all, not *really*, not *with* them, no matter how often or doggedly I might insinuate myself into their midst. (It was suppertime on Christmas Eve, and I was the only living being in my building: everyone else, even Gordon, had *somewhere* to go.) So I stomped the malignant cassette into splinters of plastic and ribbons of tape, and listened instead to the *Moonlight* Sonata — I'd had the inspired idea of borrowing that disc from Gordon at the end of our first chat, after praising his musical taste, and I'd discovered it wasn't half-bad, not when *I* decided when to listen to it. With its aid I managed, if not to elevate my mood, at least to stabilize it, to pull it out of its terrifying nosedive. That night I knew that nothing in the world — not even the glory for which Silber and I pined — was worth the curse of chronic, mind-destroying solitude to which *Sudden Noises* so chillingly attests. And when, a week later, Gordon invited me upstairs to watch some big New Year's Eve broadcast in his room, on his tiny TV set (usually concealed — as if it were a chamber pot — in a tasteful little cabinet), I accepted. I don't know how Silber spent the holidays.

### 5. *Our Father*                              12:40

The year his father died, our composer wrote a batch of variations on Malotte's beloved setting of the Paternoster. Though the seven variations vary more in mood and key than Silber's other sets, I find it significant that this batch is the only one in which the theme is recognizable throughout. The title is significant as well: not *Variations on "Our Father,"* just *Our Father.* The variety is a part of the portrait.

Solomon Silber had been a star piano student at a top conservatory (where he met his future wife, also a pianist) when a sobering second-place finish in an intramural competition convinced him that — no matter what a zealous teacher had once told him — he wasn't "the next Horowitz" after all. His failure to live up to such prophecies was due, no doubt, to nothing more dire than the thinning of the ranks inevitable when a thousand prodigies all vie to be the most prodigious, but Mr. Silber chose instead to blame the spottiness of his early training: his parents hadn't started him on the piano till he was nine, and hadn't hesitated to snatch him away from his lessons and his (largely self-enforced) practice regimen to traipse around Europe.

At the age of twenty-one, in any case, Silber's father transferred out of the conservatory into a good teachers college. In a way, he was to spend the rest of his life ruminating on his failure as a musician. Why, he kept asking himself, does one prodigy grow up to set the world on fire, while so many others fizzle like wet firecrackers? Why, of a group of ten outstanding child violinists, say, is it so hard to guess which one will stand out ten years later? Must we assume that the one who goes the furthest was the most gifted to begin with, even if the slight but crucial difference was initially impossible to hear? Or can it be that there are millions of babies born every year with as much innate ability as anyone is granted, and that it is nurture, not nature, that decides which of those babies will prevail?

Mr. Silber thought so, and he had for years by the time the twins were born. Earlier, around the time of Helen's birth, he'd set to work developing a pedagogical method to ensure that child prodigies would blossom into prodigious adults, rather than going to seed as coulda-beens. Mr. Silber had first tested and refined many aspects of the Preparation on Helen, but only to conclude that she'd been born with as *little* musical talent as nature ever gives an intelligent child, and though she hadn't shaken his faith in his theories, it was obvious long before the twins were born that Helen wasn't destined to make her father famous.

The decision to subject just one twin to the Preparation was a choice their father would regret after the Erlenmeyer meltdown. Even back in 1958, he'd known that not even the strictest upbringing could eliminate altogether the element of chance, and that by submitting both twins to the method he could double his odds of producing a genius. But he had so much confidence in the Preparation that his main fear wasn't of dropping the basket he put all his eggs in, but rather of watching all credit for his son's success go to the son's innate ability. He was afraid, in other words, that history would remember Silber's father, if at all, as it remembers Beethoven's — as a tyrant to be blamed for his son's bad temper, but seldom celebrated for his interest in the son's career.* For it must be stressed that Mr. Silber was *not* driven by a craving for vicarious success, but rather by a hunger for firsthand recognition as a visionary educator. His first concern was that posterity acknowledge *him* — acknowledge that no matter how gifted the pupil, it was the Preparation that had made the crucial difference.†

So the birth of twins had been a godsend.‡ On learning from a sonogram that two were on the way, their father had busied himself with devising a battery of tests — of neonatal IQ, personality, and physical ability — whereby to determine which twin would get to be the greatest pianist of his time. Mr. Silber was of course hoping that the twins would be genetically identical, but he thought that even then, their intrauterine experiences might differ enough, in the course of nine months, that by the day of birth one infant would already be more likely to succeed. The tests had proven inconclusive, though, and finally Mr. Silber had picked Simon, the first to emerge from the womb, as if it stood to reason that the fetus in the bigger hurry to get out of there was the one who — as they say — was going places.

Mr. Silber predicted that his method would be "generalized"

* Judging by his journal, Mr. Silber venerated Johann van Beethoven even more fervently than he did Ludwig — though I'm happy to report that unlike Beethoven's father, Silber's never came in from carousing at one in the morning, dragged the young genius out of bed despite his tearful pleas to go on sleeping, and forced him to play the piano all night long for drinking buddies: Mr. Silber didn't drink, and doesn't seem to have had any buddies.

† Silber's father was by no means the first educator to test his theories on his son: Norbert Weiner's father, Mill's father, Pascal's father, and the father of William and Henry James — to name just a few — all did the same.

‡ God helps those who help themselves, though, and when they decided to improve on Helen, Mr. Silber forced his wife to take fertility drugs in hopes of inducing just such a duplication.

one day and adapted to everything from figure skating to chess. Readers who are hoping to produce a Silber of their own, though, will be disappointed to learn that I cannot give a thorough account of the Preparation: Silber didn't like to talk about his childhood, and one of his father's last actions had been to burn "The Preparation," the monumental treatise that toward the end had bulked as large (and represented as many years of toil) as the score of *Day.* He didn't bother, though, to burn his journal, a single yellow legal pad, wonderfully bedraggled, whose entries, in a cursive so minute I used a magnifying glass to read them (with Silber's reluctant permission — otherwise he would've had to tell me all these things himself), run from 2/28/58 ("Elsie pregnant!") to 5/31/80 ("Bungled it: too lenient, too lax"), and treat exclusively of the Preparation, either because Mr. Silber kept another journal for everything else in his life, or because nothing else mattered.

As far as I can tell, the hallmark of the Preparation was its ruthlessness (Mr. Silber's word, possibly his *favorite* word), especially with regard to motivation. That, at any rate, was the selling point by which Mr. Silber distinguished his method, with pride, from a certain wildly successful rival that he never tired of deriding. Right around the time the twins were born, a Japanese student at Oberlin College astounded music teachers with a film of *one thousand* Japanese children playing Bach's Double Concerto. Mr. Silber wasn't at the screening, but his journal shows that even before its American premiere, he knew about the film and envied the success of the educational method for which that film made such a striking case, the method developed by Shinichi Suzuki. Again and again, Mr. Silber denied any debt to Suzuki, but in fact their methods had a lot in common: both promised to yield outstanding musicians by starting very early and enlisting what some would call a pathological degree of parental involvement.

Mr. Silber, though, preferred to emphasize the differences, and the single biggest, as I say, was his approach to motivation — an approach that didn't flinch at corporal punishment, starvation, or sleep deprivation, but ideally took the form instead of a sort of brainwashing that rendered such measures unnecessary by rendering the child incapable of wanting anything its parents didn't, or taking any pleasure in anything that didn't please them too. As for Suzuki, his approach was "much too namby-pamby ever to produce a genius." Silber's father found it "very telling" that the rival method was designed to be enforced by *mothers,* a class of people he believed contemptibly incapable of ruthlessness and thus of genius-rearing — for the only way to rear a genius, he insisted, was by "ruthlessly destroying the young one's capacity for independent happiness," and instilling in its place an all-consuming obsession with pleasing the parents:

> A child prodigy is a child programmed by its parents to please them and not itself. To spend its life OBSESSED with pleasing them, with "being good." Obsessed, even after their deaths, with succeeding on their terms, and unable even to CONCEIVE of success — or, indeed, of goodness — on any other terms. Every notable prodigy in history, from Mozart to J. S. Mill, has been forged by this dynamic, his own happiness subsumed in a parent's — and the crucial parent has almost always been a FATHER: mothers are TOO SOFT. (10/17/62)

According to Mr. Silber (whose journal often reads less like a journal — though it does say JOURNAL, in his microscopic hand, at the top of the first page — than like a series of outtakes from his treatise), parents must be ruthless with themselves as well, and ruthlessly honest:

> To the degree that the parent lies to himself (or more likely HERself — eh, Mr. Suzuki!?) about the essential SELFISHNESS of wanting a prodigy, to the degree that the parent yields to sentimental worries about the child's "happiness" (except as that so overvalued intangible bears on the MUSIC) — to that degree the child's regimen will lack the rigor necessary to produce a genius. Of course, this rigor will take different forms in different cases — not every child needs or even benefits (as Beethoven's did) from frequent beatings, for example, or from confinements of the type

I'm finding so useful with Simon. But the parent who BALKS at such measures, in cases where they ARE indicated, should turn the TV set back on and forget all about prodigies. (10/18/62)

Even when it didn't mandate frequent beatings, Mr. Silber's idea of rigor entailed a lot more than long and grueling practices. Silber's father was convinced that everything that happened — every encounter, every impression, every *sound* especially, but also every outing, meal, hobby, birthday present, pet, etc. — was either good or bad (most often bad) for a budding musician; all else being equal, the kid to go the farthest would be the one whose keepers exposed him or her, in the formative years, to the fewest "unpropitious impressions." Mr. Silber followed to their logical extreme — which of course means to the point of madness — the consequences of a fact that no sane parent would dispute: some events can change a child for better or worse. For that matter, Silber's father didn't go as far as the psychotic Dr. Schreber's (another visionary educator who, for instance, anxious to prevent lopsidedness, forced his son to sleep on alternate sides on alternate nights), and that may be why Silber never went as mad as Schreber (who became convinced that sunbeams shined out of his anus — though now that I think about it, Silber may have cherished the very same delusion, for all I know, but kept it to himself). But in his own way Silber's father was almost as extreme, to judge by the piano lessons he inflicted on his son.

Mr. Silber boasted that his way of teaching kids to play was "radically unlike all previous approaches"; your commentator — almost forty at the time of his first lesson (see *Digression*) — can't evaluate that claim, not even with the handy list of "helpful exercises" (dated 1/1/62) in Mr. Silber's journal. For all I know, Silber's father may not be the only teacher ever to require three-year-olds to slap themselves in midperformance for each finger slip (and — on pain of harsher penalties — without breaking their musical stride). Other teachers, too, may encourage pupils to play with more feeling by having them alter their facial expressions — sometimes note by note — to reflect the music's mood, and by punishing "unbefitting faces." Other teachers too may inure their pupils to the distraction of audience noise by standing directly behind them, as they practice a delicate passage, with an overinflated balloon in one hand and a pin in the other, and popping the balloon at some unforeseeable moment, punishing pupils who jump. Other teachers too may train their students' judgment by forcing them to vary the dynamics of a piece (one the teacher considers uneven) not according to the composer's own instructions, but in sync with dips and rises in the merit of the music (so that it gets louder or softer as it gets better or worse), and by punishing errors of taste.* In any case, Mr. Silber did all that.

To really understand his treatment of his son — his embrace of ruthlessness not just in theory but in practice — one must bear in mind that Simon's father saw him as a magnum opus. No matter how well our father expounded his theories, he knew the proof was in the pudding, and that history would rate him only as great an educator as Simon was a musician. It should also be remembered that Mr. Silber was reacting against his own upbringing — against the haphazard musical tutelage on which he blamed his own failure as a pianist. His son's insanely ruly and rigorous training seems to have been conceived by Mr. Silber partly as an elaborate reproach to his jet-setting mother and father: *See, if you'd done things right, I could've been as good as your grandson.* Whether the subsequent catastrophic failure of the Preparation enabled Mr. Silber to forgive his parents, Simon didn't know.

Given that his father's botched experiment left our composer with a lifelong and finally lethal hatred of noise, it's fitting that *Our Father* is Silber's loudest work. All but one of the seven variations is played with a lead foot on the custom-

---

* Silber refused to tell me what form these punishments had taken, and his father's journal is infuriatingly vague on that score. All I can say for sure is that the corrective didn't involve electric shocks, since in later years Mr. Silber berated himself repeatedly for having *failed* to use that "clean, effective means of discouraging slovenly playing." At several points, it looks like he first wrote "mild electric shocks," but then on second thought crossed out the adjective.

rigged "loud" pedal that replaced the customary "soft" one on the concert grand in Silber's studio. More than once I heard my friend assert that all other pianists played "too loud," but he admitted that that was in part the fault of their instrument as usually configured. Back in 1980, he had spent a day modifying the left pedal on his Steinway so that the "soft" position was its *default* mode, and only on those rare occasions when he *wanted* to play loud was it necessary to step on it.

## 6. *Wrong Number*                                        1:22

Someone who hates noise as such, and sudden noise especially, is going to hate strangers who cause his phone to ring by dialing his number in error. For a while in 1982, Silber made a point of asking all such callers what number they'd meant to dial, and of jotting down the numbers on a special pad after slamming down the phone. His original purpose in keeping this list was revenge — he planned to call all those numbers, some night at around four A.M., and punish one disruption with another. This may strike the reader as irrational: instead of punishing the misdialing callers themselves, Silber punished their associates, for the crime of having numbers similar to his. Back in 1982, of course, it wasn't as easy as it is now to trace a phone call to its source.

I'm happy to report that before he could carry out his vengeance, our composer found a different and more constructive use for his list when, in January '83, he finally broke his phone — one of those basic-black unbreakable rotary-dials — by slamming down the receiver once too often, and replaced it with a touch-tone model of which his favorite feature was a switch enabling him to turn the ringer off. *Wrong Number* is a sort of numeric counterpart to the *"Babbage" Permutations'* alphabetical shenanigans: a transcription of all those wrong numbers, as performed on a touch-tone keypad, though not in numerical order but in the order our composer had jotted them down. Well, he didn't actually transcribe them all, but confined himself to numbers differing from his in only one of their seven digits — but then, there are $9^7$ or 4,782,969 possible wrong numbers meeting that condition. He also allowed transpositions of successive digits (e.g., "83" for "38"), one of the most frequent dialing errors, but since his number began "555-" (as, come to think of it, all phone numbers did in Forest City), and since no one ever transposes the third and fourth digits — transposes across the hyphen — that added only three more permutations, for a grand total of 4,782,972. For the purposes of his composition, though, Silber required that (except for transpositions) the wrong digit be adjacent on the keypad to the right one, horizontally or vertically, which narrowed the field some, though by exactly how much I'm not enough of a mathematician to say. Silber's list, in any case, recorded only twenty-seven different numbers, though some of them appeared on his list several times (the worst offender was the Warthog, whose drunken belligerent patrons and their shrill, accusatory girlfriends tended to call at around two A.M.), so several of the seven-note motifs repeat. But most of them would've repeated anyhow, since the biggest problem facing the composer in this case was that — as anyone who has ever tried to pick out a ditty on a touch-tone phone has found, before accidentally dialing Chad or Iceland — there are only three tones on that keyboard, C, D, and E, one for each of the vertical columns in which the buttons are arrayed; nor is it possible to produce chords by pressing several buttons simultaneously. Instead of trying to make music that would move the listener the way a Schubert song does, then, or a Mahler symphony, Silber wisely confined himself here to concocting a maddening brainteaser: knowing the rules by which the piece was composed, deduce the composer's phone number.

I had an unusual telephone encounter — or rather, near encounter — with my employer, one January day, even as I was trying to solve the riddle in question. I was at the Bean in my new reading glasses, which — together with the big mustache I later traded for a beard — made me look like Nietzsche. By then I was a regular — if not a mainstay — at the Bean, though it wasn't the best place to write. The acoustics were too live, the tables too close together; when the coffeehouse was full, it reminded me of Schopenhauer's parable about the porcupines huddling together for warmth on a winter's day: it was loneliness that drove me there, a need to be with people, and yet my misanthropy always seemed to flare up in those surroundings. That day, though, I succeeded — in spite of or because of these distractions, and the added distraction of the pay phone on the wall behind me — in concentrating on my writing in a way I seldom did in the Quiet Room at the public library, or even in my rented room, though now that I had Gordon's only classical recording, I didn't hear much music from upstairs, since my neighbor was ashamed of his other CDs, and played them only when he thought I was out. (Sometimes he ascertained my absence the same way I ascertained his: that very morning I'd watched through the Bean's front picture window as Gordon emerged from our building, bent down to read my meter, and went back inside.)

At about noon, I decided I'd done enough work for one day. Without needing to leave my chair, I pivoted and used the pay phone to check my messages, something I could do from any phone now that I'd replaced my answering machine with the automated service offered by the phone company. *You have no new messages,* said the recorded woman's voice, with a note of sadness that, depending on my mood, I heard sometimes as an apology, sometimes as a reproach, and sometimes — when, awaiting an important call, I'd been checking every fifteen minutes — as barely restrained impatience. I sat back down and, after furtively eating the homemade sandwich I'd smuggled in, wasted a few minutes reading the first chapter of a bestseller I'd checked out of the library, but its very easiness made me uneasy. I felt like the tractor of an eighteen-wheeler hurling down the highway without its trailer: I wasn't pulling enough of a load to give me a sense of *prevailing*. And that morning I had rashly spent an hour reading aphorisms — a use of my eyes that always fatigued them, as if they were protesting my haste: I knew I ought to pause and savor every sentence, but instead turned pages rapidly and greedily, like someone gulping down fancy mixed nuts by the handful. Only rarely would I linger over an especially brilliant formulation, and fantasize that I had written it myself, and that *this* time Dad would *have* to be impressed — a fantasy that dated back to adolescence. (Lately Silber had replaced my father in this fantasy, though his indifference to books made me doubt that even as Nietzsche I could've impressed him.)

And so I put down the book and picked up *Wrong Number.* Silber had lent me the score the day before, saying he'd give me a tour of his basement if I could derive his telephone number from all those near misses. "Think of it as an IQ test," he'd told me, adding, "I'm not sure you're *smart* enough to be entrusted with my secrets." Throughout the year I knew him, he made many such "playful" remarks anent my education, taste, intelligence, and overall ability. He had retained some of his father's pedagogical jargon, and once informed me that, as a biographer, I was "trainable, if not quite educable." I recognized the terms as ones that had been used once to distinguish between moderate and mild mental retardation — between imbeciles and morons — and I wasn't flattered. Sometimes he would break off an anecdote in midsentence to make fun of me: "So I got up from the piano, turned to the heckler, and — and what did I do next, Norm? Can you guess? *Tom* guessed." Or else he'd tell me what he'd done in a given situation, and then ask me why: "Why'd I do that, anyhow? Can you tell me? I'm not testing you — I'm just curious. *Tom* could tell me why I did something even when I didn't know myself." I didn't really mind the comparisons to my predecessor: I consoled myself by picturing our employer's face when he read my other, unauthorized biography, and realized that I had been much smarter than I'd seemed, that till then I'd kept the shrewdest of my guesses to myself. In any case, I didn't have much self-esteem invested in my job as a biographer for hire — to my way of thinking, a humiliating job to be good at. I was an aphorist, an artist in my own right; I was allowed to be bad at everything else. At that point I still believed that Silber too considered me an artist, and in that regard his equal, and that it was precisely this unspoken understanding that enabled him to tease me about my competence as a biographer. I even came to see his teasing as welcome evidence of his underlying respect: if he *hadn't* taken my aphorizing seriously, he would've been more tactful about my shortcomings in other areas.

Even so, I sometimes felt as if he were belatedly conducting the job interview he'd forgotten to conduct the day he hired me. I'd heard of interviews where the candidate is asked to open a window that has been nailed shut beforehand, and after two hours I began to suspect that with his latest brainteaser Silber was subjecting me to just such an impossible task. Even with the advantage of already *knowing* his number, I was unable to see how anyone could deduce it from Silber's idiotic composition. And yet Silber claimed that he himself had deduced the number that way; that prior to composing *Wrong Number* he'd never known — or had forgotten — his own number, since he never had occasion to call it. (Afterward, he said, he'd sometimes dial his number absentmindedly when meaning to phone someone else, which strikes me as emblematic: although he claimed that he wrote music in order "to communicate," the sad truth is that in opus after opus he just dialed his own number and got a busy signal.)

At around two P.M., having worked myself into a state, I gave up and returned to the phone to check my messages again: I'd reserved a new release from the video shop, and they were supposed to call the minute a copy came in. This time there *was* a message, but from Silber. In the course of a long and intermittently musical monologue (whose gist I no longer recall, if it had one), he mentioned that he was calling from the Bean at "about one P.M." — or smack in the middle of the two-hour brainteasing session I'd just abandoned. My employer, who detested coffeehouses, must have come in just to use the phone and so, as all but the most brazen will do when slipping into a place of business to use some amenity (pay phone, rest room, water cooler) meant for paying customers, had made a beeline for his destination without surveying the room. He was capable of greater feats of absentmindedness, of even more elaborate sleepwalks — though just as capable, at times, of a *present*-mindedness that made his scowling townspeople look like the sleepwalkers.* It was harder to understand how *I* could have been so oblivious as not to register him at the pay phone right behind me, chatting away (and sometimes breaking into song) for at least five minutes. I decided he'd been wrong about the time, or maybe the place. Replaying his message, however, I heard *myself* in the background, whistling the Sousa march I'd been whistling, off and on, all day, against my will — it drove me up the wall. So I *had* been there, at my table by the pay phone, feverishly writing about Silber, while he, a few feet away, was trying to telephone me, and neither one — each blinkered by his single-minded purpose — had noticed the other. Silber may even have come in looking for me — he knew this was one of my hangouts — but failed to spot me because of my new glasses, just as no one recognizes Superman in his Clark Kent disguise. In that case, though, I wondered what he saw when he did see me, if a pair of horn-rimmed glasses was enough to render me invisible.

I used another quarter to call Silber, and of course got *his* machine: back in 1983 he had switched off his ringer once and for all and modified his answering machine to record calls silently, for him to listen to later at his leisure. The length of his recorded greeting may have been intended to discourage callers from leaving messages; and to discourage certain callers even

---

* Once he came into the Bean to tell me about his new lawn chair; we'd chatted for a few minutes and then, at his suggestion, gone outside, where he proceeded to repeat — verbatim, seriatim — three other unrelated conversations that had been going on at neighboring tables at the same time as our own. He said he liked to do that kind of multitrack eavesdropping just to keep his contrapuntal faculties limber.

further, it contained personal submessages to each of his siblings, almost like voice mail, except that in Silber's case, neither caller was told to press such and such a button for additional instructions, but only to hang up and not to call again: "If this is Helen, mind your own damn business — I don't give a crap about your "reputation." If this is Scooter, no you *can't* have any more money, and no you *can't* stay with me, no not even for one night, and no not even in the carriage house." That afternoon, though, right in the middle of the preemptive strike on Scooter, someone on Silber's end picked up and started dialing.

"Hey!" I shouted.

"Oh — I was just calling you. What do *you* want?"

"I — well, what do *you* want?"

And neither of us could remember why he'd been calling the other.


## 7. *Look, Dad — No Hands*        1:07

My name is Norman Fayrewether, Junior. Norman Senior was a professor of aesthetics at a tiny, overpriced, overrated private college in a region better known for its skiing. He himself was known for his book-length disapprovals of contemporary culture — diatribes with titles like *The Agony of Abstract Art, The Fallacy of Free Verse,* and *The Collapse of Architecture.* Nowadays I find his books embarrassing, but as a boy I thought my father was a genius and wanted nothing so much as to please him, and one day to be him. (As for my mom, I knew she'd love me all the same if I became a garbageman; she was too easy to please, and I tended to take her for granted.) Now I'm ashamed to have landed so close to the tree I came from, like a defective helicopter that, though it *looks* airworthy, unaccountably drops from the maple straight to the ground without spinning. I did manage, early on (and unlike Silber), to put some *physical* distance between myself and my father, leaving Colorado for an

East Coast school on a merit scholarship when I was just sixteen, but it was a boy's need to impress his dad that prompted me to major in philosophy.

I didn't make a single friend at college. All I wanted in those days was to be smarter than everyone else, or at least to enjoy the illusion that I was — not as easy at college as it had been in high school. I was so terrified of *not* being smartest that I shunned the other smart kids, lest one of them outsmart me; and since I also shunned the dumb as not worth talking to, there was nobody left to befriend. What I did instead was read, developing the eyestrain that would plague me ever after, leading me finally to focus my interests, as a reader and a writer, on the humble aphorism.

I graduated with honors at twenty, eager to continue my studies somewhere else, but either because of my youth or because I'd been libeled by professors I had asked to recommend me, I was awarded a fellowship by only one of the eleven graduate philosophy programs I'd applied to — my father's. It started as a teaching fellowship, but after one semester of Great Ideas 101, I was deemed unfit to teach: my impatience with stupidity was "simply unacceptable" (to quote from a note from the dean) at a school whose only *raison d'être* was to cater to the children of the rich.

So my father arranged for me to help him with *Heritage,* the quarterly journal of cranky opinion he edited from his big corner office in Spengler Hall. Instead of wading through freshman essays, forcing myself to write "YES!" or "GOOD POINT!" next to any sentence marginally less inane and inept than its neighbors, I suddenly found myself reading submissions by actual grownups. It was heady work for a twenty-year-old thinker, and I soon decided that I was as good as some of the people we published. On February 1, 1981, I set out to prove it with an essay in my father's manner. Neglecting my coursework and even my hygiene, I spent a month lamenting "The Malfunction of Modern Music." In those days, I didn't give a damn about music, modern or not; I chose the subject only because it was one on which my father hadn't yet pronounced at any length, though I later learned — may even have known at the time, to be frank — that he was bemoaning *The Malady of Modern Music* (a jeremiad published in 1983) even as I was dashing off *my* diagnosis. I didn't say a word to him about my work in progress; I wanted to surprise him (I almost wrote "surpass him"), and though I hoped to say the things he would have said himself, the fun for me was to *anticipate* and say them first.

I was born on leap year day in 1960; in off years we celebrated my birth on March 1. On March 1, 1981, as soon as my parents had finished a loud and out-of-tune duet of "Happy Birthday" (while, a thousand miles away, Silber winced and reseated his earplugs), I blew out twenty-one candles and presented a twenty-eight-page single-spaced essay to my father, expecting him to read it on the spot, and praise it to the stars, and publish it in *Heritage:* that was all I wanted for my birthday. I don't recall what I did get that year; all I know is that my dad took *a week* just to glance at my piece, and even then he got no further than page four. Maybe he'd already read too many unsolicited manuscripts that week. Or maybe it was too much trouble to pretend an interest in my work. His own career was going well enough that he had no need for vicarious success, and it must've been embarrassing to hear his own opinions — which already sounded archaic in *his* mouth — coming from someone my age.

I see now that my worshipful impersonation of Norman the First — his stilted locutions, his byzantine syntax, his programmatic grumpiness — resulted in an inadvertent parody more damning than anything a detractor could have written. At the time, though, I dismissed his impatient reaction as a fear of being outdone — a father's sense of being superseded by his son. In pique, in rage, almost in tears, I submitted the piece to *Patrimony* (another, newer quarterly my father considered an upstart, though it espoused the same dyspeptic sentiments as *Heritage*), omitting the "Jr." after my name — *not* in order to mislead the editors, but because I suddenly no longer wanted to think of myself as a junior version of my father: his rejection of my essay was the trauma of my life, and it triggered a belated rebellion, the one I'd been too busy doing homework to get around to as an adolescent.

My father was at school when an acceptance letter came to our house a month later. I signed the enclosed publication contract — again omitting the "Jr." — and sent it back to *Patrimony*, though it was clear from the letter that they thought they were dealing not with me but with my father. Why I didn't say anything to him — well, by that point, though I lived beneath his roof, I was no longer speaking to him: I was still enraged by his spot-on criticisms of as much of my essay as he'd read, and even more enraged by his ongoing refusal to read the rest of the essay, of which the birthday copy had been lying for weeks on the floor beneath his desk, behind his wastebasket, in what looked like an unsuccessful effort to throw it away. And the part of me that hadn't yet renounced my father altogether still hoped to surprise him, and to show him — with the irrefutable proof of publication — that my essay was better than he'd admit.

When the Winter 1982 issue of *Patrimony* came out in January with my essay batting cleanup, I wasn't as excited as I had expected: by that point, I'd recanted all the convictions expressed in the essay — they were *his,* not mine — and set about acquiring new ones. My father, though, did get excited when he saw his name on the cover. In response to his threats of a lawsuit — he claimed they couldn't possibly have thought the piece was *his* — the editors sent him a photocopy of the contract I had signed. Considering that I had wanted to write like my father ever since I'd learned to write, it was only natural that I had modeled my very penmanship on his; but needless to say I had never consciously forged his signature, as he claimed the day he ordered me to move out (February 26, 1982, according to my diary, which goes back almost as far as Silber's). The following day, the head of our department informed me that my fellowship would not be renewed next year — ostensibly because I'd been neglecting my coursework.

On February 27, 1982, I cleared out my little office (a miniature of my father's) and slammed the door to Spengler Hall behind me. By that point I'd already moved out of my parents' house — out of the same big, bright, and sunny bedroom I'd had as a kid — and into a tiny, dark, and stuffy studio apartment of the kind I would come to know so well.

I never spoke to my father again. I still haven't forgiven his refusal to take me seriously — to treat me, if not as an equal, at any rate as a *potential* equal. He died in 1993, but even now I get incensed when I relive our quarrel. And even now my attitudes and tastes are consciously and almost systematically opposed to his. (Only first-generation intellectuals can choose ideas freely; the rest of us are always either pleasing or paining our parents.) One reason I'd responded to Silber's help-wanted was that, although he hadn't merited as much as a footnote in *The Malady of Modern Music,* I'd made a point of liking living composers ever since falling out with my father, who'd been fond of saying "There *are* no living composers." And after my first talk with Silber, I already sensed that he embodied everything my father disapproved of.

Once I asked my employer if *his* father had ever rejected any of *his* compositions in a similarly callous manner. "All of them," said Silber. He told me that his father had done everything he could to convince the budding composer that he had no talent in that direction, apparently fearing that it would only distract the pianist from his first and fated vocation; and indeed the elder Silber went to his grave insisting that his son's "preposterous pretensions" as a composer were the real reason for his premature retirement from the concert stage.

Till adolescence, a presentiment of his father's disapproval had prevented Silber from composing. When I asked if his career might best be understood as a protracted adolescent rebellion, Silber looked offended. But it is the duty of the true biographer to consider every possible explanation, even the most demeaning, for why the life in question turned out the way it did. Silber claimed that only once had he composed a piece specifically in order to annoy his father. In 1976, when our composer was seventeen, Mr. Silber criticized a four-handed piano sonata so harshly that, for better or worse, Simon destroyed the only copy of the work. The following day, though, he composed a sort of reduction-to-absurdity of his father's comments — comments whose gist, according to Silber, had been: "*Four hands? Why not eight? You can't even handle two yet, maestro. You can barely manage one.*" Silber's riposte was the minute of arrhythmic, amelodic thumping on your disc — the sound of the composer (as caught by the same tape recorder used a few months later to record the *"Chopsticks" Variations*), hands in his pockets, strenuously working the pedals of his Steinway: "*Look, Dad — No Hands!*" (The title alluded to another sore point too: when he wrote the piece, Silber had been begging to drive for more than a year, but his father kept saying "Drive? Why do *you* need to drive? You already have a perfectly good bike.")

Though Silber had more sense than to dignify this joke with an opus number, and though it is arguably neither "piano" nor "music," and though our cyclist isn't *going* anywhere, just popping wheelies, I've included the piece in your set as a brief intermission, as we approach the midpoint of this compilation, which I trust you are enjoying, or rather will enjoy, as soon as you finish reading my notes (though it wouldn't hurt to read each note again as you listen to the corresponding composition).

### 8. *Helen* 13:13

This exuberant work is unique in the annals of classical music for being composed as part of an out-of-court settlement with its title character. Though the composer disparaged the piece as "garrulous," "brash," "needlessly noisy," "consistently annoying," and "obnoxiously insistent," many more-impartial listeners will join me in finding it his most exhilarating composition. Silber told me once that he'd set out to write the ugliest possible piece of music that would still strike his sister as beautiful, and that he'd been appalled by just how ugly that turned out to be, so great was the gulf between his sense of beauty and hers. The truth, I think, is that he was unwilling to admit that someone he hated as thoroughly as Helen could have inspired one of his best works, and one that argues the existence, musically, of virtues he refused to grant her otherwise.

Silber claimed that both his siblings had been "out to get" him since the day their father died and left all the money to Simon; Scooter had gotten nothing at all, and Helen nothing but a share of the big red-brick house, which Silber was determined not to share. He had offered Helen a hundred thousand dollars for her stake in the house, but she'd refused, sensing how desperate Silber was to have the place to himself and demanding the whole of his inheritance — almost a million dollars — in exchange for that privilege. Though the two had somehow managed till then to coexist under one roof for their entire lives, things became increasingly ugly in the months after their father's death and the sudden absence of his arbitrating presence. Helen not only refused to move out, or to whisper and tiptoe in the vicinity of the genius, but proceeded to make more noise than ever before. On that point — that she had gotten louder — their versions concurred, but only to diverge a moment later: Silber claimed that Helen's noise was a weapon in the war of nerves she was waging against him, while Helen insisted that she was merely turning up the volume in a house whose volume dial had been set unnaturally low all those years, *morbidly* low, by a father who'd decided early on to sacrifice for Silber's sake the happiness of the other children.* Their

---

* It was amusing to compare her memories of the acoustics of their childhood with Silber's — to hear *him* tell it, the house had been as clamorous as a bowling alley below a discotheque from the day (October 27, 1966; see "Selections from *My Life*") when their father decided to raise Simon's RDA of noise.

father's favoritism had been especially galling for Helen because she was eight years older than the twins and had been stuck from the age of eleven with the role of surrogate mother. (As a rule she refused to speak to me about her family, but on January 1 she made an exception and told me her side of the big quarrel, after I'd hinted while handing her my rent check that Simon had just told me his.)

Things had come to a head one cold December evening. The composer had been upstairs all day, walking up and down the hallway, talking softly to himself and trying to compose a twelve-part fugue. At eight P.M., he ran downstairs and demanded that Helen turn off the TV, which he claimed he could hear even up on the third floor. When Helen refused, the composer picked her up (in what he later described as a "fireman's carry") and pitched her through the big living-room window. Helen was unharmed, but Silber spent the night in jail, the fugue remains unfinished, the window cost almost a thousand dollars to replace, and Silber's sister began proceedings to have him committed to a private mental hospital. Though in the end she relented (when, according to Silber, she discovered that she wasn't in line for his inheritance even if he *were* certified insane), the threat of a committal had been enough to panic him into buying his sister the small rooming house into which she had moved after the assault — the one where I now lived (though *she* no longer did), the one that had become the cornerstone of her real-estate empire. My employer had also been obliged, as part of his plea bargain, to help dispel the townwide rumors of war among the Silbers by composing a musical homage to his sister on the occasion of her thirtieth birthday, and then to come out of retirement long enough to perform the piece at a big party in her honor, where he was also made to play duets with Scooter until a disagreement over tempo led to an unseemly shoving match between the twins.

Nowadays, though Simon and Helen no longer spoke when they could avoid it, they were no longer at war. But Simon and

Scooter still were. They had squabbled constantly even while their father was alive, and with his death the brotherly hate between them had swollen to biblical dimensions. In January '81, Scooter had gotten out of jail and — having learned by then that Simon had inherited all the money — come to town demanding some and, when the composer refused, issuing his first death threat. Silber had finally given his brother five thousand dollars on condition that Scooter never bother him again. When, a week later, Scooter returned to demand another "loan," Silber chased him away with the Smith & Wesson he'd bought in the meantime; he told me that only his fear of noise had prevented him from putting a bullet in Scooter's head. The next day he'd obtained a restraining order against his twin brother and had also sent him a copy of his — Simon's — will, which left everything to a famous charity too well endowed already to kill Silber for his million (as he'd been convinced his siblings were about to do when he drew up the will in September 1980). These measures had warded off Scooter for about a year; the next time he showed up on Silber's doorstep, Silber had brandished the pistol again, but this time Scooter — who of course knew all about Silber's allergy to noise — had stood his ground and called his brother's bluff. Finally the composer had put down the gun, picked up the baseball bat he kept by the front door, and with that relatively quiet weapon had broken his brother's right arm. By the time the cops appeared, Scooter had managed to scoot, leaving town in the stolen car he'd arrived in (which must have had an automatic transmission), and he hadn't rung the composer's doorbell since, though whenever he returned to Forest City — once or twice a year — Scooter made a point of phoning in a death threat, as he was too frugal to do, evidently, from outside the local calling area.

I gathered that Helen spent almost as much time and energy managing the Silber family image as she did running her business. As much as she must have resented her wealthier brother, she was even more anxious than he that my portrait hide his warts. The whole time I knew her, she regarded me with a wariness verging on hostility. Even after Silber's death, when Helen elected me to write these liner notes and to determine which pieces to put on which disc in what order (since she herself had bigger fish to fry), she refused to grant me access to the master tapes from which your discs were made, forcing me to make do with low-fidelity copies — something the reader must bear in mind if I sometimes seem to hear less in Silber's music than I should.

Helen's animosity may have been a reaction to mine, since I'd hated her from the day we met. No doubt I would've come to hate her anyhow — as I come to hate all hard-nosed, frowning, blazer-wearing, sensibly shod businesswomen in a position to boss me around — but what enabled me to make up my mind so quickly was that she reminded me so uncannily of Martha, the woman who'd replaced my aunt as head of the Tacoma library, and who had barely learned the names of her employees when she fired me.

Silber's sister, nonetheless, was for all I knew the only living person who recalled his early years, and once a month I forced myself, in the name of research, to put a smile on my face and do my best to win her over, chat her up and draw her out. Her office was a few blocks from my rooming house, and I made a point each month of dropping off my rent in person.

At ten A.M. on February 1, I was surprised to find Silber standing with his back to me at the Dutch door across whose countertopped, never opened bottom half his sister transacted her business. He wore an especially garish and ill-fitting yellow tuxedo, and was saying, "Maybe *this* time I *won't* go away. Maybe I *like* it here."

"You ungrateful little shit." Neither one had noticed me. "I ought to cut you off right now."

"C'mon, Hellie, all I'm asking —"

In the room beyond Helen the telephone rang.

"Shit," she said. "Hang on." She went into the inner office, shutting the top half of the Dutch door behind her.

"Silber?"

"Yeah?" He turned around slowly and insolently, then broke into a big smile. "Hey, it's the Professor."

"Scooter? Why the tuxedo?"

"Tell you later. Can you meet me at the Warthog in ten minutes? Great — now fuck off before she sees us talking. Oh," he added, spotting the check in my hand, "just leave it with me."

Walking to the Warthog, I marveled at how eager I was to get drunk with Scooter again. Was I so hard up for companionship as to get excited at the prospect of talking with a ne'er-do-well like him? Even *Gordon* was better-read than Scooter, and I never looked forward to talking to Gordon. Could it be that book learning wasn't what I wanted in a friend after all? Or was it rather that a *little* learning is worse than none (and Gordon didn't even wear his little lightly)?

When Scooter finally showed up half an hour later, he had changed back into his ratty leather jacket (the one with BAD-ASS on the back) and the greasy jeans he favored; as for that egregious tuxedo, he confessed that he'd been planning to scam on Simon's bank account by impersonating him at the teller window and withdrawing all his money, but he'd chickened out because he didn't know Simon's account number, or for that matter his bank. (He was disappointed to hear that I didn't either.) I wondered if it had been wise to entrust him with my rent check.

According to Scooter, he and Simon had been impersonating each other all their lives. He regaled me that morning with all sorts of mistaken-identity stories (some of them suspiciously resembling certain episodes of certain situation comedies). Although life (i.e., their father) had made them very different, and their differences had begun to show early on, he and Simon shared a gene for impersonation, and by the time they were five could both imitate Helen, for example, well enough over the phone to fool at least some of her friends. And when it came to imitating each other, they could fool everyone but Helen.

Sometimes they cooperated in these deceptions. Part of what makes the time-lapse film of Silber's face so eerie (see *My Face*) is that it isn't the history of a *single* face after all: according to Scooter, he had sat for Simon's nightly photo shoot dozens of times. Once when they were seven, they had swapped identities every day for a week, Scooter staying home to bask as Simon in their father's favoritism, and Simon satisfying his curiosity about the school that all the other kids in town attended;* he'd had no trouble passing for Scooter, since Scooter — though much more outgoing than Simon — had been prone then as now to gloomy spells in which he didn't speak, or acknowledge even his best friends.

Sometimes, inevitably, the twins had played doppelgänger pranks on each other. Throughout their childhood, Scooter had given his name as "Simon Silber" whenever he was caught sniffing glue or stealing hubcaps. One day when the twins were ten, Scooter had stayed home from school insisting that he was Simon, though Simon too claimed to be Simon that day. Not till Helen got home that afternoon was their father able to determine who was who. After that incident, Mr. Silber hadn't beaten Scooter, just carved a large "2" in the sole of his foot; the scar was still visible thirty years later, as Scooter insisted on showing me.

My favorite case of mistaken identity, though, occurred when the twins were seventeen. One of Scooter's girlfriends had stopped by the house, stinking drunk, when no one happened to be home but Simon — and Simon, by that point fiercely envious of his brother's love life, had impersonated Scooter, sitting down with the girl on the big living-room sofa and getting as far as "second base" (whatever that means —

---

* Our composer later confirmed this story, adding that he'd had recurring dreams about the elementary school ever since. Had their father known about this swap — which had exposed his favorite son to all kinds of distracting and counter-Preparatory influences, foremost the idea that lives other than the one his father had ordained for him were possible — Mr. Silber would no doubt have cited it as one more extenuating circumstance explaining why his failproof method had failed to produce a great pianist.

I was too embarrassed to ask Scooter to define it) before his ignorance and dread of sex had tipped her off. Scooter said their father had punished both twins for the fistfight that ensued: Scooter for beating up Simon, and Simon for throwing a punch or two himself, at the risk of injuring the hands that were supposed to be his ticket to glory. (Mr. Silber seemed not to care about Simon's imposture, except insofar as it suggested that the boy wasn't focusing on his destiny.)

Though Scooter's usefulness as an informant was impaired by his reluctance to discuss any event in which he couldn't give himself a starring part, he did provide me with some of my juiciest facts about his brother. No doubt a fear of such disclosures was exactly why his sister had forbidden him to talk to me. One reason for her wariness was that the first biographer had befriended Scooter too (as he'd befriended Gordon), and had somehow gotten Scooter to give him a guided tour of the walk-in closet where the family skeletons were kept. I later obtained a copy of Tom's manuscript, despite my employer's best efforts to keep me from seeing it, and I remember my hurt as I read and realized that Scooter had been "holding out" on me. Somehow Tom had won Scooter's utter trust, or utter enough for Scooter to blurt out things that later he wouldn't tell me. Thus, though he maintained to *me* that he wasn't bitter about the brilliant career he'd been denied, and that he'd never wanted to play piano anyhow, or not since he was four or five — not since he'd first understood the horror of his situation — he confessed to Tom that the day his father died, he had vowed to resume his career, but that by then he hadn't touched a piano in almost seven years (except for the one he'd attacked with a shoe), and found he had lost too much ground: any chance he might have had of fame and fortune was long gone.

Since then he had failed at everything he'd tried — paid employment, marriage (three times), junior college (dropping out after a week), etc. — either because the Silber twins had no innate ability for anything *but* music, or because poor Scooter's childhood had been one long intensive training in futility, and he'd learned his lesson well. For most of his adult life he'd lived off a meager allowance from his sister (though that was one more secret he told Tom but never me), a subsidy he supplemented with small thefts. Now and then — guided by "classic rock" as others by voices — he stole something big enough that for a while afterward the government provided him with room and board, since crime was one more thing he'd failed at, if always getting caught amounts to failure.

It was thanks to Tom's knack of worming his way into people's confidence that he — while failing in his six months as biographer to unearth material *I* dug up the week I started — had admittedly managed to turn up a few amusing facts I hadn't yet discovered for myself when I came upon his notes.* Though I am (as the reader has already gathered) a witty and well-spoken person, the sort to whom anyone ought to be grateful to talk — so you'd think — when granted the chance, I can't deny that Tom had better luck with some informants, maybe because he got to them first (and before Helen told them *not* to talk), like the first to hunt on an island where the animals haven't yet learned to fear man. According to Silber, moreover, Tom had been a private eye before deciding to impersonate a writer, and so had certain skills I don't. I'd like to report that detection's loss was literature's gain, but no, it was a setback for literature too: Tom's manuscript was embarrassingly bad.

I had another bout of carousing with Scooter the following morning, though I had to cancel a date I'd reluctantly made a few days earlier with Gordon: he'd won a hundred dollars with a scratch-and-win lottery ticket, and we'd arranged to celebrate with coffee at the Bean.

Instead it was beer at the Warthog — and, as always, Scooter

---

* Somewhat of a pedant, he'd also gone to the trouble of ascertaining the exact dates of certain events in our composer's life, such as the death of his sister's canary, and though I have better things to do than double-check these datings — and in any case I doubt their relevance — I see no reason to doubt their accuracy.

was late. People are said to count up the faults of those who keep them waiting, but for some reason I found myself counting up Gordon's instead. He was filling in that week for the eighth-grade English teacher, and all he could talk about was the stone-dead Junior Classic they were reading in Honors English: his taste in books was that of a clever eighth-grader. If Scooter was a stray, a big friendly pet gone feral, then Gordon (I decided) was the tame bear at the circus, proud of its tutu and desperately intent on not falling off its little bike.

I recount these unkind thoughts to provide a context for the unkind thing I did a little later, after two hours of laughing and drinking with Scooter. Now, I am not proud of the scene I'm about to relate. I would pay a lot, in fact, to be able to rewind and erase the length of tape in question. And yet I confess to an amoral exultation at the time, at being on the winning team, for once, in a two-against-one.

Scooter and I had just emerged from the Warthog when I heard my name. "Norm! Hey, Norm! Hey — look what I just got!"

"Shit," I said, and turned to see Gordon approaching with a cheap electric keyboard and a book of *Immortal Melodies for Beginning Pianists.* Reaching me, he gazed up eagerly, but I stared back with less friendliness than he'd come to expect — with no friendliness at all, in fact — and without responding to his eager tidings. Although I didn't consciously *refuse* to speak to him (something I have never done to anyone), I may have lost track of time as I stared, trying to see him as Scooter must see him. I don't know if Gordon (no longer smiling) knew about Scooter, or if he assumed he was seeing another side of Simon, an alter ego who appeared to find poor Gordon even more contemptible than the familiar Simon did, and in whose presence I too was ashamed to know Gordon. Either way, my hapless neighbor finally got the picture and — without another word — turned and slowly walked away with his self-improver's purchases.

"Who the hell was *that*?"

"Oh, just some loser who lives in my building," I said, evidently speaking louder, in my unaccustomed drunkenness, than I had intended, since I saw poor Gordon wince at that point (though without looking back).

I wound up getting drunk with Scooter every morning for a week, and it may have been the best week of my term in Forest City. For a few days there, I — Norm — was a regular at a biker bar, on a first-name basis with people with names like Crusher, Wolf, and Horst. I was toying with the idea of buying a motorcycle myself when Helen called one frozen morning to ask why my rent was late. I told her that I'd given it to Scooter and that according to my balance the check had cleared already. She said she'd never seen it, and that Scooter had left town the night before.

### 9. *Sirens* 4:04

The reader has already guessed that the sirens in question are not the mythological creatures whose singing lures sailors to their doom, but rather the prosaic horns on fire engines — and guessed, as well, that Silber hated sirens.* In this case, however, his usual hatred of noise was complicated by his morbid fear of fire: he was neurotically afraid that *Day* would go up in flames before he had a chance to finish it. Several times that winter, in the course of an evening walk bejeweled with colored lights and scented with woodsmoke, Silber suddenly froze in midstride and midsentence, scrunched up his face in concentration as if trying hard to place a half-familiar tune, then gasped and

---

* It occurs to me that he had much in common with the crafty Odysseus, who stopped his ears (or was it just his sailors' ears?) with wax in order to behold a spectacle that would have destroyed him if he'd also had to listen to it, except that in Silber's case the spectacle was life itself, the earplugs were not wax but silicone, which has a higher Noise Reduction Rating — when used as directed, between twenty and thirty-seven decibels, depending on the frequency — and in the end the noise destroyed him all the same, so ineffective are even the best earplugs compared, for example, to eyelids.

ran off up the street in the direction of his house. A minute later I would hear the siren that his morbidly sensitive ears had already detected — even before the dogs did — and I knew that he had run off to check a horrifying hunch that his house was on fire, and more specifically that *Day* was. This fear had been especially acute since October, when a small kitchen blaze had destroyed the master tape and the only manuscript of his most accomplished aleatory composition* to date, the *"Que Será, Será" Variations.* Throughout his career, Silber was intrigued by methods of harnessing chance to drive his compositions, in this case with the aid of the Pop-o-Matic dice agitator from an old Milton Bradley game called Headache. He told me the piece was an homage to the Doris Day classic, though in only three of the twenty-four variations had I been able, the night that Silber played the whole thing for me over the phone, to hear a trace of the original tune. He'd entrusted me with his only other recording of the work the day before the fire; when he asked for the cassette back, I had to tell him I'd lost it. Actually I'd taped a talk show over Silber's composition, guiltily reminded as I did so of a story I had read in junior high, about a lonely housewife who gives a peddler a pot of chrysanthemums one morning and then, out driving with her husband later the same day, sees her flowers and a flowerpot-shaped clump of dirt — but not the reusable pot itself — lying in the middle of the road.

Sirens, then — composed in February '94 — had the dual role of accommodating a hated noise (à la *Crows*) and assuaging the neuroses activated by that noise. There is no theme to speak of:

---

* Incidentally, another of his recent random works, a microtonal ramble called *As Luck Would Have It,* had also been whisked off by fate, almost as soon as it was finished, blowing out an open kitchen window and away after Silber carelessly left the manuscript on the windowsill like a cooling pie.

Insofar as so peripatetic an artist could be said to have a headquarters, it would have been the kitchen: that was the room he most often wound up in at the creative height of his pacing sessions, maybe because it was connected by the back stairs to his third-floor pacing lane, and by the butler's pantry to the room enshrining his beloved Bösendorfer.

while the left hand rumbles ominously in the bottom octave, the right repeats a four-bar phrase that climbs from a′ to e″ and then falls to a′ again. The phrase is repeated (with a legato meant to simulate a real siren, though Silber admitted that almost any other instrument — a violin, a trumpet — would have been better suited to that mimetic office) over and over, louder and louder, so that in the course of two minutes the warning sound swells from *pianississimo* to *fortissimo;* but then over the next two minutes it fades gradually back to inaudibility. As far as I can tell, the "message" of the piece is: Something bad is happening, right now, somewhere, to somebody, but not *here,* not to *you* — not *this* time.

At around the time that Scooter skipped town with my rent, Gordon lost his job. By that point he was no longer speaking to me (when I went upstairs to apologize the day after the Warthog incident, he had refused to open his door), but according to Billy, our neighbor had been fired for slapping a sarcastic seventh-grader while substituting for the music teacher.

Over the next two weeks, Gordon lapsed into a lavish depression. He stopped speaking, even to Billy. He no longer left the rooming house except for food, though sometimes late at night he'd leave his room to walk the halls. One Friday night I found him, in brown flannel pajamas, crying on the landing; when I led him back upstairs to the wide-open door of his no-longer-tidy room, he slammed the door behind him and then thanked me for my kindness by turning on his keyboard and picking out the single most pathetic passage of the *Pathétique* over and over till dawn.

Gordon's despair affected the morale of the entire rooming house. Billy took to wearing knee and elbow pads in addition to the helmet when he left his room at all. My room was a mess, strewn with clothing, books, and papers, but Gordon's room was so much messier that just the sight of it had sapped my will to straighten up. I myself was fighting off dejection — as I had to every February when my birthday loomed — and Gordon's histrionics didn't make it any easier. I found myself starting to hate him again, as in the days of the *Moonlight* Sonata. I told myself my hatred made no sense but that — for Gordon's sake as well as mine — I'd have to do something about him. Helping Gordon: that would be my birthday present to myself. (I had no one else to give me presents, aside from my mom.) Finally, on the evening of the twenty-seventh, I did my best to cheer him up as we stood in the dim and drafty hallway, grimly awaiting our turns for the common single-occupancy toilet (there was only one for the entire house, almost always occupied, though each kitchenette came with a stainless-steel sink compelled, sometimes, to serve an even humbler function than it was intended for). *It's always darkest just before the dawn:* that was the gist of my sermon, though even as I sermonized I remembered all the times I'd stayed up all night long, and how each time the heavens had gradually grown *brighter* for at least an hour before sunrise. I could see, in any case, that my pep talk didn't "take," and the next day I tried a different tack, ambushing Gordon outside the john again after his morning bath (a long indulgent demoralized soak somehow involving fortified wine but not — or so I gathered from his mounting body odor — soap) and handing him Schopenhauer's *Studies in Pessimism:* "Maybe this will help!" It was the most depressing book I owned at the time, and I was counting on its having a homeopathic action: the sheer extremity of its title sentiment,* the grotesque reduction to absurdity of the gloomy mood in which my overwrought neighbor was overindulging, would cause him to recoil from his morbid moping with manly disgust. I also recommended baking cookies as something that always cheers *me* up, and mentioned that Food Town had a special that week on those big tubes of oven-ready cookie dough.

I put in a long and productive day at the Forest City Pub-

---

* E.g.: "A quick test of the assertion that enjoyment outweighs pain in this world, or that they are at any rate balanced, would be to compare the feelings of an animal engaged in eating another with the feelings of the animal being eaten."

lic Library — not in the sober, grownup Quiet Room with its flickering fluorescents and oddly enervating *Eigenton,* but amid the happy babble of the Children's Room, in the warm glow of an old-fashioned floor lamp at a child-scaled table by a glass case displaying a local kid's collection of discontinued candy bars. Night was falling when the library closed for the weekend at 5:00 P.M. The air was brisk but not unpleasant, and I walked home whistling cheerfully. (Silber was intrigued by the possibilities of the human whistle, or whistling human, as an underexploited musical instrument; he'd even started a sonata for piano and whistler.) Back at my rooming house I paused to check the gas meters and saw with a smile that Gordon had taken to heart my suggestion to bake cookies — his "cubic feet" needle was turning faster than I'd ever seen it turn before.

I used my own oven to heat a frozen dinner, cleaned my room so thoroughly as to change its acoustics, took a shower in the unexpectedly vacant bathroom, and was in bed by 7:30. The past few weeks I'd been unable to fall asleep without earplugs, no matter how tired I was, or how quiet the rest of the house, so great was my apprehension that Gordon would suddenly shatter the silence, but that night I somehow knew that there would be no music.

I was awakened from dreams of firemen and yowling cats by the sound of sirens. Silber once explained to me (the day after one of his siren-prompted homeward sprints) that sirens — and similar urgent upward surges in musical pitch at critical moments in certain compositions — derived their meaning from the tendency of the human voice to rise during crises. And in fact my own voice rose uncontrollably when, smelling gas, I opened my door just in time to see two firemen with respirators racing upstairs.

"What's going on?"

They ignored my question, but when they came back downstairs — after clomping around overhead for at least half an hour — I stuck out my head again just in time to see them struggling with a stretcher bearing something shrouded and utterly silent. I followed them outdoors, stood by the gas meters shivering in my pajamas, and watched the paramedics load their cargo into the ambulance. After the vehicle wailed off into the night, I glanced at Gordon's meter. Ordinarily — due to the oven's pilot light, I guess — the needle on the cubic-feet dial continued to turn at about the speed of the hour hand on a clock even when no one was home, but I could somehow tell that even that minimal stirring had ceased.

# Disc Three

## 1. *Digression* 18:09

In what might almost be mistaken for humility, Silber seems here to embrace the role of commentator, presenting his own music as no more than a parenthesis in an obscure piano piece by Beethoven, "The Rage over a Lost Penny." Since the Beethoven, however, is about six minutes long as normally performed, and Silber's insertion is three times that length, we must wonder whether our composer really acts here as a conscientious annotator, or rather as lethal parasite — one that, as it gestates in the belly of its host, tears it apart at the seams. Silber himself compared *Digression* to a Saint Bernard inseminating a Chihuahua.

Just enough of the Beethoven is quoted, before and after the digression proper, to indicate the point — roughly midway — where Silber wanted his interpolation. Beethoven's piece is intentionally petty, petulant, and puny: a comical musical tantrum. Silber ennobles the rage with thundering chords and long, slow, sullen interludes of unbearable intensity. The "point" is clear, and not original: the most trivial events can provoke magnificent emotions; true art can grow from tiny irritations, as pearls grow from grains of sand.

In Silber's case, of course, the initial bit of grit was more apt to be "The Rage over a Honked Horn" or (to cite the biggest nuisance of his brief career as a concert pianist) "The Rage over a Cleared Throat." For all his faults, our composer was not a penny-pincher. He may not have paid me much, but more than I was in any position to demand, and his canceled checks reveal that over the years he gave a lot of money to assorted charities (including, on several occasions, the local humane society — in atonement?). No, my friend was stingy only with his time, which he hoarded, gloated over like a miser, heartlessly refused to spend with me. And here, notwithstanding my determination to keep myself in the background of these notes, where some would insist a biographer belongs, I must say a word or two about my loneliness in Forest City.

I had found few friends in my thirty-eight years, for the same reason that my book had found few readers: I knew exactly what I was about, and made no crowd-pleasing concessions. And now I had moved to a town where the only man I considered my equal — the only one for whom I could muster the respect without which there can be no real friendship — dictated absolutely the terms of our acquaintance. My employer was a wonderful companion when he wanted company, but he could go for days at a time without speaking to me or anyone else. I, however, needed people, at least as background music, and I spent several hours a day at the Bean, watching other patrons mingle. The coffeehouse was frequented by all the misfits who for one reason or another had wound up in Forest City, or like Silber had been born there and had failed to escape — people who would have had nothing to do with one another in a *real* city, since each deviated from the norm along a different axis, and in a real city every deviation has its own subculture and newsletter; but here we were all thrown together: perverts, anarchists, unsuccessful aphorists, ne'er-do-wells, believers in elaborate conspiracies, dropouts, runaways, layabouts, psychopaths, touchers, ticqueurs, flaneurs, frotteurs, unpublished poets, unpatented inventors, and every other kind of able-bodied unemployable. I had not befriended my fellow misfits, though, and no more intended to than I intended to befriend my fellow customers at T&A Video.

Soon after Gordon's death, Helen told me that in what turned out to be her last chat with the poor man, he had referred to me at one point as his best friend and at another as his *only* friend, which gave me a pang for my treatment of Gordon, whom I'd never numbered among my friends at all, though in no position myself to be picky. (By my count, in fact, I was no more "popular" than Gordon when I knew him, since the only friend I did count was Silber — who for all I knew may not have counted me.) But maybe Gordon and I had been friends after all, since I became much more aware of my own isolation after his death. I'd grown accustomed to my upstairs neighbor, and as little as I'd liked his noise, I now felt a horrible desolation, an appalling *stillness,* as if my television set had been repossessed.

Helen, anyhow, was so moved by the idea that I'd befriended Gordon as to give me his electric keyboard, in addition to a fat manila envelope, sealed and labeled "FOR NORM" in Gordon's childish hand. Not for several days did I work up the nerve to open that envelope, and when I did I got no further than the first typewritten page of the fifty or so inside: it turned out that Gordon had been so inspired by my aphorisms as to try his own hand at that deceptively simple form:

> Sometimes they have Symbols in books — but sometimes a book is a Symbol!
> Some people say their [sic] too busy for Great works of Art — but did it ever occur to them that Great works of Art are too busy for them???*

Imitation is the most disturbing form of flattery, and (wondering if this were how my dad had felt on reading "The Malfunction of Modern Music") I stuffed the manuscript back in its envelope and stuck it in the cardboard box, beneath my bed, to which I relegated papers — time-for-a-checkup reminders

---

* Let it be said in fairness to Gordon that better writers than he have managed to go astray within the seemingly safe confines of an aphorism. No form is too small to allow for false starts, wrong turns, lost ways, dead ends.

from my former dermatologist, long letters from my mom — that I couldn't deal with but couldn't quite throw out.

As for the keyboard, it was technically a synthesizer, I suppose, since (as I'd already gathered from the sound effects of Gordon's final weeks) it was capable of many other sounds than those of a piano. After a few days, though, of experimenting with those other sounds (I especially liked a certain springy "boing-boing" setting), and feeling sorry for Silber with his old-fashioned acoustic pianos, which all at once seemed pitiably limited (just as, with the advent of bubble gum, all mere chewing gums must suddenly have seemed) — after that spree, I decided actually to teach myself to play. March came in like a wet dog that year; it rained every day that month in Forest City, and without a hobby I would've gone stir-crazy. The keyboard had come with a Schaum's piano book "for earliest beginners," and by the end of my first day, I'd already mastered two pieces in that book — the first two, "On the Seas" and "Seize the C's," both in the key of C.

I also tried my hand at composing, maybe only because it was raining, or maybe for the same reason that Silber had turned from performing to composing: relative merit is harder to gauge in a composer than in a performer. I may even have allowed myself to entertain some notion of one day surpassing my employer, though up to that point my only musical training had been group instruction, in fifth grade, on something called a recorder, a sort of rudimentary flute made of a substance (lacquered wood? vulcanized rubber? fossilized plastic?) as ambiguous to the eye of memory as its color, a dark brownish red or reddish brown verging on prune. I'd never even learned to read music, much less to write it. I found, though, one sleepless night, that by slowly playing three adjacent white keys over and over — ABCABCABC — with my right hand while picking out "Jingle Bells" with my left, at the stately tempo of the most solemn dirges, with the volume down as far as it would go, I could produce a very soothing little lullaby, one that to my ear had more to recommend it than some of my employer's compositions, for all their fancy book learning. Needless to say, my employer disagreed: I still hear him laughing stagily the day, a few weeks later, I played my Opus no. 1 for him at the Bean, where I'd already figured out about the pedals, and kept the one for "soft" depressed throughout ("flooring it," as I liked to pretend — speeding to Slumberland). Was his laughter as uneasy as I remember it? Well, if you've been practicing an art for decades, you are bound to hate beginners in the same art: not even the least talented — not that I was of *their* ilk, I trust — are *that* much worse than you, no matter how good you may be. Even the slowest of slow learners are on pace to overtake you one day, if they continue to develop — as of course they won't — at the breakneck speed of beginner's luck.

In the middle of March, wanting to learn a bit more about music — to finally find out what all the fuss was about — I enrolled for the spring quarter at Lumber Junior College. Thanks to my father, who'd listened to nothing but classical music while I was growing up, I heard that music now with the ears of a native, but I'd never learned its grammar, never even learned to speak it — never learned an instrument. The gaudy little edifice of knowledge I'd constructed as a young man while composing my tirade (see *Look, Dad — No Hands*) had washed away at once, like a sand castle built at the water's edge with the tide coming in, and while it stood had been unsound even as sand castles go, consisting as it did of overarching metamusical considerations founded on the void where a knowledge of musical basics belonged. I could impress the many who knew even less about music than I did, but I lived in terror of the many who knew more.*

---

* I can assure my readers that (in addition to my course of intensive night-study at Lumber Junior College) I've done a lot of reading since then, studying the liner notes to all 217 classical LPs in my record collection. I've also been a loyal fan (and pledge-drive supporter!) of KDOA, which may not play Silber's works but does broadcast several syndicated programs with educational ambitions. So any allusions to my "ignorance" must be understood to refer to the era *before* I embarked on this commentary.

So I signed up for five night classes, each meeting once a week on a different weeknight (neatly solving my problem of what to do in the evenings): Masterworks of European Music, Music Theory, Ear Training, Composition, and Elementary Piano. Silber took the news of my enrollment badly. He even threatened to fire me, claiming that my studies would divert time and effort that should be going into the biography, and that my "profound ignorance of music" was the only reason he had hired me in the first place; I had no more right to destroy that ignorance, he insisted, than an anchorwoman hired for her hairdo has to shave her head. But the real reason for his objections, I think, was that he was afraid I'd learn to appreciate other composers — and in fact I met one in the cafeteria during the first week of classes.

It was dinnertime on Thursday and I was eating a tuna-salad sandwich before the first session of my Composition class. The menu that evening was Salisbury steak, mashed potatoes, succotash, lime jello, and brownies, but by that point — four evenings into the semester — I'd already deemed the cafeteria fare inedible and taken to brown-bagging. I would've much preferred to sit outside beneath a spreading oak, as two students, he and she, were doing on the front of the brochure that had lured me to Lumber Junior College in the first place, but it was still raining.

I finished the first half of my sandwich (sliced on the diagonal the way my mother would've done) and was about to embark on the other (with the sad thought that my meal was already more than half over, since I'd already eaten my apple and most of the potato chips in the little bag I'd bought from a machine) when I was arrested in mid-bite by a voice too loud to be addressed to anyone but me: "Mind if I sit here?"

I looked up and saw a huge bearlike man with a full black beard still dripping from outdoors, though he'd already been through the food line. Together with his potbelly, cheap blue overalls, and heavy southern drawl, that beard made him look like he ought to be swigging moonshine from a jug and guarding the still with a shotgun — or attending night school at a junior college. Now, I don't want to dwell on the menagerie of drug addicts, wife beaters, gay divorcées, gay parolees, alcoholics, lonesome widows, sex offenders, and welfare mothers I encountered at Lumber Junior College, but I will say that they looked nothing at all like the pair on the front of the brochure, and even made the Bean irregulars look like happy clones in a eugenicist's utopia. By that point I'd already resolved to avoid all contact with my fellow students, lest I catch what they had. So I scowled as I nodded very faintly — at that point, the chair in question, the one across from mine at an unwiped formica-topped table for two — was in fact the only open seat in the entire cafeteria (all plastic and unfinished concrete), so I could hardly say no.

"Some weather we're having."

Not wanting to get trapped in a discussion of the weather — a subject on which my companion looked like he would have all kinds of strong opinions — I ignored him and continued eating. After a long minute, another table opened up, and the stranger left me in peace.

Twenty minutes later I was sitting in Room 303 of the Arts building doing my best to ignore my fellow students when the big man in overalls entered and walked over to the lectern in the front of the room, and I realized that he was none other than my Composition teacher, Cletus Pitchford — a man whom Silber would describe in coming weeks as a "nonentity," a "hick," a "half-witted clodhopper," an "inbred moron," and (I'm sorry to repeat) a "fat hillbilly retard." And Cletus, to be sure, was not a genius, or if he was he hid it well enough to pass for something almost as anomalous: a happy, well-adjusted human being. He was so easygoing, so friendly, and so charismatic that, after class, when he suggested that the group adjourn to the campus pub, I surprised myself by joining the expedition.

In the smoky cellar pub I made a point of sitting by Cletus — God knows there was no one else in our party I wanted to speak to — and of telling him all about myself, lest he mistake me (as I'd mistaken him back in the cafeteria) for just another hapless night-scholar. He, in turn, told me a bit about himself. He'd grown up in Marked Tree, Arkansas, the son of a world-famous yodeler so fat that in later years he had to be carried on-stage in a custom-built sedan chair by four burly attendants. Cletus had studied violin and composition at a prestigious in-stitute of music as a rebellion against his tobacco-chewing father (albeit a rebellion funded by the latter), but, since his fa-ther's stroke in 1991, had made his peace with the folk art he'd spurned and was now an accomplished yodeler in his own right.

I spoke to him again a few days later in the school gym, where I'd taken to lifting weights before class, figuring I might as well give my body a workout, since my brain wasn't likely to get one at Lumber Junior College. As I recall, I was wearing a fluorescent yellow sweatsuit with the insignia of a shoe manu-facturer whose actual shoes I couldn't afford. The men's locker room in the Phys Ed center was such an inferno that I pre-ferred to drive to Lumber in my sweatsuit, not showering or changing till I got back home. That meant I had to sit through class sticky with sweat, but I liked to think of sweat as a camou-flage that enabled me to move among my simple fellow stu-dents undetected.

It didn't always work, of course, that camouflage. On the af-ternoon in question, I was lying on a padded, vinyl-covered bench — getting "psyched," as we say, for my final set of bench presses — when I noticed that three of my muscle-bound class-mates from Intro Piano had finished for the day and were snickering at me as they collected their things. Wondering how much of their lifting they'd done in prison, I got up, added two more giant fifty-pound plates to my bar, and then, pretending to remember something, left the room. I went down the hall to the pop machine, bought a can of cola, and unhurriedly con-sumed its contents while scanning a bulletin board. When I re-turned to the weight room intending to remove the extra plates and continue my workout, my classmates were gone as I'd hoped, but Cletus had come in and was doggedly walking on a treadmill in what looked like a doctor-ordained workout. He nodded and smiled in self-deprecation, then raised his eyebrows when I headed for the bench press. He looked so impressed, in fact, that — with the mild delusions of grandeur a good can of cola can briefly induce — I got under the overloaded barbell, determined to lower and raise it just once.

Anybody who has ever tried to bench forty pounds more than his personal best, at the end of a long workout, can guess what happened next. Though his short sprint from the treadmill left him winded, some of my teacher's bulk must have been muscle, since when we lifted the crushing bar off my chest and back onto its stanchions, it felt like he was doing all the work. A few minutes later, as I lay there on my back — not hurt but stunned, and overwhelmed by gratitude — I decided Cletus was my friend.

For the next month, Thursday was my favorite day, especially since the after-class outing proved to be a weekly custom, and even though the rest of the class insisted on coming along. Everyone wanted a piece of Cletus. As far as I could tell, he was no better known than Silber as a composer, but he had an affability that Silber lacked, and his students found him irresistible, mobbing him every week after class in a way that reminded me a little of children welcoming their father home from work, but even more — considering how many of his worshipful students were women — of a scene in a video I'd rented recently, in which three attractive nurses press their ample charms on a lucky male patient.*

But our friendship wasn't confined to Thursday evenings.

---

* As I've mentioned, my year as Silber's lackey was a lonely one, and for the most part I was forced to entertain myself. Readers will understand why someone who earns his living by reading and writing would rather do anything but in his free time. For the same reason, I often wasn't in the mood to listen to music, or even to tickle the ivories myself. I took long walks, but sooner or later I had to return to my room. So I rented videos. I see no reason to conceal the fact that some of these videos treated of strong human passions, including the fleshly ones.

Sometimes we "hung out" in the daytime, usually in Lumber, where we mostly walked, something his physician had ordered Cletus to do more of. He was so big and slow-moving and round that once as we were skirting Bobb Observatory we pretended he was our planet orbiting the sun and I — running circles around him — the moon.

Once or twice he made the trip to Forest City, where we also walked around (I didn't want him to see my rented room). Silber disapproved. I remember his look of astonished disgust the day he ran into us on Tree Street (I confess I'd timed our walk to intersect with his), Cletus yodeling at the top of his lungs and I energetically clapping along. That was when I realized with a thrill that Silber was *jealous* of my new friendship — jealous of our happiness, as they say. All I had to do was mention Cletus and he'd get upset. Suddenly Silber, who had spurned my overtures at friendship for half a year now, till I'd come to feel like an unrequited lover, was chasing after *me,* inviting me along on walks and drives, and even inviting me over to his house (or at least his carriage house — he *still* wouldn't let me back inside the main house) on the flimsiest of pretexts: "Listen, I was just cleaning out the garage and you'll never guess what I found: my old bike. The one I had back when I was a kid. I figured you might want to see it, seeing as you're writing my biography and stuff." Usually the invitation was for coffee (which he prepared by spooning brown powder out of a jar and into a mug of hot water) but once he invited me to dinner, after I mentioned that Cletus had made dinner for me.

That unforgettable meal (with Cletus, not Silber) was my first and, now that I think of it, my only visit to his house, a much smaller house than Silber's, on the edge of Lumber. Cletus met me at the door in an aphoristic apron (ONE MAN'S MEAT IS ANOTHER MAN'S POISON) and ushered me in. I almost turned around and walked back out when I found four or five of my fellow students lounging in the living room, drinking beer and watching some idiotic program about dogs who bite their owners, but these interlopers left as soon as I arrived, and I had the teacher to myself for the rest of the evening.

While he chopped and simmered in the kitchen, I reviewed the bookcase behind the TV set, shaking my head sadly at the bloated paperback bestsellers Cletus favored. *Well, at least he reads,* I reasoned, as if reading per se were a virtue. His taste in food, though, proved to be much better than his taste in books — so much better that by the time he cleared away the herbed caviar roulade and brought in the stuffed pheasant, I began to feel sheepish for bringing a big plastic bottle of supermarket bourbon — one I'd chosen not because I don't appreciate fine wine, but in a good-natured attempt to "do as the Romans," since I'd had Cletus figured for a no-nonsense drinker. (For kindred reasons, I had made a point of dressing "down," wearing sneakers, ratty blue jeans, and my oldest sweatshirt — the orange-and-blue one with the name and gnashing cartoon badger mascot of my high-school wrestling team — only to find Cletus clad in a natty black suit beneath his apron.) Evidently, my obliging host had had the same idea, and had gone so far in *my* direction, taken such elaborate pains to cater to *my* (possibly more cultivated) tastes, that rather than meeting halfway, we passed en route, missing each other completely.

As for Silber, he made me dinner in the carriage house's tiny kitchenette: macaroni and cheese, potato chips, and little single-serving cans of chocolate pudding. I resisted the temptation to tell him that *Cletus* had served pheasant; instead, I told myself that I was getting a rare glimpse of Silber's bachelor routine in all its dinginess. (My own eating habits weren't much better, but at least I had the excuse of poverty.)

All this was fun at first, but I soon grew to miss Silber's old aloofness. Though arguably a more interesting person than Cletus, my employer was a much less skillful friend. He had no gift for friendship, and watching him strain to be gregarious was painful. My first sessions at the keyboard could not have been more inept, more ridden with wrong notes, than Silber's efforts at affability. Besides, I knew his sudden change of heart had less to do with me than with his rival at Lumber Junior College. And by that point I was accustomed to being the pest and not the pestered (every friendship has one of each). Suddenly my employer was demanding that I account for my time, for all the world like a jealous husband fearing infidelity:* "Yes, I know you had your little amateur make-believe Composition class last night, but you said the class only runs till nine and you still weren't home when I called at eleven!" He even made me start keeping a time sheet to log the hours I spent on his biography. No wonder I found myself avoiding him, and finally screening my calls.

But I digress — emboldened by Silber's own *Digression*. Our composer predicted that one day his interpolation would be included routinely in authorized scores of the Beethoven piece, just as the scores of certain concerti incorporate cadenzas added by later performers. One of Silber's unreleased recordings — from which the performance on your disc is excerpted — was a performance of the enhanced version of "Rage"; Silber reasoned that if the recording were released on CD with separate tracks for the digression and the two halves of the Beethoven piece it bisects, purists would always have the option of programming their players to skip his parenthesis with only a small track-hopping hiccup.

## 2. *Eleven to One*       5:00

Although this boxed set may be thought of as a multimedia collaboration between a little-known composer and an even more egregiously neglected author, the only time that Silber ever collaborated on a purely musical project was in July 1985, when the first-ever convention of the New Composers' Alli-

---

* But of course sex had nothing to do with any of this — to say what should go without saying but doesn't, to judge by the reactions of people to whom I've described my relationship with Silber. As far as I could tell, Silber was asexual.

ance was held in Forest City, of all places. Formed in 1969, the NCA was a group of contemporary composers that limited its membership to twelve; Silber had been admitted in 1983 with the death of charter member Hoyt Boyd. I don't know why the honor fell to my employer, among all the unallied composers in the world, but it can't have hurt that the president of the Alliance, David Altschul, had known Silber's father when the two were students at the same conservatory. As for why the convention had been held on the newest member's turf, Silber claimed that it was in honor of his preeminence among living composers, but one wonders if the number of guest bedrooms in his house wasn't a bigger factor: many of the members were too poor for a hotel — as poor as Silber himself would have been had his income derived from his art. (As poor as *me,* in other words.) In any case, fully six of the eleven visiting composers had spent the week in Silber's house. That he'd been willing to throw open his doors to half a dozen imperfect strangers is evidence of how badly Silber had wanted to host that convention, or maybe just to attend it, since his unfortunate phobia (see *Route 111*) would've prevented him from attending a convention in someone else's city. That he subsequently sealed off two rooms "defiled" by his houseguests (see *Annex to "My House"*) suggests what a trauma the invasion must've been.

For a long time I assumed that my reclusive employer had never had any contact at all with other living composers. One Thursday night, though, toward the end of March, Cletus told our class about the "speed composer" Goodenough, whose music involved so much repetition, and so many formulas for rapid expansion of shorthand notations, that he was able, with the aid of a computer program of his own devising, to write music (usually for synthesizer) in less time than it took to hear — to write a fully orchestrated thirty-minute tone poem in fifteen, for instance. "By the way," Cletus had added, nodding at me, "I think he used to be a friend of your employer's, Norm."

Silber flushed with anger when I mentioned this exchange.

Goodenough had never been a friend of *his,* he said, and even spoke of suing Cletus for slander. But he did admit to knowing Goodenough, and told me all about the band of outsiders to which they'd both belonged, and the convention at which they had met.

The NCA wasn't a "movement" or "school"; as far as I could tell, in fact, the only thing that our composer had in common with his fellow members was a lack of interest in all music but his own, including that of fellow members. Otherwise they were a motley bunch: Altschul, who had just finished the thirty-year task of composing a different suite of miniatures for every interjection in *Webster's* (twenty-four *Aah*s, twenty-four *Ah*s, twenty-four *Aha*s, twenty-four *Ahem*s, twenty-four *Ahoy*s, twenty-four *Alack*s, twenty-four *Alas*es, twenty-four *Amen*s . . .); Battcock, whose instrumental works incorporated laugh tracks every time the music did something "humorous" (though I, for one, have always been skeptical about claims of humor in instrumental music, like claims of flavor in cigarette ads); Cowlick, who for years had confined himself to the note of middle C — not just the key but the *note,* varying only the volume, duration, and instrumentation; Dunsmore, each of whose eight mammoth symphonies existed, according to their composer, merely to set up a single overwhelming moment (Silber compared them to flowering trees planted for the sake of the week or two each year when they blossom); Earleywine, who kept developing new instruments with names like the *trombonium,* the *pseudobassoon,* and the *acoustic synthesizer,* in order to be the first composer to write music for them; the psychotic Farraway (see *"Annex to My House"*); Goodenough; Hirt, of whom more in a moment; Noseworthy, concerning whom I can't recall a single fact; Pilcrow, who — congenitally deaf — wrote only *Augenmusik,* music meant to be seen and not heard; and Webb — like Silber, better known as a performer, though unlike Silber he was still performing (and, presumably, like any serious musician, practicing several hours a day, every day, on his chosen instrument, the gong).

The most nearly famous member of this club of unheard and unheard-of composers was probably Eberhard Hirt, who claimed to write the saddest music ever written. In an attempt to bolster that claim, Hirt — a Sunday inventor with several patent applications to his name — had developed a device to measure sadness "scientifically"; according to Silber, the gizmo (calibrated in "millihirts") looked suspiciously like an ordinary rain gauge, but Hirt insisted that it measured "sadness itself" and not just tears. Silber added that Hirt had once been named in a lawsuit by the widow of the horn player in the ensemble that was to have premiered Hirt's horn quartet — a work so devastating that after one especially intense rehearsal of the long slow movement, the musician in question ended his life by driving his car at eighty miles per hour into the stone wall of a passing cemetery.

Silber hadn't made a single friend at the convention (though most of it was held under his roof), but he said he'd "hit it off okay" with Pilcrow, who was mute as well as deaf, and whose fanciful, colorful scores — aswarm with hieroglyphics, algebraic symbols, pictographs, and other nonstandard notations — may well have inspired our composer's later interest in nonperformable music.

Toward the other new composers, Silber's feelings seem to have ranged from indifference to hatred. He'd especially hated Goodenough, who, in a session devoted to works in progress, had trumped his host's triumphant description of *Day* by boasting that *he* was at work on a *yearlong* composition, a massive symphony "for synthetic orchestra," in four movements corresponding to the seasons.* Needless to say, Silber disapproved of such a project. Like most of the few people who had heard of Goodenough at all (though arguably with less right than most), Silber considered his yearlong work presump-

---

* I once infuriated Silber by granting that (as he insisted) the day is the basic unit of human consciousness, but maintaining that the basic unit of *memory* — the standard pigeonhole for sorting past experiences — is not the day but the *season*.

tuous. "Music by and *for* computers," he once called the symphony, since no human being, not even Goodenough himself, was likely to listen to the whole thing note for note; that was 365 times more unlikely than that anyone would ever listen to the whole of *Day,* already unlikely. In Silber's opinion, Goodenough's masterpiece discredited megaworks in general, while also making *Day* look puny by comparison: even as an example of the madness of modern music, poor Silber now amounted to no more than a footnote.* On the final day of the convention, anyhow, Goodenough (a millionaire like Silber) had announced his plans to buy a thousand-watt radio station by the end of the year and start broadcasting *Once Around the Sun* around the clock on January 1, whether or not the yearlong work was finished yet: Goodenough was confident that he could stay a day ahead of the broadcast. The applause that greeted this announcement was interrupted when Silber lunged at his guest and had to be pulled off by the other composers.

But that was only one of many outbursts, not all Silber's. With so many big egos under one roof, it is no surprise that things got out of hand that week. The surprise is that the New Composers' Alliance survived the convention — evidently by directing most of its aggressions outward, at the rest of the world, in an appalling spree of vandalism. As I say, the president of the Alliance was David Altschul. With him at the helm, it was perhaps inevitable that the band of geniuses should name itself the Davidsbund, after Schumann's imaginary posse of true artists bound together by their fight against the philistine majority. With the exhilaration of a long-oppressed minority that suddenly finds itself for once outnumbering the enemy, the pack of frenzied composers had taken to roaming the streets of Forest City at all hours in their matching black commemorative NCA convention sweatshirts, destroy-

---

* After the convention, Silber toyed with the idea of dusting off his own primitive computer (see *"Babbage" Permutations*), and programming it to "do something musical" — juggle half a dozen notes, say — for a hundred years. The program itself would be the score, and the title would be *Century.*

ing ugliness of every kind — defacing the philistine billboards, egging the philistines' houses, and even trampling a bed of petunias, since Dunsmore was a serious gardener with strong opinions about flowers, and in his opinion petunias were a philistine bloom. At the height of the revelry, the burly Cowlick lifted a newspaper-vending unit overhead and hurled it through the plate-glass window of a record store — not the store that (catering to adolescents) spurned classical music altogether, but rather a link in a nationwide chain always vaunting its wide selection of "serious" music — a chain that so far had refused to distribute any of the various Davidsbündler recordings (admittedly not many, and most of them vanity-pressed). By the time the cops showed up, the visiting composers were en route to the airport in Goodenough's rented mini-van, and their host was left to face the music. This time he wound up spending *two* nights in jail — his lawyer happened to be out of town that weekend, and his sister (who sat next to the owner of the record store at monthly chamber of commerce meetings) refused to bail him out.

A few days earlier, before things got so out of hand, Silber and the other new composers had agreed, at Altschul's suggestion, each to write a five-minute piece of music incorporating quotations from the other eleven, hence the title of the projected hourlong collaboration (of which your disc includes only Silber's contribution): *Twelve Times Twelve.** The idea seems to have been to force the composers to listen to one another's work, since as a rule the twelve "allies" were almost as contemptuous of one another as they were of all other living — and most dead — composers. Altschul may have also hoped that if any one of them got lucky, he would take the other eleven along with him, to fame and fortune, if only as footnotes. (Once, in a gloomy though alliterative mood, Silber described the collaboration as "a dozen paupers pooling their

---

* Silber said that Altschul, an Austrian by birth, had initially wanted to call the work *Gross,* a word with different connotations in German.

pennies to purchase a lottery ticket.") In any case, Altschul's vision was never fulfilled. As far as Silber knew, only three of his colleagues had followed through on the plan, and two of those three (including Altschul himself) had been content to represent Silber with a single chord from *My Life*.

Not that Silber's treatment of his colleagues was much better. He chose eleven brief atonal phrases in the lower registers — the eleven most similar passages he could find in an hour or two of fast-forwarding through a sad heap of homemade cassettes — and then used the twelve-track recorder in his studio to record them all, over and over again, on top of one another, in a low muddy rumble. Predictably, he mixed the piece in such a way as to assure that *his* part — a pretty tune like one of the more simple Chopin *Préludes,* singing solo in the limelight of the treble clef — would single-handedly overmatch the other eleven.

### 3. *Monkey See, Monkey Do*          2:53

A shameless reprise of *The Not-So-Identical Twins* composed in March 1999, the week I started taking music classes. The two works are so similar that I include the latter only for the sake of completeness, and as evidence that the composer didn't learn a thing in the intervening years about sublimating ugly sentiments; in the case of *Monkey,* the music is as ugly as the jealousy that prompted it. As in the earlier work, the left hand endeavors and fails "comically" to duplicate the right hand's rather shallow and self-satisfied dazzle. Here, though, the composer isn't ridiculing a rival pianist but rather a rival composer — the author, though in fact I am right-handed, and Silber, of course, was a lefty.

If I *was* guilty of monkey-doing that spring, I wasn't the only one. When Silber realized that he was no longer my only friend in the region, and that his jealous anti-Cletus rhetoric was serving only to fan the flames of my new friendship, he responded in a manner that astounded me: he retaliated by be-friending Billy, the retarded man in my rooming house — the one who, though he didn't own (and maybe couldn't ride) a bike, never ventured out without a bicycle helmet protecting whatever there was in his skull to protect. Well, there are as many spite friendships as spite marriages. Silber seems to have gone to the Bean one evening looking to "pick up" a new best friend, much as other men go to bars to pick up women, or in-deed to pick up other men. I don't know how many prospects he auditioned before settling for Billy, or if Billy had simply been the first misfit to approach my employer. It can't have hurt that Billy was my next-door neighbor. Once or twice the composer visited him in his room, and (though he'd never deigned to visit *me* there) he clearly knew that the adjacent room was mine. As far as I could tell, the sole purpose of those visits was to laugh so much — have fun so noisily — that I would hear and feel jealous. Once, with my ear pressed to the wall, I heard Silber say, "Tell me the one about the milkmaid again," and then heard Billy respond with an inept recital of a dirty joke no able-minded grownup could consider funny, a joke whose inaccuracy on matters of female anatomy suggested that neither the teller nor his listener had ever seen a naked woman, or even a good picture of one. Billy picked his nose, smelled a bit like pee, drank a lot of pop, and watched too much TV; and for a while I wondered if Silber was laughing at *him* and not at his jokes, but soon ascertained that the mirth was for my ears. One evening, pressing one to the wall, I real-ized that my employer had his hands cupped to the wall on the other side, the better to project his laughter through to me. The common wall was thin enough that even without eaves-dropping I could clearly hear each burst of laughter, but most bursts were preceded by an indistinct mumbling that led me to fear they were laughing at *me*. It was such an obvious attempt to make me jealous and even paranoid that I'm embarrassed to say it succeeded. Dim as he was, Billy wasn't *that* much dimmer than the "friends" that Silber had been accustomed to before I came along and — in all modesty — brought up the average (or, as we said in night school, "wrecked the grading curve").

There are people whose biographies can be written by listing their friendships over the years, but Silber was not one of those people. His lifelong list of friends was short, with little to elaborate on. His real life was lived in solitude. Till I came along, he'd never had a friend who understood him, something he'd always wanted but always dreaded. His behavior in the year I knew him — from our first self-conscious meeting to his stagy final exit — was nothing but the sweating, blushing, stammering, and stumbling of a private person suddenly receiving unaccustomed scrutiny. Or if that attributes too much sheer humanity to Silber, think of his behavior as the hopeless writhing of a centipede that has become aware of its hundred legs and is trying to coordinate their movements consciously, the better to impress the entomologist watching it walk. (Even bipeds, after all, can have difficulty walking when they think too much about it.)

Still, a catalogue of friendships, such as they were, can't hurt: they represented the only significant contacts that Silber managed to make, as an adult, with the rest of his species.

SILBER'S FRIENDSHIPS

| Name | Occupation | Flourished |
| --- | --- | --- |
| Dexter Eggers | mechanic | 1975–1978 |
| Harley Pitts | drywall installer | 1981–1988 |
| Mike Kowalcek | bricklayer | 1985 |
| Earl Kickham | animal control officer | 1993–1994 |
| Norman Fayrewether | philosopher and aphorist | 1998–1999 |

Silber's first biographer (of whom more soon; for now it will suffice to note his absence from the list) saw these unlikely friendships — as he saw so much else — as evidence of homosexuality. I, however, favor Schopenhauer's explanation for why a man as accomplished as Silber, lacking a friend in his own cerebral weight class, would associate with grease monkeys and dogcatchers: "Men of very great capacity will, as a rule, find the company of very simple people preferable to that of the common run, for the same reason that the tyrant and the mob, the grandfather and the grandchildren, are natural allies."

And speaking of transgenerational alliances: in April, Cletus got involved with one of my classmates, a tiny teenager named Candy who by that point hated me because once or twice in class I'd been unable to suppress my harmless mirth at her amazingly dimwitted questions ("Is the second movement in piñata form too, Mr. Pitchford?"). From one day to the next, my new best friend became too busy for me, and even if I'd been willing to share him with his little companion — to sit on his left at the movies, for instance, while she sat on his right (a compromise I actually proposed, one Friday night, in my abject need for company) — Candy made it clear to Cletus that she didn't want me around at all, and did her best to turn him against me. To his credit, Cletus seemed to feel bad about cutting me out of his life, but when push came to shove, he wanted what she had to offer more than what I had to offer.

"And after all," he reminded me, one Thursday in his office before class, "there's always the Lion's Den." He referred to our weekly adjournments to the campus pub, an outing I'd come to look forward to all week long, even though I had to share the teacher with my fellow students. I'm ashamed to say I didn't have enough self-respect to refuse this insulting consolation prize before it was retracted, as I should've known it would be. The world never gives you as much as you ask it for, and if you ask for next to nothing, you wind up with less than that. At the pub that night I drank more than usual and may have talked more too, and louder — compensating for Cletus himself, who appeared preoccupied and kept glancing anxiously down the long rough wooden table at his sulking concubine (I'd beaten her out for a seat by the teacher). The following week after class, Cletus announced that his "schedule" would no longer allow him to accompany us to the pub, but that the rest of us — and here he met my eye (defiantly? apologetically?) — were encouraged to continue the custom without him.

"He hates me now!" I blurted when Silber called to check up on me an hour later (needless to say I *hadn't* gone to the pub).

"Wait — who hates you?"

"Cletus!" And I burst into tears.

Silber didn't hide his pleasure, but it wasn't altogether a malicious pleasure. I even had the sense, for once, that he was capable of something like compassion; and though he stopped courting me now that he no longer had a rival, he did make a bit more time for me, from week to week, than he had before the Cletus episode. Not enough time to keep me from embarking on a long and misanthropic suite of aphorisms on the Impossibility of Friendship (*Like to be liked? Get used to getting used!*), but enough to remind me, now and then, that however impossible on paper, in real life friendship is merely extremely unlikely.

4. *Aphorisms*                                     0:59

| Follies and Foibles | 0:05 | The One and the Many | 0:12 |
| Customs and Mores | 0:06 | The Battle of the Sexes | 0:08 |
| Self-Love | 0:03 | Good and Evil | 0:04 |
| Self-Knowledge | 0:03 | Greatness | 0:07 |
| Self-Deception | 0:03 | Live or Learn | 0:05 |
| Solitude | 0:01 | Life and Art | 0:02 |

Everything that Silber wrote in his last year bears traces of my influence, but never more glaringly than his *Aphorisms,* a work composed — he boasted — in less than fifteen minutes, and one that takes no longer than a minute to experience, if one omits (as I have) the rather pompous fifteen-second pauses Silber specified between successive miniatures, pauses meant ostensibly to give each thought a chance to register, but actually to pad the piece and so conceal its true puniness. Silber wrote these *morceaux* on April Fools' Day in what I trust the reader will concur with me in finding an unsuccessful effort to prove that (in Silber's words) "anything words can do, notes can do better." The subtitles are section headings stolen from my book of real — verbal — aphorisms, *So I Gather*. I'd given the composer an autographed copy that morning when we met at the Bean to discuss the latest chapter of the biography. (By that point, at Silber's insistence, I had switched from scrawls on index cards to monthly typewritten installments. "That way," he'd explained, "even if I fire you I'll still have *something* to show for my money, and not just some crappy notes.") In its subject's opinion, the chapter (which I'd given him the day before) failed to do justice to the breadth and depth of his intellect. And in fact I had forgotten that not all idiot savants like to be described as such (he also objected to the chapter title, "Simple Simon"), but in calling Silber "pretty much illiterate," I was only paraphrasing his admission that he hadn't read a book in years because, if you please, reading gave him the sensation of being stuck on a narrow road behind a slow-moving vehicle. As for my claim that he was "shockingly uncultivated" — well, he was. Of the three Silber children, only Helen had gone to college (Radcliffe — where, a true Renaissance woman, she'd pursued a triple major in Business, Management, and Economics). Our composer had earned the equivalent of a high-school diploma at home, under the tutelage of his eccentric father, but the ordeal seems not to have disposed him to further adventures in learning. (Scooter, deemed unworthy of home-schooling, had dropped out of Forest City High at age sixteen.)

Silber's upbringing wasn't *quite* as one-sidedly musical as that of the brilliant Hungarian pianist Nyiregyhazi — who, though he started composing at age four, was still unable at eighteen to feed himself or tie his shoes. But music was the only area in which my employer's education wasn't notably deficient, and even there, despite his occasional cogent remarks, I couldn't help thinking he knew less than I would if my whole life had been devoted to the art, to the exclusion of everything else — of life itself, almost. Certainly he knew no more than Cletus, who managed to find time for living too. As far as I could tell, in fact, Silber knew no more than any clever nonmusician might've gleaned by reading the jackets of all the LPs in Silber's collection. Sometimes his pronouncements on music were shamelessly lifted from those jackets, just as his opinions on life were often echoes of mine — though where life was concerned, Silber could've raised his grade by cribbing almost *anybody's* answers, let alone a leading aphorist's.

It was partly with a view to supplementing my employer's education that I gave him my book that day at the Bean. He called two hours later to say he'd just composed a piece inspired by the book, though he'd gotten only as far as the table of contents. I was flattered: he had been so eager to read me that he'd opened the book as soon as he got home; and if he'd then been sidetracked by an inspiration of his own — well, by definition, an artist is a person who prefers producing to consuming works of art. It takes me awhile to know when I've been insulted, and I continued to feel flattered at having inspired a piece of music even after Silber — choosing to construe a gift as a loan — returned the book unread on April 2, with no other comment than a paraphrase of what Wagner said about Nietzsche's books: that collections of aphorisms always made him think of trained fleas.* (I resisted the temptation

---

* I'll admit that Silber knew a thing or two about the great composers. On deciding, at fifteen, that he would be the next one, he'd developed an obsession with that pantheon, and had done more voluntary reading in one year — furtively, by flashlight, since around that time his father had forbidden books — than in all the years before and since, racing through biographies of all the greats and all-but-greats. (At fifteen, he had had an adolescent's sureness as to who'd been great and who not quite, and had been so certain of his own nascent greatness as already to disdain the merely very good.) At last his father had prevailed on the public library to revoke young Simon's privileges — a measure the composer never bothered to reverse; by his own admission, he hadn't read a book since 1974. (That may explain why his notion of "greatness" had remained so adolescent, however sophisticated his musical tastes may have grown.) Before his father cracked down, though, Silber had acquired a broad if shallow knowledge of musical history from which he could still fish a fun fact now and then.

to retaliate by quoting one of Nietzsche's remarks about Wagner — for example, the one about "lava which blocks its own course by congealing, and suddenly finds itself checked by dams which it has itself built.")

I won't waste the reader's time with an extensive discussion of a work on which the composer himself expended no more energy than on a series of after-dinner yawns. The three "self"-titled aphorisms are identical except for the final note. "The One and the Many" is a sort of microconcerto, with the right hand picking out a melody of single notes which the left hand, or rather the left forearm, echoes with ugly, muddy clusters. "The Battle of the Sexes" also allegorizes the treble/bass duality, as indeed do "Good and Evil," "Live or Learn," and "Life and Art." Silber's hubris and his fondness for the number twelve have deafened him to the fact that he simply doesn't have a dozen inspirations here; indeed, one could get the sense that the composer hadn't added at all to his bag of tricks in the twenty-six years since *The Not-So-Identical Twins*. In any case, though hardly aphorisms, these tiny, jumpy nuisances — vaguely reminiscent of Schumann, as certain farts of certain foods — are more flealike than anything ever to spring from *my* pen. I have no idea why Silber chose to record this work for posterity while excluding worthier efforts, such as the first seventeen hours of *Day*.*

Speaking of recording for posterity, there was one ray of sunlight in that endless rainy spring: I resumed my aphorizing. And for that I suppose I have Silber to thank, though in a different way than he had me to thank for *his* "aphorisms." The day I met him (see *My House*), he'd given me the little tape recorder that was to revolutionize my writing habits, though at

---

* Except for the brief excerpt on Disc One and another even briefer on Disc Four, Silber never recorded a minute of his unfinished masterpiece. As a rule, he never recorded anything unfinished: recording for him was an assertion of completion, like a painter's signature. Of course, a painter sometimes paints one picture over another, and whenever Silber returned to and revised an officially finished composition, he made a point of rerecording the work, taping the new version over the old.

first I had dismissed it as another needless gadget, something along the lines of an electric blanket or a battery-operated toothbrush, and for months I'd used it only as a paperweight. But then one night — in March, I think — as I was drifting off, I thought a thought that struck me as *almost* worth preserving, if only I didn't have to get up, turn on the light, etc. If only I could record the idea without the physical effort of jotting it down — say by snapping my fingers. Snapping my fingers, I jumped up, got the recorder, and started taping my ideas over Silber's guided tour of his house.

Soon I was taking the recorder with me everywhere, and dictating bright ideas all day long. In recent years, I'd wistfully accepted that my brain was not as fertile as it once had been, but now I saw that I'd been wrong. If it took me longer to fill a notebook nowadays, that was because where once I'd clucked ecstatically over every new idea, like a hen for whom each egg is cause for celebration, I no longer got quite so excited about my brainchildren. Even the most doting parents, after all, take fewer photographs of each successive baby. It was so easy to blurt an idea to my tape recorder, though, that just a trace of excitement was enough. No doubt the day would come when even the effort of raising the recorder to my mouth would seem like too much trouble, too arduous a labor for the brainchild in question; and in the end I'd be too listless even to think the thoughts in the first place, much less to utter them; but I wasn't that far gone just yet. And actually, the chances were that I would give up thinking — as most people have already, by my age — before I gave up speaking; I *liked* speaking. I liked the sound of my own voice, and the feel of my vocal cords at work. Often as I spoke into the tape recorder, I felt a surge of gratitude: if I was Silber's Boswell, it was mine, and unlike me it worked for free. I even felt remorse for having used it as a paperweight: if anyone could empathize with a precision instrument put to a cruder use than its intended one, *I* could.

I especially used the gadget during walks. Like Silber, like his hated father figure Beethoven (who composed, at the top of his lungs, on long hikes through the German countryside), like Nietzsche ("Never trust any idea that occurs to you indoors"), I did my best thinking on foot. At first I worried a bit about looking — like Beethoven, Nietzsche, and Silber — insane. Only the gregarious are supposed to make noise in our culture; solitary thinkers are expected to keep their thoughts to themselves. When I started taping and transcribing my peripatetic ideas, I found that those ideas had a different rhythm and indeed a different structure depending on when and where I walked, and thus how many people I encountered — how often I had to hit PAUSE and hold my tongue. Soon, though, I realized how silly it was to care what people thought in Forest City, of all places. By that point, though I still bathed, I had otherwise ceased to bother about grooming, almost as I would have on a desert island; and if I'd taken now to talking to myself, that was because there was no one else worth talking to — no one but Silber, who was usually too busy communing with Silber. In a town where there's nothing to shave for, there's no reason to hit PAUSE, not when your thoughts are racing.

And even when my thoughts were nothing to write home about, when in fact I had nothing to say, I would chatter to my tape recorder anyhow: it was company, an ear as nonjudgmental as the perfect analyst. Sometimes, when I had babbled for an hour without accomplishing a single aphorism, I would repeat some lines I'd read in an old anthology:

> *Wherefore, unlaurelled Boy,*
> > *Whom the contemptuous Muse will not inspire,*
> *With a sad kind of joy*
> > *Still sing'st thou to thy solitary lyre?*

When I first started dictating on walks, I reused the same tape every day, conscientiously sitting down every night to transcribe its contents so that it would be ready to go again in the morning — a process so laborious, however, as to offset the ease of dictation. Before long I realized that it was simpler to keep buying blank cassettes, especially when my walks became so garrulous that a single sixty-minute tape was insufficient to see me through the day. Needless to say, I soon developed a huge backlog of untranscribed tapes. I still have many hours of dictation I haven't found the time to listen to, and it's safe to say I never will: for better or worse, the thoughts on those tapes are buried alive.

(It occurs to me that, strictly speaking, that whole business about me, my walks, and my recorder is a digression; and also that I'm in no hurry to finish these notes. Indeed, if not for Helen breathing down my neck, I'd probably waste years of unpaid labor on the task, and wind up writing several thousand pages, if only to postpone as long as possible the laughable release of this absurd, unwarranted, misguided set — *how* misguided, you, misguided buyer, may judge for yourself. And these notes may be my only chance to tell posterity that I, too, once existed: last week — Christmas '99; now it's New Year's Eve — I finally abandoned my almost lifelong plan of one day writing my own memoirs, after nary a nibble of interest from any of the twenty-seven publishers I'd queried back in June. I've also been unable to interest any editor in my luridly unauthorized biography of Silber. Readers will forgive me if this little book of liner notes — the only thing of mine that anybody wants to publish — salvages a page or two from *those* books. As for the charge of "digressing," Montaigne said it best: "We should jump over plebeian rules in the name of truth and freedom. I not only dare to talk about myself but to talk of nothing *but* myself. I am straying from the point when I write about anything else, cheating my subject of *me*.")

Several times in the spring of '99, Silber allowed me — his solitary liar — to join him on his after-dinner walks. We'd stroll along in silence till one of us had an idea, verbal or non-, and blurted it to his recorder. Actually we never walked along in *silence:* Silber was constantly singing or humming, as if anxious to disturb the peace before someone else did. Even when he paused to take his temperature (as he did, once or twice a walk, with the oral thermometer he kept like a pen in the pocket of his shirt), he continued humming, though not walking. But he taped only the tunes he intended to keep.*

Some evenings he was the inspired one and did all the dictating; on those occasions I felt as if we were fishing side by side from a bridge, and Silber, with his better rod, fresher bait, longer cast, and sharper hook, was catching all the fish. But some evenings it was my turn, much to his annoyance. Once he even made me cross the street and walk down the other side, claiming that my aphorisms had been triggering his tape recorder, which had a voice-activated option he refused to switch off.

Sometimes we were both inspired, though, and dictated simultaneously as we walked abreast — jeered at by children and sneered at by their elders — so that afterward when I transcribed the tape (in the special notebook where I was assembling *By the Way,* the sequel to my first collection), my aphorisms were accompanied by background music, just as some of Silber's melodic memoranda must've been enlivened by background aphorisms. Sometimes the jeers were also audible. We must have made quite a sight, what with our matching gadgets and mismatching gaits: Silber was a full head taller than I, and so freakishly long-legged that I had to take three steps for every two he took; but I knew that I could bench more.

Even on those perfect evenings, though, when we were both in top form, one of us would finally realize — with as much relief as disappointment — that the well was dry, and would wait impatiently for the other's well to dry up too, so we could talk. (The artist is never more desperate for company than after the departure of his muse.) I remember one particular talk that

---

* Though he claimed to have a "phonographic" memory for finished works of music, Silber was surprisingly unable to remember his own inchoate musical ideas (not even, evidently, by humming them aloud and then remembering the hum), maybe because those ideas were all so *evitable* and ungainly. It occurs to me that our physiques — Silber's sprawling, gawky, and loose-jointed; mine compact, well knit, and muscular — reflected the difference between his ideas and mine.

took place on April 15, at the end of a prolific walk for both of us. The day had been warm for that time of year in that part of the world (spring in Oregon can be hard to tell from winter), but by eight P.M. it had cooled down enough for me to need a sweatshirt — as usual, a red one with white words across the front: THINKERS DIGEST. Though I'd been unable to interest any publisher in my first book of aphorisms, I had gotten several of its component thoughts printed in the "Tidbits" column of the newsletter whose name I wore with pride, though less pride than I'd have worn it with if the shirtmaker had splurged for an apostrophe. I had seven identical sweatshirts in my closet — one for each thought *Thinkers' Digest* had used. As for the one I was wearing, the oldest, I'd earned it by pointing out that *In the kingdom of the blind, what you see is what you get.*

On the evening in question, anyhow, when Silber finally quit dictating bits of music to his gadget, I tried to ask about Tom. That morning while hunting for the W-2 from my library job, I'd come across the packet Gordon had bequeathed me, the one containing his own aphorisms, and in my frantic need to put off my taxes for a few more hours, I started reading. There turned out to be only one page of Gordon's wit and wisdom; the remaining pages comprised a long typewritten text by someone else, to judge by a felt-tip scrawl on its first page: "Gordie — I'd be greatful for any comments on grammar, spelling: ect. Thanks a million, T." The first sentence — "People like Simon Silber aren't born every day"* — was enough to grab my attention. Realizing that I'd lucked onto my predecessor's biography of Silber, I read the eighty-eight-page manuscript from beginning to end that afternoon, wondering why Gordon hadn't shown it to me sooner. Though barely literate, the document had piqued my curiosity about its author and his relationship with the composer, since it revealed secrets that Silber still hadn't told me but must've told Tom (in

---

* The author had originally written "are," but at some point, with more districts reporting, had crossed it out and written "aren't" instead. Or had Silber himself made that emendation?

addition to all kinds of facts, if that's what they were, that I couldn't see Silber telling *anyone* — see *Annex to "My House"*). Evidently our employer had been more candid with Tom than with me. It was hard to know, though, since Tom had the sense to keep himself out of the picture, evidently realizing what a nonentity he was, and how little claim on readers' attention his own actions and emotions had.

That evening, anyhow, as we headed south on Tree Street, I suddenly said: "So tell me a little about the first biographer."

Silber stiffened momentarily, then said, "Okay. What did you want to know?"

What *did* I want to know? "Well . . . did you two have the same arrangement we do?"

"Yes, I'm paying you as much as I paid him, if that's what you're worried about."

"And you made him give you a chapter a month the way I do?"

"No — like an idiot I trusted him and let him wait till it was done to show it to me."

"But then why — ?"

"Because I learn from my mistakes."

I was silent for a minute, then found the nerve to blurt: "Were you guys friends?"

"Pssh! Anything but. Look, why are you asking all these questions anyhow? You almost sound . . . *jealous.*" When I didn't answer, he astounded me by saying: "Okay, so you heard from Edna or somebody that he used to come over for dinner on Sundays — is that it?" I'd heard nothing of the sort, of course, and it was one fact about my subject I'd prefer never to have unearthed. I must've looked as stricken as I felt, since Silber added: "Look — it's nothing personal. I couldn't stand the guy, to tell the truth. It's just that back then I was too trusting. I found out the hard way [smile] not to trust biographers." I let the subject drop, too crestfallen to do otherwise. We finished the walk in silence, parting as always in front of the house to which I was forbidden entrée, though evidently Tom had been a weekly guest.

Back in my room, I grabbed his manuscript and marched it over to my stove, planning to burn the document a page at a time. The stove was an electric, though, and by the time the burner was hot enough to set fire to paper, I'd thought the better of such a melodramatic gesture. After all, it wasn't Tom's fault if Silber felt most at home around his fellow illiterates.

### 5. *Annex to "My House"*         9:02

| | | |
|---|---|---|
| 1. | Boyhood Bedroom | 2:54 |
| 2. | Practice Room | 1:41 |
| 3. | Guest Bedroom | 1:29 |
| 4. | Conservatory | 2:01 |
| 5. | Master Bedroom | 0:57 |

By including this suite of rooms in your set, I make an exception to my rule of selection, since our composer never recorded *Annex,* as he made a point of doing in his little studio with every composition, large or small, the day he finished it. So I suppose I "fibbed" earlier when I said that all the performances in this set were by Silber: I performed four of the five sections of *Annex* myself, maybe at a slower tempo than even our *largo*-loving composer would've chosen, since when the recording was made last month I'd been taking piano lessons for less than a year. The tricky second section — unsafe for me at *any* speed — was performed by Ed Edwards, a terrific pianist in his own right, as well as the teacher in charge of Elementary Piano at Lumber Junior College.

I realize that I am violating Silber's will, which prohibits anyone from recording his music, but since he's dead now I don't see what difference it can make to him. If he really wanted his recording of each work to be the only time that anybody ever played it, he should've destroyed each score as soon as he'd recorded it. Instead, he saved the manuscripts of all his compositions (or all but *Day*, which again had a room of its own) in the locked top drawer of a tall green file cabinet in his studio. He insisted, nonetheless, that those manuscripts were nothing more than byproducts, that his *real* legacy was on the master tapes shelved alphabetically in gray metal canisters* on a gray metal shelving unit next to the green file cabinet. Though he'd never recorded *Day* or *My Life* (both unfinished, after all), his oeuvre bulked much larger on those shelves than it does on your CDs: Silber, who could afford such waste, allotted a separate sixty-minute tape reel to every opus, including the four-second *Crows*. Even so, his oeuvre looked puny next to many, but that paucity seemed not to bother Silber, who saw the finished compositions in your set as no more than hors d'oeuvres to keep his guests happy till *Day* was finally ready to pull out of the oven and bring to the table.

So *Annex* may be thought of as a plate of crudités (cruder than most, since abandoned unfinished). The work dates from 1990 and consists of paraphrases and quotations, most of them from other people's music, as if Silber would've found it too upsetting to express in his own notes the feelings sealed away in the five rooms omitted from *My House*. I include the suite not for its intrinsic value — only Section 4 has any to speak of — but because it is as close as Silber ever came in his music, or (as far as I can tell) in *any* medium, to discussing certain restricted areas of his past. That, no doubt, is why he didn't give the work an opus number or record it for posterity: he didn't want to call posterity's attention to the episodes in question. He was sufficiently convinced of his own destiny, his inevitable — no matter how belated — recognition as "the only great American composer," already to feel harassed by an adoring future's curiosity.

---

* The canisters were painted the same shade of gray as the metal wastebaskets in the library where I worked for fifteen years — an unfortunate coincidence that may subliminally be affecting my assessment of the opuses inside those canisters.

In the case of the forbidden rooms, I'd been happy to accede to Silber's wish for privacy, especially after I discovered that Scooter had no idea why those particular rooms were now off-limits even to the homeowner. Tom, however, seems to have been obsessed with the Secret of the Missing Rooms (as he might have put it, with his boy-detective sensibility), maybe to the point of larceny: the manuscript of *Annex* — the original, as far as I could tell — was stapled to Tom's manuscript, evidently as an appendix. As long as chance has handed me a copy of Tom's monograph, and as long as I've gone to the trouble of perusing it, I see no reason not to share his "findings," such as they are, with the reader. As for Silber's privacy — well, I used to tell him that every detail of a great man's life, no matter how trivial or even compromising at face value, is of interest to posterity; that the same accomplishments that make a great man great also transmute his daily habits, even the not-so-great ones; that, like Midas, a great man can't pick his nose without striking gold. But maybe Silber wasn't as convinced of his own greatness as he always claimed to be; maybe he was one of the borderline great, able to believe in their magnificence only by suppressing all evidence to the contrary. That would explain why he had forbidden me to mention that his middle name was Gary, so hard was it for him to associate that name — even as a middle name — with greatness. Maybe *Beethoven* could've gotten away with "Gary" — maybe even as a *first* name — and so changed the world's idea of Garys once and for all, blazing a trail for others to follow, but Silber was barely making it up the slope of Mount Parnassus as it was; if he left the beaten path for the untrodden wilderness, he'd lose all upward momentum.

1. It was just this sense of his own damning *normalcy* that led Silber as a young man first to abandon and then to seal off his boyhood bedroom. At least that's how I take his claim that at one A.M. on his sixteenth birthday, as he lay in bed, half asleep, half listening to Schumann's *Humoresque,* he'd been visited by a

terrifying vision of his own "mortality, futility, nonentity." (His words, from a letter to David Altschul, not long before their quarrel. Note that even in this hypnagogic trance, Silber's self-love was sufficiently alert to steer him away from a less extreme and so — one might suppose — less terrifying word: *mediocrity*. He may have dared to gaze into the abyss, but not to accuse himself of something as plausible as *that*.)

His musical portrait of this room is a bouncy rendition of "Happy Birthday" that veers off on a long atonal tangent at the point corresponding to "dear Si-mon" (if you sing along), never to return to the initial tune. And Silber was never to sleep in that room again: the very next day, he moved out to the carriage house, though there were many spare rooms in the main house. But he'd reached an age when most boys want to flee their boyhoods. Like most boys, he didn't get too far, but I think the carriage house, with its exciting cars downstairs, was associated for him — all his life — with dreams of further flight. In any case, he spent his nights out there until his father's death in 1980, at which point Silber took possession of the master bedroom. Half a year later, on taking possession of the house itself with Helen's departure, one of his first acts was to seal off his boyhood bedroom (and the practice room — see note to Section 2). Helen told me once that when, in the years between abandoning and erasing the room, Silber had to go back in to fetch something, he would always hold his breath, as if the very air in there were poisonous.

2. Despite his reticence about the sealed rooms, Silber, who was proud to own so many grand pianos, couldn't resist boasting* first to Tom and then to me that in addition to the four we'd seen (three in his house, one in his studio), and the one in the off-limits basement, there were two more in rooms

---

* He was the sort of artist who — nagged by the sense of having failed to fulfill his promise — needs to supplement his principal claim to fame with all kinds of subsidiary claims. He even boasted that his great-aunt Audrey had served as the model for the Mrs. Butterworth's bottle.

he'd sealed off, for a total of seven. He added that one of the two was the instrument he'd practiced on throughout his years as an aspiring pianist — up to the age of twenty, then — in what he still thought of as the practice room. But he refused to tell us why he had later immured that piano, his best. Tom suggests that Silber sealed off the practice room (first floor, southeast corner) because he'd been in there when it dawned on him that he wasn't and would never be a world-class pianist. As Tom reconstructs it, this traumatic "revelation" would've occurred at an especially inconvenient time — as Silber was warming up for the final round of the Erlenmeyer Competition, a few hours before he assaulted the judge. Tom may be right for once, though *revelation* is too strong a word. Even *inkling* might be overstating it: if Silber had really faced the truth, once and for all, before that evening's concert, he wouldn't have gone berserk during the concert itself. No, what Silber felt beforehand in the practice room would've been no more than a faint shudder.

In the weeks after reading that microfilmed account of Silber's Erlenmeyer breakdown (see "Selections from *My Life*"), I managed to gather a little background information. Every odd-numbered year, the nearby town of Lumber (the same town, some dozen miles to the east of Forest City, where I now attended junior college) held a competition for pianists twenty-one and under. Though not as prestigious as some competitions, the Erlenmeyer (endowed by a music-loving local lumber baron of that name) was lucrative enough to draw contestants from across the country, and even one or two from over- seas. Silber had wanted to enter in 1977, but his father had deemed the pianist — then eighteen — not quite ready.

In retrospect, his father regretted that decision; even if Silber had lost in 1977, the experience might have made a difference the next time around. As it was, the '79 competition was not only Silber's first of any kind, but the first time he had ever heard other serious pianists of his own age. It was also the first time he'd ever performed outside of Forest City. Till then, with some misguided notion of allowing genius to germinate in the dark, or perhaps of selling no wine before its time, Mr. Silber had kept the prodigy under a sort of hometown arrest: prior to the Erlenmeyer, Silber's recitals had all taken place in the basement meeting room at the Forest City public library, three blocks from Silber's house. Mr. Silber seems to have thought of the competition as his son's debut on the national scene: following his triumph in Erlenmeyer Hall, Simon would be invited to perform all over the country, and then the world.

Notwithstanding some enfant terrible airs (pausing between sections of *Kreisleriana* and glaring at his audience until the coughing, clearing of throats, and unwrapping of candies subsided), and despite his brother's disgraceful antics, Silber did well in the preliminaries. He had enough sense to stick to relatively orthodox tempi for the Liszt and Scriabin he'd chosen, and he managed nonetheless to stand out among a field of young virtuosi all playing similarly ostentatious music as flashily as possible. (It can't have hurt that he was the hometown favorite.) In the final round, contestants were confined to Haydn, Bach, and Mozart — to works where sheer flash would be exposed as such, where insight, intelligence, and sense of structure counted more than technical pizzazz or violent emotion. This should've been the point at which Silber pulled apart from the pack, since the average virtuoso is as vapid as the average diva; I doubt that any of the other finalists had thought as much about the inner workings of the music — of music per se — as our composer. Unluckily for Silber, he drew the final slot (in a lottery he later claimed was rigged), which meant he'd be playing for ears that were already sated, and hands already raw from clapping. Worse yet, the *next*-to-last contestant — Young-Seong Oh, the nineteen-year-old Korean man who wound up winning (and whom Silber had already heard the day before in the preliminaries) — chose as his featured presentation the same piece as Silber, Mozart's *Fantasy in*

*C Minor,* and dispatched it in such a masterly fashion that another masterly performance would've amounted to replaying the same record, with diminishing returns for the listener. I'm trying to reconstruct the logic that led our contestant to opt for a tempo so slow it would've trapped the judges in their seats till after midnight if he hadn't interrupted his performance to lunge at one of them. Tom suggests that Silber had known he was going to lose the minute he heard Oh in the preliminaries, and so had purposely chosen a ridiculous tempo, in order that afterward he could deny, at least to himself, that he had lost because somebody else had simply been better. Again, I disagree. I think the truth of his inferiority hit Silber later, in the finals — he would've had a lot of time for undisturbed reflection between successive notes of his slow-motion rendition of the *Fantasy'*s slow passages. He must've sat down at the piano that evening believing that iconoclasm was the only way to overcome the handicap of not being the first to do what he was doing. When one of the judges — an octogenarian who may have heard too many brilliant young eccentrics in her day — began to yawn, young Silber must've felt that the entire senile, arthritic, liver-spotted classical-music establishment was yawning. *That's* when he would've opted to disqualify himself with a calculated act of madness, preferring disgrace and even incarceration to the inexorable process by which the establishment was about to relegate him once and for all (so it must've seemed to Silber at the time) to the status of an also-ran.

As for his tribute to the practice room, where he happened to be (if Tom is right) when he first began to stir from his lifelong dream of glory, the piece consists of two runs through the same passage from the Mozart *Fantasy.* As performed by Ed Edwards, in accordance with the score, the first take is very polished, well behaved, law-abiding, inoffensive; the second is highly unorthodox with regard to tempo, dynamics, pedaling, etc., and is cut off with a bang a few notes shy of the end — cut off, as the score instructs, with "the sound of the lid slamming shut," as it were on the pianist's fingers, and presumably by another hand (that of officialdom? of prevailing taste?), since both of his were busy playing.

3. Though Silber once told me that "in one way or another" all five of the sealed rooms had been "defiled," only one had been defiled in the strictest sense. It was the only one that Silber would talk about. In 1985, in the course of the NCA convention, one of his houseguests, Arthur Farraway, had ruined a guest bedroom by covering the walls with all sorts of bodily substances. Farraway, said Silber, was easily the craziest of the Davidsbündler twelve — though the most gifted of the other eleven — and had spent most of his life in institutions; only through Altschul's intercession had he gotten a weeklong pass (from the same psychiatric ward where Silber had once spent a restful week himself) to attend the convention.

Over the years, Farraway had perfected ways to compose without paper or pen, since his behavior in custody was evidently such as to merit frequent reprisals, and the best way to punish an artist, of course, is to prevent him from setting down his ideas. During his week as Silber's guest, Farraway had scored the walls of his room with what must've been a razor blade — maybe the same one he would use a few years later to slit his throat — and then filled these makeshift staves with makeshift musical notation, writing with feces, semen, blood, and what looked like earwax. The marks composed a work of music, or a part of one: a single movement in sonata form. (You need more space to write with feces than with a fine-point pen.) Silber hadn't discovered the movement till after his guests had left. His homage to the room is a delicate and eerie miniature exhibiting a sensibility found nowhere else in Silber's music; I take it to be no more or less than a direct quotation from Farraway's opus, which Silber, with his photographic memory, would of course have memorized while scrubbing down the walls. (He told me once that although Farraway had approached genius in his choice of *which* substance to use for which notes, the actual music had been nothing special. It was clear, though, that my friend had been impressed, for once, by someone else's art. I even remember feeling jealous: these infrequent reminders that Silber was in fact capable of admiring another mind made his ongoing refusal to admire mine all the more galling.)

I have changed a few notes here and there to make the piece sound more like one of Silber's; I see no point in denying that I've made similar minor emendations to the other parts of *Annex*. In the first, for instance, the composer specifies *maestoso* (or majestic) for the birthday theme but *I* found through trial and error that *doloroso* (sad) is more effective. It was perhaps in fear of just such liberties that Silber insisted on recording an "authoritative" version of each of his piano pieces for posterity, but that always struck me as a wrongheaded attempt to control the life of his works beyond the womb of his workshop. I'd like to think that *my* performances, in their very roughness, and indeed in their departures from the score, will lead listeners to use their imaginations in a way that a flawless performance doesn't — will lead you to intuit an ideal version of the piece in question, an ideal that not even so accomplished a player as Silber could realize in real life on a real piano.

4. In January 1986, Silber sealed off the second-floor conservatory because six months earlier he had rashly played an hour of *Day* in that room for a fellow composer, during the same convention that also resulted in Farraway's defilement of a guest bedroom. Silber's audience was David Altschul, the head of the NCA and — after Farraway — the living composer whom Silber seems to have respected most at the time. There is no record of what Altschul said when Silber pushed away from the piano, but he must've spoken tactfully — so tactfully that not for half a year did Silber understand his colleague's comments as a criticism, and a devastating one. Once he did reach that conclusion, Silber wasted no time in firing off a twenty-one-

page hate letter to Altschul — a letter ostensibly announcing Silber's withdrawal from the NCA, but devoted mostly to raving. Tom somehow obtained a photocopy of this furiously scribbled document, in which Silber keeps saying things like this: "A hundred years from now, *you'll* be no more than a footnote to *my* biography. Your great-grandchildren won't even know that you ever pretended to be a composer, only that their great grandfather, whoever the hell he was, once met the great composer Silber." What makes the letter even more embarrassing is that two months earlier, Silber had sent a much friendlier (and briefer) letter to Altschul, and Altschul had promptly responded in kind: the rage of Silber's second letter stems from something that happened before the first was written, but that took six months to germinate.

Silber's musical allusion to the episode in *Annex* is simply a minute from *Day* (11:59 A.M. to noon, though under my unpracticed hands it takes a little longer) interrupted repeatedly, at shorter and shorter intervals, by a single chord deep in the bass register (according to Tom, Altschul sang bass in a barbershop quartet), always the same chord, louder each time. The piece ends with the passage from *Day* falling through a long diminuendo into silence, while the chord sounds over and over, deafening now: Silber's delicate music has been drowned out by Altschul's misgivings, as they resound deafeningly in our composer's head.

5. In October 1988, Silber was rejected by perhaps the only woman he had ever loved, an eighteen-year-old cleaning lady named Conchita, who at the time had been working for him for one month. According to Tom's sources, Silber made a pass at her on his thirtieth birthday after calling her into the master bedroom — formerly his father's room, but Silber's at the time of the incident — on the pretext of pointing out the dust balls under the bed. Conchita didn't say (or Tom didn't relay) the exact nature of this pass, whether verbal, tactile, or both, and if tactile which part of Silber had touched what part of Conchita

and how, and for how long, and to what effect, but it isn't hard to picture several plausible scenarios. (Conchita did tell Tom that the "creepiest" thing about the incident had been the thinness of their voices in that bedroom, which was lined with anechoic panels. The room had always frightened her, she added. She didn't even like to vacuum in there — hence the dust balls.) From that day on, in any case, Silber slept in the basement.

His incidental music to the incident in question is simply a quotation from *Carmen* — from the "Habanera" — that stops in midphrase, maddeningly unresolved. Not a very inspired memorial, but a suggestive one — at least to this suggestible biographer, to whom it says that Silber's attitudes toward Conchita (toward all women?) were molded by art and annihilated instantly on contact with real life. The musical quotation is also ominous, given Carmen's fate. (According to Tom, though, Conchita is alive and well in San Diego.)

Most of Tom's information about the incident came from Edna, the septuagenarian hag that Silber hired to replace her, no doubt determined not to let another temptress into his house. Now, like most people, I've never gone out of my way to ingratiate myself with cleaning ladies, and by the time I came across Tom's notes to *Annex,* Edna and I were no longer on speaking terms. She had in fact mistrusted and disliked me from the start, like so many people in Silber's sullen, stolid, narrow-minded town. Nonetheless, I kicked myself, as I read Tom's manuscript, for not having recognized Edna as a potential source and treated her accordingly. It had never occurred to me — as it had to Tom — that as stupid and malignant as she was, she might still have stories to tell. Who knew what she'd learned about our employer from a decade of emptying his wastebaskets, laundering his sheets, even defrosting his Frigidaire?* It was humiliating to think that in this respect —

---

* I understand, by the way, that she made her own ketchup — and, as I observe in the aphorism that gives my second collection its title, *What isn't by the way is* in *the way.*

humoring eyewitnesses to the disaster that was Silber's life —
Tom had been better at his job than I was. One reason I'd become a writer in the first place was that I'd thought it one profession where I wouldn't need the demeaning "people skills" of
the extrovert. I'd soon realized how wrong I'd been about that;
even a form of writing as pure as the philosophical aphorism
demanded — if one wanted the aphorism published — all the
arts of the practiced sycophant: a convincing phony laugh, a
no-less-fraudulent solemnity, an ability to climb over people
without stepping on toes, etc.

Tom — who considered him a homosexual — claimed that
Silber had contrived the whole Conchita scandal in order to
mislead his less astute biographers; that in fact Silber fired the
girl not for rebuffing his advances but precisely for allowing
them, for reasons of her own, and thereby calling his bluff. In
Tom's scenario, it was Silber who finally rebuffed Conchita
that day in the master bedroom, after hiring her the month before in order to give rise to the very rumors of red-blooded het-
erosexual shenanigans that had in fact arisen in the wake of her
departure. Maybe so. If our composer did have homosexual
desires, though, he hid them from posterity, and maybe from
himself as well. I'm convinced, as I say, that — in practice, anyhow — Silber was *a*sexual, and I'd be happy to leave it at that.
But no longer are biographers allowed, alas, to gloss over a subject's sexlessness with adjectives like *pure, ascetic,* or *austere.*
Modern readers want to know what the problem was.

Silber's problem, I suspect, was that he never figured out
how to operate the air lock between fantasy and reality. Tom
may well be right about what happened with Conchita, but
he's wrong about the reason. I suspect that — like most men —
Silber defaulted to thoughts of naked women any time he
wasn't straining to think about something else, but as potent as
his lust may have seemed in solitude, it buckled under the
weight of an actual flesh-and-blood woman in his lap: anything more solid than a daydream was too heavy. A perfection-

ist like me,* he preferred the fantasy — odorless and antiseptic — to the real thing.

It may also be that he had waited too long: like any other language, sex is easier to master the earlier you start. Silber's musical development outstripped his psychosexual. By the time he took a fleeting interest in the other sex as such (in his late teens, according to Tom), he was too accustomed to being the best at what he did to start doing something else, something to which his contemporaries all attached supreme importance, and at which he knew he would never excel. It had proven easier (after a few fiascoes, perhaps?) to withdraw into his music altogether — to get even better at the thing he did best. After all, it's hard enough for an adult just to admit he never learned to swim.

Silber hadn't sealed off any more rooms since 1988, but in '94 he'd gotten out his trowel once again to plaster over his front door from inside. Right around that time, according to Tom (who heard it from Edna), Silber had also stocked up on more than a thousand dollars' worth of canned goods, as if intending to spend what remained of his life in what remained of his house, as if he didn't plan to venture out ever again, as if the whole outdoors were just another place where something bad had happened.

Incidentally, Tom came up again in conversation in the middle of May, or roughly a month after our first discussion of the subject. Like that first discussion, the second took place at the end of an after-dinner walk, and once again I wore a THINKERS DIGEST sweatshirt, or rather doffed it and donned it repeatedly, since the evening was really too warm for a sweatshirt, if still a little chilly for the T-shirt underneath. (The

---

* Luckily, biographers are not required to explain their *own* sex lives or lacks thereof, but I will say that my defeats in that arena, and my status since the age of twenty-seven as a noncontender, are due to difficulties not so very different from those I'm imputing to Silber.

sweatshirt was a bit too snug, moreover, though the tag said LARGE. But maybe I was large for a thinker; maybe shirt sizes are smaller in the realm of the intellect, just as parking spaces — and shirt sizes too? — are smaller in Japan. Or maybe the loud red shirts had shrunk in the wash — I always laundered them in hot water, hoping in vain to turn down the volume.)

By that point I'd gotten over my pathetic jealousy of Tom, but I had another more practical reason for wanting to know more about him. His manuscript contained, as we have seen, all sorts of lurid allegations, some of which I wanted to include — as facts, if possible — in the unauthorized biography, but Tom was as lax about documentation as about grammar, and seldom bothered to explain just *how* he knew the things he claimed to know, or who his sources were. Rereading his biography that afternoon, I'd resolved to track him down and pick his brains. That evening at the corner of Tenth and Tree, I tried to ask Silber about Tom's current whereabouts, but carefully — he didn't know that I had found Tom's manuscript.

"So — whatever became of that other biographer, anyhow?"

"Why?" demanded Silber, jerking to a standstill and pivoting to stare at me, as if he knew exactly what I had in mind. "What do *you* care where he is?"

I shrugged and said I was worried that Tom would "scoop" us with his own, unauthorized, biography of Silber. And I *was* afraid that it might occur to Tom, if it hadn't yet, to sell to the highest bidder the secrets he'd been fired for unearthing. (At that point, I tended to forget — what I've since been forced to remember — that Silber was not a household name and that any publisher to whom Tom pitched his book would be apt to answer "Simon who?") That in fact was one reason I wanted to track him down — to find out if he had plans for a book of his own, though without putting the idea in his head if it wasn't there already. I told myself that Tom couldn't write to save his life, but that didn't mean he couldn't publish. More reassuring was the knowledge that the story *I* was selling was the tale of *two* men, and one of them me: the account of how two artists of our stature came to meet, and how it was destined to be, just as the two best boxers in a given weight class are destined to meet, by and by, even if they start out on opposite sides of the globe. Surely *that* story had more human interest than the story of Silber alone, no matter how much muck poor Tom had managed to rake up.

Evidently reassured by my quarter-truth, Silber tried to reassure me too: "Oh, don't worry about Tom. *He* won't be publishing anything any time soon." After a moment, he added, "About me, I mean."

"How do you know?"

"I just do." And abruptly he resumed walking — and dictating to his tape recorder too, though I could have sworn that he had finished for the evening.

## 6. *Route 111*                                              36:00

We've already seen the sports car Silber received on his twenty-first birthday,* after years of begging for a car he could actually drive. Silber had spent his adolescence tinkering with junkers, but hadn't been allowed to take them out of the garage: he'd been obliged to put them up on cinderblocks, surrendering the wheels to his father. Mr. Silber feared that Simon, given half a chance, would try to flee his future as a world-class pianist and be lost forever in the traffic jam of normalcy.

By the time his father finally relented, Simon's adolescent wanderlust had given way to a view of the world as one enormous minefield. Soon after the Erlenmeyer Competition, he developed an odd phobia: suddenly he was unable to go anywhere he hadn't been already — to venture onto any unfamiliar road, or travel any farther down a known one than he'd traveled with his father on one errand or another. One effect of this

---

* Yet another reason for his siblings to resent him: Scooter — whom his father no longer acknowledged — had received nothing that day, and Helen had merited only a hat on *her* twenty-first birthday.

phobia was to confine him to Forest City and vicinity, since Mr. Silber had confined his son to that vicinity, and not from lack of funds or dislike of travel, but in order to keep him focused on his music. Anxious to prevent the boy from seeing any more of life than necessary — any more of the world with all its enticing alternatives to the lot of a concert pianist — Mr. Silber had never taken Simon more than three miles from home prior to the competition, and had managed to keep him from venturing any farther on his own by frightening him daily, from the day he started crawling, with this dire warning: *If you go somewhere new, something bad will happen.*

Tom believed that Silber's phobia, which made it so "conveniently impossible" for the vanquished virtuoso to move on to larger halls and worse defeats, was nothing but a sham to fool Silber's father, and the press, and in due time posterity — everyone, in fact, but Tom, who blamed Silber's sudden career-ending inability to travel on his insanely belated discovery of the greater world out there where the standards were higher. Up till then, Tom speculates, Mr. Silber had succeeded in keeping that world a secret from his son.

Though I'm convinced that Silber's phobia was real, I'll grant Tom that Silber's nervous breakdown was precipitated by his first encounter (at least since his brother dropped out of the running) with a better pianist his own age. It was ultimately to save his self-esteem that Silber's psyche resorted to the desperate measure of a neurosis that made a career as a concert pianist impossible. To put it another way: the incapacitating fear that Silber felt each time he thought of turning onto a new road, or following an old one into terra incognita, was in fact anxiety for his self-image. He was like a man who develops hysterical blindness at the instant he incurs a disfiguring injury, so desperate not to see himself that he stops seeing altogether.

Mr. Silber did everything he could to help our composer overcome his fear of traveling and get his show back on the road. For a while, a psychiatrist made house (or carriage house) calls, seeing Simon thrice a week. When that failed, Mr. Silber threatened to disown our composer, but the threat had no effect — and far from making good on it, Mr. Silber changed his will, a month before his death, in Simon's favor. Maybe, in the end, he decided that his son had simply not been destined for great things in the first place, and that he, the father, had done Simon a great wrong by ruining his chances for a normal life without successfully "preparing" him for any other kind. Maybe the convertible was not an attempt to get a concert pianist back in the saddle — back, as it were, on the horse that had thrown him — but an invitation to the mindless, happy, noisy, unambitious life that till then had been denied him.*

Either way, the gift had failed: Silber never did outgrow his phobia. His father's death in 1980 seems to have arrested our composer in midcrisis. In the nineteen years since then, in any case, Silber literally *hadn't been anywhere new.* But considering that back in 1979 the day had seemed near when he would refuse ever again to leave the carriage house at all, I suppose the car had been a success of sorts. I don't deny that Silber seemed almost as rapt while driving as he did composing (even when he didn't manage to combine those hobbies), though I can't agree with Tom in seeing Silber's little outings as evidence that the phobia was a "fraud." On the contrary: Silber's weekly drive was no more or less than a compulsive and meticulous line drawing of the labyrinth in which he'd been trapped all his life. So few and short had been his sorties beyond Forest City limits in the first twenty years — the years when he was able to go places he hadn't been already — that later it was possible, by driving around for two hours, to revisit every place he'd *ever* been, which is what he did, and all he did, on his weekly

---

* On second thought, that seems improbable. It's true that Mr. Silber's final year was given over to regrets, but as far as I can tell, all of them were variations on the same remorseless theme: he should've been even *more* ruthless and strict. There is no evidence that he ever regretted the pain he had caused.

jaunt.* He'd follow one road as far as he had followed it as a passenger with his father at the wheel, and then he'd turn around and double back. On nights when he was feeling bold, he might forge ahead another fifty feet or so, into unfamiliar territory, before slamming on the brakes in panic, but the next time out those fifty feet would seem just as alien and forbidding as they had the first time. In nineteen years, he hadn't added an inch to the maze in which his father's death had stranded him.

Almost as pathetic as his inability to leave Forest City were the places he wanted to go: Cincinnati, Brooklyn, Queens, Milwaukee, Minneapolis. His father's home-schooling curriculum had eschewed geography, with its enticements to wanderlust, and Silber himself had never been much of a reader. Most of what he knew about the world, he once joked, had been gleaned from television — from the sitcoms of his youth. At least I'd *thought* he was joking, but possibly not. He often spoke with longing of some indifferent city, though he wouldn't say *why* the city enticed him. It occurs to me now (I've been watching a lot of old reruns) that his unlikely list of daydream destinations was no more or less than a list of cities where his favorite sitcoms had been set.

*Route 111* was composed in 1992 as a sort of soundtrack to Silber's favorite part of his invariable drive. Starting on Main Street, at the south edge of town, the music crosses First Avenue (whereupon Main becomes Route 28) and heads excitedly north for half a mile to Route 111, then breathlessly east for eleven, slowing down and shifting from a major to a minor key as it turns off at the first exit, where after some brief but complicated maneuvers (too complicated to detail here) through the streets of Forest City's larger neighbor, Lumber, the compo-

---

* "One night when we got back I said to go a different route next time," writes Tom the Eloquent (who also rode along with our employer once or twice), "and show me *other* places that he went when he was little, but Simon said, 'What other places? I just showed you every place I ever went in my whole life.'"

sition pulls dejectedly into the parking lot of Erlenmeyer Hall and sits there for a moment in dead silence under the midnight sun of the halogen lights while the composer wonders whether he wasted his life, whether he's in the process of wasting it right now. It is a silence reminiscent of — if not outright stolen from, for silences too can be plagiarized — the one in Schubert when Gretchen, overwhelmed by unrequited love, momentarily allows her spinning wheel to stop. Then the key turns in the ignition, the wheels resume spinning, and the music turns around and — at a much slower tempo now — heads back home the way it came, because that was the route that Silber's father had taken to and from Silber's final concert. The homeward stretch is a note-perfect retrograde version — a mirror image — of the corresponding outward passage, but averages thirty miles per hour instead of sixty, and has a very different character and effect. The difference between the breathless outward leg and the sober homeward leg is the difference between tobogganing down a hill and trudging back up.

Like *My House* (though not *My Face*), *Route 111* is composed in "real time." If Silber had played the piece on his tape deck during one of his drives, starting the tape when he crossed First Avenue and passed the sign that said YOU ARE LEAVING FOREST CITY (an announcement also scribbled on the score, above the first measure), the work would end, exactly thirty-six minutes later, just as he passed the sign that said (as it says above the final measure — a mirror image of the first) YOU ARE ENTERING FOREST CITY. Silber insisted that there was a moment-for-moment correspondence between the music and the route itself. He claimed that for any note I singled out, he could tell me exactly where on the route he was. Otherwise, it's hard to see how *Route 111* "represents" the drive; the music doesn't always, or only, swerve where the road does, for example, nor do the tempo changes correspond to speed limits. All the composer would say on the question was "But can't you see — it's *obvious*." My sense is that *Route 111* is less a topological than a psychological portrait: the piece exists to evoke the sequence of feelings that Silber felt on every drive, a sequence of feelings as immutable as the drive itself. They were — if my hunch is right — the same feelings (though refined and stylized by years of repetition), and in the same order, as the ones he'd first experienced on the evening of January 14, 1979, heading to the finals of the Erlenmeyer Competition, and then heading back home in disgrace.

On our drives, my moods tracked Silber's for the most part, either because his excitement was exciting and his depression depressing, or because *any* late-night joy ride is more fun during the first, outbound part, before that adolescent sense of boundless possibility on the open road reveals itself to be an illusion.

Aside from my first and last rides with Silber, in September 1998 and August 1999, the one I remember best took place at the end of May. It had been the warmest day so far that spring, the first to hint at summer, and even late at night was warm enough that for the first time since September, Silber put the top down. When we were about midway between Forest City and Lumber, Silber stopped the car along a lonely and unlit stretch of 111 and stared off into the blackness of the pines on his side of the road.

"What's up?"

Ignoring my question, he sat there, face averted, for several minutes. Finally he started the car and told me, as we continued to Lumber, that at the age of ten, at a little picnic spot among those pines, he had made the biggest decision of his life, the one compared to which all subsequent decisions — even the one to be a composer — were no more than aftershocks. The whole family had gone there for a picnic, and like all family outings this one had made young Silber wretched, since he had no family feeling and could never be happy as part of the group, only as the sole focus of his father's praise and love. At some point that afternoon his father yelled at him (Silber had squirted charcoal lighter at Scooter) and the future composer had taken his paper plate and sat on an old tree stump, apart from the others. When his father didn't apologize or call him back to the table, but continued eating and laughing with the other children, both of them ignoring their brother, Silber had felt first panic, then detachment, as if watching his family through soundproof glass. It was then that he had had his big epiphany: he'd realized that to be special meant to be unhappy, and yet as he sat there on that stump eating potato salad, he'd vowed once and for all to be special.

And he'd kept his vow, and he'd been unhappy. Though he sometimes claimed to love the odd, sad life he led in Forest City, he once confessed that he was only ever really happy outside city limits, and specifically outbound on 111, where his fantasy of leaving town was most intense: by the time he turned off at the Lumber exit, he was already admitting once again that tonight, at any rate, he wasn't going anywhere. It was in Lumber, after all, that his life had been sidetracked in the first place. He told me that he'd gotten the idea for *Route 111* while speeding eastward through the night, watching the familiar scenery rush past, and telling himself — as he did on all these drives, right up to the moment when he turned off at Lumber — that for all he knew, he was seeing that landscape for the last time: *Last week I chickened out,* he'd tell himself, *but tonight . . . who knows? Maybe this is the night I'll finally escape my childhood's gravitational pull once and for all.*

# Disc Four

## 1. *Ice Cream Rag*                                             4:58

As I begin the liner notes to the last disc in your set, it is January 12, and twenty-eight degrees outside, and what's left of last week's snow is black with soot; but I just turned up the heat, and pulled down the window shades, to pretend that it's my favorite season, summer. Silber always said that summer was his favorite season too, the time of year, year after year, when he felt "most alive," but — like life itself, alas — feeling more alive is a mixed blessing. In Silber's case it also meant more easily annoyed — since, unfortunately, summer was of course the *loudest* season: the cats went into heat; the crows found more to crow about; the neighbors left their dogs outdoors to bark all night; they left their windows and their front doors open in the evenings, as if to share their raucous sitcoms with the neighborhood; their children set off firecrackers, cherry bombs, M-80s; they dribbled basketballs on backyard courts, played loud games out front till well after dark — and the days kept getting longer. Everybody, not just Silber, seemed to idle higher, like crickets chirping faster, as the days grew warmer. The crickets were a nuisance too.

The summer noise that Silber dreaded most, though, was the ice-cream truck, or rather the tune that blared from its speaker, over and over and over and over, as the tiny clown truck threaded slowly up and down the side streets. Every afternoon, all summer long, poor Silber had to listen to it — now approaching, now receding — for at least an hour. In 1999, the ice-cream season opened on June 5, the day after classes let out for the summer at the elementary school. I wasn't too surprised when Silber called me on June 6 to say he'd just composed an old-time piano rag based on "that obnoxious tune the ice-cream truck keeps playing," by which he meant the first eight bars of "The Entertainer." Luckily for Silber, that work is in the public domain: his development of the theme is *identical* to Joplin's, down to the last grace note, even though Silber claimed never in his life to have heard "The Entertainer" in its entirety.

Afterward he would dismiss both his own rag and Joplin's as "jingles," but when he first announced the composition of the *Ice Cream Rag,* he thought more highly of it; he even said that "note for note," it might just be the best thing he had ever written. I remember my excitement as he sat down to play it for me at the Bean, and then my nervous laughter, as the piece unfolded, at what I took to be a joke. I remember his astonishment when I lured him across the street and up to my room long enough to play him an old recording of "The Entertainer"; somehow he'd never thought of the ice-cream-truck theme as part of a larger piece with a known composer.

He soon recovered, claiming that the theme he'd borrowed was so "limited" that only one composition could follow "logically," like an algebraic series from its first few terms; he also compared himself and Joplin to scientists independently cloning identical organisms from the genetic matter of that theme. (He still insisted, though, that *his* version was "better.") I have another explanation: at some point in his life, Silber *must* have heard "The Entertainer," maybe decades earlier, and perhaps subliminally, while paying attention to something else, or even in his sleep. One day the ice-cream truck had finally jogged his memory, and he had mistaken the music he remembered for sheer inspiration.

When I persuaded Silber that the *Ice Cream Rag* was an unconscious plagiary, his hatred of the truck intensified. Over the years, he had written several letters to the *Forest City Ranger* to complain about the truck. He had circulated a petition, though no one but Edna had signed it. He was even rumored to have assaulted the driver — not the current one, but his predecessor. He still recalled with glee a weeklong interruption of the music, several years ago, due to a salmonella outbreak at the dairy that supplied the truck: Silber was *against ice cream*. Silber, to be sure, was opposed to anything that made the world louder, but I can't help seeing this particular antipathy as emblematic of the distance he had traveled, and without ever leaving his hometown, from the innocent pleasures of childhood — emblematic, indeed, of the sheer perversity of his whole life's project.

The *Ice Cream Rag* debacle had a sequel. I've mentioned our creative walks, dictating side by side in our respective media to our respective tape recorders. The last such walk took place on the evening of June 14 and ended on such a discordant note that all my diary says on that date is "S and I no longer friends." That evening I was in top form, uttering some of the best aperçus I'd apperceived in years. Silber was making a lot of noise too, though of the nonverbal variety. His *spoken* noises during walks were few and far between — so few, so far, they always came as jarring interruptions of the music, like the Food Town manager's voice overriding the instrumentals to page a cashier or encourage the purchase of a particular product. So I was caught off balance when, as we passed Forest City Elementary, he said, "Quick — give me your recorder!"

"What?"

"My batteries just died and I've got an inspiration. Quick!"

Reflexively submissive, I ejected my cassette and gave him the recorder. He inserted his own tape and started singing.

"But *I* was having inspirations too," I said a minute later.

Silber, busy dictating, didn't seem to hear me.

"Okay," I said after another minute. "Okay, I need it back now."

He continued singing.

"Silber —"

"SHHH!" He stopped, spun around, and bared his teeth before resuming his walk and tune in tandem. When he finally finished and returned the gadget fifteen minutes later, it was with a quiet admonition: "Don't ever interrupt me like that again."

I was too angry to say anything, but I told myself, back at the rooming house, that I was through with Silber, through with Forest City: I would return to Tacoma in the morning, and pick up my old life, such as it was, where I'd left off. After reviewing my bank balance, though, and the terms of my lease, I decided to stick around till the end of the month — long enough for one more paycheck.

Looking back now on my year as Silber's flunky, I wonder how I put up with him as long as I did. It was by far the longest I'd ever managed to hold down a job, not counting the Tacoma job, which — as it turned out — didn't count, and not only because I'd been working for my aunt Lucy. I've mentioned her successor, the Helen look-alike who'd looked askance at me from day one, as if she'd been *told* about me, as if, before we'd even met, she'd known something that had predisposed her to despise me. The day she fired me for being arrogant, belligerent, contemptuous, etc., I'd made the mistake, on my way to the door, of suggesting a few adjectives for *her,* and she'd retaliated by finally telling me — and everyone else in the building, since we were shouting — just *what* it was she'd always known. It turned out to be something I hadn't known myself: for the past fifteen years, my mother had been subsidizing my job — secretly paying my salary, that is, and even paying my ostensible employers an additional "processing fee" to let me sort their books in a back area where patrons wouldn't have to interact with me.

What made my discovery even more humiliating was the knowledge that my father must have funded the arrangement till his death in 1993, since my mother didn't have any money of her own till then. I kept picturing his sneer as, once a month, he authorized her to make out another check to Lucy; and I found myself resenting him afresh. (He didn't leave *me* a cent, by the way.) I was still in shock when Silber hired me, still chastened, shamed, and on my best behavior, desperate to prove that I could keep a job without my mother's help. I probably put up with more on-the-job indignities in the year that followed than in the fifteen before.

After the recorder incident, however, I resolved to have as little as possible to do with my employer. And indeed I didn't talk to him again for a week, not till the morning of June 20, when he phoned to say he needed my help with *Day*.

Flattered, I forgot my resolution to be proud and cold if and when he ever called. "I — I'd love to — if you think I'm competent." And after all — I told myself excitedly — why shouldn't he? He knew I had taken a class in composition. Of course I might not know as much about the art as he did, but I'd have the advantage of approaching *Day* afresh. Two decades back, my friend had set himself an impossible task; there was no shame in admitting that he couldn't go the distance, that he simply wasn't throwing with as much force or accuracy as he'd had in the first inning. Why shouldn't there be relief composers? Silber would still be credited with a win (assuming the thing was successful), and I would get a save.

Or maybe I'd be more like a backup quarterback sent in for one game-winning play while the starter takes a breather. Yes, it sounded like he needed me for only a minute, but the critical minute, the one he'd been stuck on for years. He'd been stuck on *Day* before, he said, but in the past he'd always been able to break through "by paying close enough attention," at the time in question on the day in question (June 21), to "the time of day itself," whatever that meant. Though this strategy had failed him at 5:00 P.M. for three years in a row now, he blamed his failure on chance distractions at exactly the wrong moment: one year a dog had started barking, one year a motorcycle had roared past, one year Mrs. Talbot, his hated next-door neighbor, had paid someone to mow her lawn at that hour. My friend was terrified that one of these disruptions would repeat, or that something else would come along — a crow, a car, a string of firecrackers (and how many times had he kicked himself, over the years, for choosing a date so close to the Fourth of July!) — to break his concentration. He was especially worried about the ice-cream truck, which as luck would have it had adopted a new route that brought it to Silber's block right around five. And that, said Silber, was where I came in: he wanted me to "ward off" the truck the next day, though he was unable to tell me what form the warding should take. I pictured myself setting up traffic barricades and DETOUR signs, rear-ending the truck with my car, flinging tacks in its path. I pictured all that and more, and said no. I told him I was only the biographer; I could omit certain events from my account of his life, but I couldn't stop them from happening in the first place.

"You're fired!" And he slammed down the phone. (Silber fired me that summer six or seven times, though without officially rehiring me in between. The firings themselves may have been informal, but at least they were *explicit*. The reinstatements were so subtle that I was apprised of each only by the firing that subsequently ended that term of reemployment.*) An hour later, though, he called again and — in what sounded like a shameless bid for sympathy — told me that his father had died at 5:00 P.M., had clutched his chest and fallen to the kitchen floor even as the hour was tolling from the tower of the Episcopal church that in those days had stood at the

---

* By that point I was vaguely assuming that the childless composer had written me into his (frequently updated) will, and every time he fired me, I thought of myself as not so much unemployed as *disinherited*.

corner of Fourth and Tree (it burned down a few years later). Ever since, Silber said, he'd felt "funny" at that hour, and *that* was why he couldn't get beyond that point in *Day.*

"Well," I said, "that's too bad about your dad, but I still won't stop the ice-cream truck."

"I'll give you anything you want."

*Could* he give me anything I wanted? All I really wanted was respect: I wanted him to treat me as an equal, as an artist in my own right. But respect is not a gift that you can *choose* to give someone. (If it were, I would have been more generous with mine, and I might have had more friends.) And against all evidence, I still deluded myself that I already *had* Silber's respect. In any case, I wouldn't earn it by serving as his thug.

"I'm sorry — no."

"You're fired!" He hung up again.

After thinking it over for an hour, I called and told his machine that I would flag down the ice-cream boy at the start of his route and buy up all his wares if Silber would foot the bill and would promise to read my book of aphorisms — not just the table of contents this time — and give me a written response of the sort I'd once required from my students to confirm that they'd done *their* required reading. I said I'd look for him that evening to work out the details.

"Sure, sure," said Silber that evening — the evening of the twentieth, the eve of the big day — when I intercepted him at the corner of Meadowbrook and Seventh and thrust my book at him defiantly. He took it but looked so preoccupied that I doubted his good faith. I could already hear him indignantly denying that he'd ever agreed to such a bargain. I almost demanded that he read the book and return his typed response *before* tomorrow's caper, but I didn't have the nerve, especially as my preface was an exhortation to read slowly, to *digest* each thought before advancing to the next. (I even recommended a walk around the block after every aphorism.) And at least he too had come prepared, handing me a check to cover my expenses. I did get him to assure me (if "sure, sure" is an assurance) that he'd have his book report ready by the twenty-third.

The next day the temperature hovered around ninety. At 4:35 P.M., I sat in my car in the insufficient shade of a young ginkgo at the corner of Fourth and Main — the point at which, each afternoon, the ice-cream truck slowed to a crawl and turned on its loudspeaker. I'd been there since four. I had the engine running and the air conditioner on high. On the seat beside me was a big blue insulated plastic chest I had borrowed that morning from Billy. In the park across the street, two junior-high kids were exploding model tanks and G. I. Joes with firecrackers. Would the noise impair our composer's perception of five o'clock — less than half an hour away — as it revealed itself in his back yard, less than half a mile away? Not my problem — my assignment was the ice-cream truck. If it came along before 5:00, my orders were to flag it down and buy up the entire stock. If the driver balked, I was authorized to offer him a fifty-dollar bribe. If he still refused, or complied but then continued on toward Silber's anyhow, music blaring, with his empty truck, as Silber thought he might do out of simple malice, I was to stop him by any means necessary; Silber promised to post bail.

At 4:36 P.M., I saw the truck approaching and got out of my car, leaving the motor and the AC running. The driver looked a little frightened by my request, as if only a pervert could want that much ice cream, but he sold out without a fight — it would be the easiest shift he'd ever worked. The only hitch was that there turned out to be a lot more ice cream than Silber and I had reckoned on; in addition to the ice-cream money he had given me, I had to use most of the bribe (which I'd been planning to keep so that even if Silber didn't uphold his end of the bargain, I'd have *some* compensation for my demeaning mission). I wondered, as I watched the driver switch off his loudspeaker and head for the beach, what on earth to do with the mound of frozen novelties I'd heaped by the ginkgo, in a tiny oasis of shade on the searing sidewalk. Billy's cooler held no more than a quarter of the inventory, and the freezer in my kitchenette was already full of fish sticks, TV dinners, toaster waffles, and other bachelor fare. As I pondered, the delinquents who'd been blowing up their toys came out of the park and traded me a cherry bomb for all the ice cream they could eat, but that barely made a dent. Finally I shoveled the surplus — already softening ominously — into the back seat of my car, planning to race over to the Bean and treat the regulars to as much as *they* could eat. Let them retaste their childhoods at Silber's expense — they seemed like people for whom the advent of adulthood had been a disaster. No sooner did I put the car in gear, though, than the engine died. I'd known I was low on gas, but had forgotten how much the AC squandered. I got out again, opened the passenger door, and hurriedly, furtively, transferred the deliquescent ice cream back to its spot at the foot of the ginkgo. Just as I finished, a police car pulled up behind me and a huge policeman ordered me to clean up my mess, indicating a green fifty-gallon drum at the edge of the park, catty-corner across the busy intersection. "No jaywalking, either. I'll be watching."

It took me four trips with many long and law-abiding waits for traffic lights to change, delays that I spent blaming Silber. ("He *better* read my goddamn book," I said aloud at one point.) Soon I was sodden with trickles of vanilla ice cream, smears of chocolate coating, and rashes of syrupy popsicle colors. After the second trip I abandoned all hope of salvaging some of the haul — the only way to move the goop to the dumpster was by using Billy's cooler as a bucket.

"Good enough," said the bighearted cop from his air-conditioned squad car, when all that remained was a hard, shiny glaze where the ice cream had baked onto the pavement. He drove off to fight crime elsewhere, and I walked back to my rooming house, sticky and sunburnt, to shower — only to find Billy tying up the only bathroom, beating the heat with an all-day bath.

I hoped my employer had noticed the silence.

## 2. From *Day:* 5:00–5:01 P.M.  1:00

Readers will gather from the title of this track that in the end the composer overcame his block on *Day* long enough at least to add another minute. Those who go on to listen to that minute will find it an excruciating one — "cacophonous" doesn't begin to suggest the torments in store for you — and will wonder, long before it's over, how such gasps and groans, such dissonant death agonies, were produced on an ordinary piano. They weren't: the noises were extracted, like so many wisdom teeth, from a specially modified instrument, and that instrument — the same Steinway concert grand used to record most of the other works in your boxed set — was further modified, and more specifically demolished, in the course of the performance.

Silber had promised to call me on the evening of the twenty-first. When he didn't, I assumed that once again the independently wealthy composer had failed to grasp the essence of quitting time long enough to set it to music. When he hadn't called, or returned my calls, by the evening of the twenty-third, I became obsessively convinced that he was avoiding me because he hadn't read my book and didn't intend to. I don't know why this breach of contract upset me as much as it did, but for a couple of days there I had to steer clear of the public library: the sight of people reading was a galling reminder of Silber's refusal to read *me*.

My obsession was full-blown by the next time I saw him, on the morning of the twenty-sixth. The night before I'd gotten up at three to use the bathroom and then had worked myself into such a state rehearsing my case against Silber that I couldn't get back to sleep. I was still awake at six, when the Bean opened its doors, and rather than lie in bed stewing any longer, I got dressed and crossed the street for coffee, vowing in all earnestness to heave a brick through our composer's living-room window that evening if I hadn't heard from him by sundown.

Twenty minutes later, I was reading Boswell at an outdoor table when I heard a noise and looked up in time to see Silber loping past with his eyes shut and his head thrown back, quietly singing the *vivace* from Schubert's final piano sonata. Silber had forbidden me to interrupt these transports — to do so, he insisted, would be wakening a sleepwalker — but I was so angry that I welcomed the chance to defy and disturb my employer. I jumped up to shout his name but then had a better idea, ran over to the rooming house, and fetched the cherry bomb I'd been keeping on my desk, a cherry red reminder of the last humiliation I had undergone for Silber's sake. I also grabbed the matches I used to light my stove.

Silber sleepwalked slowly, and I found him not a block away, still headed west on High Street (my street). I overtook him on the far side of the street and hid myself in some bushes, or ambushes, in front of the vacant house at the corner of Fourteenth and High. The shiny thick green fuse contrasted prettily with the matte red bombshell; it would be a pity to burn up the one and blow up the other, but the contrast in Silber's demeanor — Before and After — should be even better. When he neared the intersection, I lit the fuse and lobbed the bomb across the street, not *at* my employer but in his direction. Or if I did throw at him, I was trusting that the poorness of my aim would guarantee a miss. And miss I did, but not by much: I threw with more precision than I'd ever thrown before, and the bomb had barely cleared Silber's head when it exploded, in midair, not three feet from his left ear.

A moment later my own ears were ringing — I'd forgotten just how loud a cherry bomb can be — and I hadn't even seen the cartoonish startle response I had hoped for: Silber had frozen for a moment in midstride (seeming briefly to debate spending the rest of his life on that corner, in a catatonic stupor), then turned and — eyes wide open now — walked slowly back home, not even looking around to see where the noise had come from.

He finally called me the next morning, as if my firecracker

had succeeded (as less drastic measures hadn't) in getting his attention — though I later ascertained that he had no clue who'd thrown it. He announced that he had made progress on *Day* — that he'd gotten over the five-o'clock impasse.

"Hmm. Did you get a chance to read my book yet?"

"What?" He sounded annoyed. "No. I've had other things to do." *More important things,* his tone implied, and I wished I'd thrown a bigger bomb.

We hadn't spoken since the eve of the ice-cream debacle, so I tried to tell him about it, but he wasn't interested. As a rule, he was bored by *my* misfortunes. If he complained about the crickets and their pointless racket, and I parried with an evocation of the slamming doors, creaky stairs, flushing toilets, thumping music, blaring television sets, shouted hallway conversations, and other nuisances that made my rooming house so noisy night and day, he would wait impatiently until my mouth stopped moving, and then resume his case against the crickets. So now, when I embarked on my account of the ice cream and the cop, Silber interrupted me at once to say that though he had added only *one minute* to his daylong sonata, it was the most important minute to date, the one that had been holding things up: "I've still got a lot of work to do, but for the first time in years, I'm convinced that I'll finish the thing — I'm finally over the hump." He invited me to a premiere of the big minute.

I drove over to Tree Street, my resentment yielding to curiosity. As always, I parked out front and walked around back, where I found a mountain of debris in Silber's yard, not far from the garage. It took me a minute to recognize the wreckage as that of a grand piano, maybe because its modification had somehow involved magnets, pulleys, clothesline, bells, and whistles — components which by that point, with a full trimester of group piano lessons under my belt, I knew enough not to expect among the ruins of a concert grand. Had my employer been playing so hard that the instrument had crumbled under his fingertips? Or had he just gotten sick of his constant companion and taken a sledgehammer to it? And did he plan to bury the piano in his yard, alongside the casualties of other tantrums?

I noticed a trail of debris — black and white keys, shards of lacquered wood, levers, dampers, wire — leading from the yard to the side door of the garage. As I gazed, the door swung open.

"Hi, Norm," said Silber. Instead of a tuxedo he wore a grimy gray-green jumpsuit with SIMON stitched in cursive over the breast pocket.

"What's all this?" I indicated the wreckage.

"A busted piano. Last night I decided — goddammit!"

"What's the matter?"

"Don't you hear?"

Perking up my ears, I heard a distant frantic barking. I've mentioned lurid rumors about Silber killing pets, but for me those rumors were rebutted single-throatedly by Sentinel, the Websters' Border collie, which for thirteen years now its owners (hard of hearing) had left outdoors to bark all day, day after day, all summer long. But old Dr. Webster was the obstetrician who had brought our composer into the world, and maybe for that reason — simple gratitude — Silber refrained from killing *his* dog, notwithstanding Dr. Webster's previous and concomitant deliveries, respectively, of Silber's two unwelcome siblings.

More than once on our walks, the composer had bemoaned the popularity of dogs among the rich: a rich man like Silber, who *didn't* like dogs, couldn't get away from them — as from most other bothers — by living where rich people lived. "It just isn't fair," he said now, as we stood in his back yard, harking to Sentinel's barking. "No matter how well off you are, or how good a house you have, all it takes is just one stupid goddamn dog next door to ruin everything. I might as well be living in your goddamn rooming house."

Though the lament wasn't worded in a way to inspire pity for the poor beleaguered rich man — and the dog responsible for Silber's fulminations was *not* next door but several blocks away and barely audible — I forced a sympathetic smile. Later I learned that Silber had almost been arrested, back in 1994, for making a series of menacing anonymous phone calls to the Websters. It was a good thing they *didn't* live next door, or there would've been a showdown long ago.

"Well, c'mon in," said Silber. "Let's get away from that racket."

Since my last visit, Silber had cleaned out his attic or basement or both, to judge by the mountain of junk on the grimy concrete floor of the garage, a mountain whose highlights included a blender; an old red tricycle with red, white, and blue streamers hanging from its handlebars; a four-slotted toaster; a manual typewriter with a sheet of typing paper in its carriage (the sheet — an abandoned autobiography? — was blank except for the words: "This is the story of my life. I was born"); a bicycle pump (the old-fashioned kind that looks like the plungers they use in cartoons to set off big red bundles of cartoon dynamite); a black rotary-dial phone with what was still Silber's number printed in black characters on a white disk of paper beneath the clear plastic hub); a phonographic turntable with a well-worn recording of Schubert's "Unfinished" symphony; an electric carving knife; a yellow pogo stick; and an automatic coffeemaker.

"What's all this?"

"Never mind all that. C'mon." We followed a trail of piano debris — like a path of bread crumbs through a fairy-tale forest — upstairs to the skylit studio. On my other visits there had been a grand piano, but now there was only the bright unfaded silhouette of a piano on the faded carpet, underneath the skylight.

"What happened to the piano?"

"Not so loud," said Silber. "Why are you shouting today?"

I hadn't been shouting. "Sorry," I said.

"The piano gave its life," said Silber, "for a worthy cause." He took a reel of magnetic tape out of a gray metal canister labeled "5:00 P.M.–5:01 P.M." and threaded it onto his player. He hit a switch, said "back in a minute," and left the room, shutting the door behind him. I heard a few seconds of silence, and then the minute of "music" on your disc. Another minute passed before the composer ventured back in, as if the clamor needed time to dissipate. "So what do you think?"

"So you wrecked a grand piano —"

"Shhh!" said Silber, though in fact I'd spoken softly. "Not so loud! You think I'm hard of hearing?"

"You wrecked a piano," I persisted, sotto voce, "for the sake of a one-minute recording?"

"Not just *any* minute. That was my farewell to music you just heard. Or music as *you* know it."

"But —"

"I think you better go now. You're beginning to annoy me."

So I went. As far as I know, Silber never touched a piano again. At any rate, he never recorded another note for posterity, though for his own purposes, increasingly obscure, he continued to croon to his hand-held recorder. Whether the Steinway's destruction really was his farewell to music as we know it, though, or just a wanton gesture allying the composer with a thousand electric-guitar-smashing cretins — well, I'm still not sure.

## 3. Selections from *My Life*                1:00

| | | | |
|---|---|---|---|
| August 26, 1978 | :03 | May 4, 1988 | :03 |
| December 11, 1980 | :03 | May 5, 1988 | :03 |
| December 15, 1980 | :03 | May 6, 1988 | :03 |
| December 18, 1980 | :03 | May 7, 1988 | :03 |
| December 19, 1980 | :03 | July 14, 1994 | :03 |
| October 25, 1983 | :03 | July 15, 1994 | :03 |
| October 28, 1983 | :03 | July 17, 1994 | :03 |
| October 29, 1983 | :03 | July 19, 1994 | :03 |
| October 31, 1983 | :03 | December 25, 1997 | :03 |
| May 3, 1988 | :03 | August 5, 1999 | :03 |

Something tells me that even the self-sufficient listener who up to this point has disdained to read my notes — as stubbornly as Silber refused to read my book — has joined us now in hopes of learning why our second sampling from the composer's diary consists of twenty instances of the same unpleasant chord. To that belated reader, I say: welcome aboard, but go back to the beginning of the booklet and read your way up to this point fair and square.

Toward the end of June, Silber's lifelong sensitivity to noise intensified. He took to wearing earplugs night and day. He started whispering. He made me address him in a murmur barely audible to *me,* and told me to wear sneakers in his presence. He quit eating crunchy foods or ones in noisy packages (brittle cellophane, vacuum-sealed jars) and tried to interest me in ghostwriting a book about the special Quiet Diet he'd devised, though that diet tended to give him indigestion, a condition he could no longer treat with the deafeningly effervescent antacid tablets in his medicine cabinet. He forbade Edna to run the vacuum cleaner — such an affront to her sense of things that she forgot her animosity long enough to call and urge me to "have a word with him," as if he were wise and a word would be sufficient. He no longer flushed the toilets, Edna said, but he didn't seem to mind if she did once he'd left the area. Though it was one of the hottest summers on record, with temperatures pushing into the nineties almost every day, Silber would neither open the windows, according to Edna, nor use the house's central air conditioning.

According to Silber, it wasn't his first attack of hypersensitive hearing. He'd had four already, each lasting a few weeks, and all following the same basic course, starting harmlessly but growing more and more severe and finally incapacitating Silber — more than once he had been housebound, even bedridden, for days — before subsiding like a fever, after which recovery was rapid. What made this latest bout uniquely bad was that for the first time in his life, even the noises that *he* was to blame for had become unbearable. Till now, he'd always been oblivious to them, as so many people are to their own noises, or for that matter their own odors. Silber's customary tread and his normal speaking voice were if anything louder than most, as if he were trying to drown out the world's hubbub with his own. Now, though, he could barely breathe without wincing at the noise.

He started having nightmares in which the tiny sounds he was unable to exclude even from the soundproof basement where he slept — the roar of his own blood coursing through his veins, the gusts of his own breathing (luckily he didn't *snore*), the grating of his eyelash on the pillowcase — would find their way into the dream, though without quite waking him, just as other dreamers will sleep through louder noises (power mowers, motorcycles, squalling babies, barking dogs) by painting them into the picture. He was no longer able, he lamented, to escape the world's noises even in his sleep — since of course his body was as much a part of the world as anything else, and by making noises it lost its one distinction: that unlike the rest of the world, it did what he wanted.

He said that though he finally knew exactly how to finish *Day* — a hypersensitivity to noise meant one to music too — he couldn't compose for more than a few minutes on end because "the racket" was unbearable. At the time I didn't know how unorthodox, how *loud,* his latest method of composing was. So I wondered just what "racket" he meant, since he'd said he didn't plan to demolish any more pianos, and of course the actual mental act of composing is silent. Maybe he meant that he couldn't pick out tunes at the keyboard (as he sometimes liked to do) even with his lightest touch — and he'd been famed, in his day, for the lightness of his touch; one of his favorite stunts as the local enfant terrible had been to take some famously clamorous showstopper like the *Hammerklavier* Sonata and play the whole thing *pianissimo.* Or maybe even the sound of a pen scratching on manuscript paper was too much for him to bear. One night in July he did take his tiny voice-activated tape recorder to bed with him, in order to capture the sounds that were giving him nightmares, but the resulting document is of course omitted from this all-piano compilation.* In any case, not even Silber considered it music, though he did remaster it to high-end two-inch tape. Judging by the volume at which he played that tape for me (once again leaving the room while I listened, as if he were an x-ray technician ducking behind his leaden partition), its purpose was to let me know how it felt to have painfully sensitive hearing. Because of the volume, and the poor quality of the original recording, there was a lot of tape hiss between eye blinks — as if, during these attacks, silence itself were deafening.

As the summer wore on, Silber's condition grew worse. By mid-July he was enlisting me — with no raise in pay — to do all sorts of tasks that were now too loud for him, like shopping for groceries or mowing the lawn with his rusty old push mower. (He'd removed the motor from his power mower, evidently lest I even think of using that one.) Though I'd vowed to quit at the end of June, I felt duty-bound as his biographer to stick around and lend a hand, as a doctor might be bound by an epidemic to cancel his vacation plans. And just as that doctor, no matter how saintly, would be motivated not only by compassion but also by a scientific interest in a new disease awaiting its first expert, and promising to make him famous if it didn't kill him too — so it was with me and Silber.

I was also motivated by guilt: Silber had mentioned that in the past each bout of hypersensitivity had followed — and presumably been triggered by — exposure to some unusually loud noise: in December 1980, the screaming match that culminated in his throwing Helen through a picture window; in October '83, a jackhammer; in April '88 a thunderstorm too close to home; and in July '94 a car crash at an intersection, a few

---

* Aside from *My Life* and *Day*, the only other notable omissions are the *Fantasy for Pitch Pipe and Tuning Forks* (Opus 2), a violin transcription of "I've Got a Right to Play the Blues," the *Six Sonatas for Unaccompanied Gong* (Opus 10, commissioned by the great gong-thumper Webb), and *Red Fugue* (Opus 14), an eight-part fugue for string quartet composed, one night in 1990, in a bright red room (a feat I would not have thought possible).

feet from Silber's idling convertible. As for his current attack, he wasn't sure, but mentioned that he'd heard a loud noise on one of his walks. I often felt the nibble of remorse that summer, though it wasn't certain that my cherry bomb had triggered the attack. After all, the demolition of a grand piano can't have been a quiet process.

Silber still took walks — he said they kept him sane (!) — but they were skittish, fearful walks, those of a one-legged soldier through a minefield. Although I didn't join him on these walks — that chapter of our friendship was over forever — sometimes I tailed him at a respectful distance. He no longer followed a fixed route, but veered down side streets, doubled back, froze in his tracks, or broke into sprints as needed to avoid sudden unforeseen noises. In commercial neighborhoods, he kept to the back alleys, though even those were rife with perils. One night he came upon a vagrant poking around in a dumpster behind the steak house on Main Street. With the merciless eye for human weakness so many winos seem to cultivate, this one had not only noticed Silber's skittishness, but had somehow understood at once its etiology, and had amused himself by shouting raucously as Silber passed. Silber had winced and lunged at the vagrant in rage, but the latter had been able to defend himself simply by clapping his hands, an ovation that sent our composer reeling off down the alley in pain.

As for foreseeable noises, Silber had drawn up a detailed Noise Map of his neighborhood, indicating bawling babies, barking dogs, blaring stereos, etc., and consulted the map when debating which way to go to avoid a "noise obstacle." But there wasn't always time to deliberate. One evening he was walking up Meadowbrook when a moped rounded the corner and came roaring his way. Silber froze for a minute, then ran up the nearest driveway in order to be as far away as possible from the moped when it passed. Just as it did, though, a dog started barking, and Silber rushed back down the strangers' driveway: he'd forgotten, or hadn't had time to consider, that according to his map, those strangers kept a German shepherd fenced in their back yard. A few days later, another dash onto private property caused the owner to call the police, who caught up with Silber a few blocks away — taking his temperature at the corner of Fourteenth and Tree — and commanded him to identify himself, as if he hadn't lived in Forest City all his life. By that point he looked (and, for the record, smelled) like a vagrant himself: in an ominous reprise of Gordon's final weeks, he had started to neglect his hygiene, though in Simon's case it wasn't depression but an inability to tolerate the pelting of a shower, or the plashing and sloshing of a bath, that led him to go without bathing for weeks on end, and during a heat wave. Judging from the scruffy beard he'd started growing (and assuming that it wasn't just an homage to *my* beard), the scraping of a razor was intolerable too.

As for my obsession with inducing him to read my book, that had gone into remission: Silber was suffering as much as I could possibly wish — not that I did wish, of course — if I'd been in a position to punish him for his failure to keep his end of our bargain, and for the immense arrogance and callousness and self-absorption that were to blame for that failure. Only once, when he complained that he couldn't "do anything" because everything made too much noise, did I say, "You could always read a book. For example, *mine*."

Silber rolled his eyes. "I mean anything I *want* to do. And even books make noise."

I controlled my anger, which was more than he could do. Every living thing infuriated him, and inevitably I did too. Though I trained myself to murmur in his presence, and not to sniffle or blow my nose (I had hay fever), and never to crack my knuckles or click my fingers or snap my gum, I knew it was only a matter of time before I slipped up and committed some unforgivable noise. It finally happened on the afternoon of July 31, at the corner of Seventh and Thrush, where we'd met to swap the penultimate chapter of his biography for my penultimate paycheck, since Silber could no longer tolerate the clamor at the Bean. I had expected our meeting to be brief, but to my annoyance Silber wanted to talk. He didn't want *me* to talk; I was required to listen in silence, and nod in comprehension, while he maundered on beneath his breath, since I was no longer able to speak softly enough for his ears. That afternoon, as I recall, I had just rented a new release, and the strain of listening to Silber's whispered monologue made me all the more eager to get away from him and back to my VCR. As he was telling me about his plans to have his ears surgically "disconnected," I yawned aloud and winced as I reopened a tiny wound at the corner of my mouth — I had cut it the day before on a tortilla chip.

"Shh!" said Silber, also wincing. I was allowed to yawn in his face (no insignificant "perk" for an as-told-to biographer), but not to accompany my yawns with a canine howl (as I'd been doing since adolescence, when boredom was a torture too excruciating to suffer in silence).

"*Sorry!*" I whispered.

Silber glared at me, but resumed his monologue. The operation (one he'd fantasized about for years) would be irreversible, he said, like some vasectomies. He'd already heard all he wanted, he said. He no longer listened to music and, in any case, so little of what cluttered the sound waves *was* music — so low was the signal-to-noise ratio of everyday life — that it would be a small price to pay. And after all —

At that point I interrupted him again, this time by sneezing. He recoiled as if socked in the nose. Admittedly, my sneezes are the loud cartoonish kind; as an adolescent I had gotten into the habit of enunciating them — "Ahh-CHOO!" — and Silber wasn't the first to find that habit annoying. He was wrong, though, in assuming that I'd *meant* to be annoying, that my sneeze had been a conscious effort to torment him.

Without thinking, Silber bellowed, "GODDAMN YOU!" and then grimaced, clapped his hands to his ears, doubled over in pain.

"SILBER!" I shouted in panic, "ARE YOU OKAY?" Another shock of pain ran through my employer. *"Oops!" I added in a whisper. "Sorry!"*

*"Shut up!"* hissed Silber. *"Get away from me! Don't ever talk to me again!"* He staggered back up Tree Street toward his house.

After that unfortunate incident, Silber dropped out of sight. By that point, he'd discontinued the walks that kept him sane, and now no longer left his house at all. Concerned, I started routing my own walks past his house, always rising to tiptoe when I got within a block, and always passing, with my breath held, on the far side of the street. For a week I walked past several times a day, but I never once saw a sign of life. I left several messages on his machine, but he didn't return them. (I did hear again from Edna, who called in tears on August 2 after she too fouled out of our employer's favor: she'd been unable to restrain herself from vacuuming the living room while she thought Silber was in the garage, but he'd come down the front stairway instead and chased her out of the house with a wrench, threatening to kill her if she ever ventured back into earshot.)

I assumed I'd been fired again, and this time for good. I didn't mind: I was sick of Forest City. I had more than enough dirt for my unauthorized tell-all biography. I worried about Silber, though — if his condition continued to worsen, what would become of him? I began to think he might be dead, and on August 7, instead of walking past his house, I crossed the street and tiptoed around to his back door with the stealth of a Navajo scout. I raised my fist to knock but couldn't: Silber had trained me that well.

As I stood there staring at a red five-gallon gasoline can on the back porch and wondering what to do next, I was startled by a sound from Silber's garage, the sound of metal striking metal. I tiptoed over. It wasn't the first time that summer I'd heard such noises in the vicinity of his house; I always listened up when I walked past, hearing noises with the composer's ears, and more than once I'd heard a distant clanking, grinding, revving, but I'd always assumed that a neighbor was tinkering in some other garage.

As for Silber's, its door — the one for people, not for cars — was just ajar, and through the chink I saw the composer with his back to me. He was wearing his gray jumpsuit and a pair of ear protectors — the bulky plastic kind that look like headphones used to. Behind him the heap of old appliances I'd seen on my last visit was still visible, but visibly diminished.

As I watched, he raised a ball-peen hammer overhead and swung it, striking metal, and shuddered with pain, though in fact the clang had not been loud. (Schopenhauer praises Beethoven's ability to "thunder on a flute," but only *our* composer could murmur with a hammer.) He reeled as if dizzy, and then raised his face to the rafters, maybe supplicating for the courage to continue. And sure enough, a moment later, he lifted his hammer and took another crack at whatever he was building or destroying now. Again he recoiled in pain. I turned away puzzled — and also a little annoyed, I admit, that the subject of my book was still alive and enacting new enigmas for his biographer to solve and record.

Several new patches of green — some of them as big around as garbage-can lids — polka-dotted Silber's mustard-colored lawn. Since my last visit, the heap of piano debris had traveled to a spot by the back porch, near the sunken garbage can, whose lid was now wide open. It looked like the composer had stuffed as much as possible of the piano *into* the can, though he would have to drag that can out to the curb on garbage night if he expected the garbageman to empty it. Gazing at the can and shaking my head sadly, I noticed a thick, rumpled score among the shards of wood and snarls of wire. *My Life.* I knelt and snatched the yellowing manuscript out of the trash, as if it might be worth a lot one day. Why was Silber discarding his *Life,* a musical diary almost as old as the diarist? It seemed a little ominous. Like anybody for whom consciousness itself is an ordeal, our composer was obsessed throughout his life with suicide, or at least throughout the year I knew him. The day we met he told me that at his most ecstatic, when *everything* seemed wonderful, suicide — that option — seemed wonderful as well. At his most despondent, he saw it as the answer to all his problems, even that of artistic neglect. He had insisted on one of our last walks that he — his continued existence — was the sandbag that kept his reputation from soaring; he was clearly meant, he said, for *posthumous* success, and by remaining alive was only postponing his induction into the composers' hall of fame. On that occasion, I'd agreed that some of the greatest artists hit the charts only after death, and that a visionary like Silber, so far ahead of his time, was no doubt of their number; but didn't it bother him that when his fame did come, he wouldn't be there to enjoy it?

"Yes," he had said, after a moment. "That does bother me."

The day after I rescued *My Life* from the trash, Billy knocked on my door after lunch to say that someone had set fire to the Websters' collie. I recalled the gas can on Silber's back porch, and the green spots in his back yard, and Helen's canary, and Mrs. Talbot's beagle, and it occurred to me that the composer had been killing animals — especially dogs — for decades now. The reader who arrived at that conclusion pages ago must remember that I wrote those pages — as he or she is thereby reading them — with the benefit of hindsight. Even at the point I've now reached in my account, it was by no means clear to me that my latest hunch was anything *more* than a hunch. What proof did I have that the rumors weren't just rumors, that Silber had ever done more than shoot a few crows?

So I drove over to the public library to check my hunch the same way I'd checked others. The rumors that concerned me now, though, were harder to date — that was why I hadn't checked them sooner. The microfilm archives for the *Forest City Ranger* went back to May 1978, and I scanned them all in chronological order, looking for news about animal killings. I wound up spending eight straight hours at the microfilm viewer, developing the worst case of eyestrain I've ever incurred, and one from which I still haven't recovered: I did lasting damage to my eyes by forcing them to peruse twenty years of daily news in a single day. I finally left the library at closing time with a reader's headache verging on nausea and a folder of twenty-one photocopied items about murdered animals, most of them dogs, most of them strangled. Only one item named Silber as a suspect, and his accuser — poor Mrs. Talbot — had retracted her accusations when he threatened to sue her for slander.

But I wasn't done yet: back at the rooming house, I strained my eyes still further checking every article against the corresponding image in the time-lapse film of Silber's face — that is, the image dating from the day *before* each item (since the *Ranger* was a morning paper, the kind that tells what happened yesterday) or even, in the case of late-night crimes that might've missed the paper's deadline, *two* days earlier.

Not all items lent themselves to this forensic method. The first pertinent story I found, for example, dealt with the belated discovery of corpses that, according to authorities, had been dead at least a month: on February 14, 1981, in a disused picnic area on Route 111 between Forest City and Lumber, a hiker had found the carcasses of four dogs, apparently strays, and all badly decomposed. Nonetheless, I wound up with thirteen "hits," murders acknowledged in *My Face* by a certain unforgettable scowl — a pursing of the lips, a flaring of the nostrils, and above all by a demonic redness in the eyes. As I think I mentioned, the film began in black and white but then, when our composer was ten, switched over to color.* I understand that at that time, or long before red-eye reduction became a standard feature on cameras, Mr. Silber had modified his flash device to flicker before the actual flash, causing pupils to constrict and thus reducing the amount of light reflected redly off the retinas. In general, Mr. Silber's gadget had worked well, but not on the days when his son had murdered something.†

---

* As I later took the trouble to determine, the switch occurred on Labor Day in 1969. Could *that* have been the day of Silber's epiphanic picnic?
† I later found similar scowls, but minus the bloodthirsty eyes, on November

Those murders had occurred in three clusters, each coinciding (as I later noticed) with one of Silber's "noise attacks": four in October '83 (when one of the victims had been a cat in heat), five in May '88 (including Mrs. Talbot's beagle), and four in July '94.

On a hunch, I fetched the bulky manuscript of *My Life,* the chord-a-day diary I had taken from Silber's trash. Sure enough, his bedtime chord was identical on the thirteen days when I'd convicted him of murder: at some point, in other words, he had designated a "murder chord."*

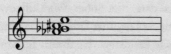

On another hunch, I scanned the passage in *My Life* corresponding to Silber's first attack of hypersensitive hearing, the one in December 1980 following his fight with Helen, and found four more instances of that same chord (which Cletus helpfully describes as a "half-diminished seventh chord in third inversion") on December 11, 15, 18, and 19 — presumably the dogs discovered two months later in the picnic area.

As successful hunch succeeded hunch, I checked to see if Silber had played the murder chord the day his mother died — though he'd been three at the time — or the day his father did. The reader will share my relief and disappointment on learning that on neither day did our composer enter a plea of guilty. (For the impassive chord he did play on the first occasion, see the first selection from *My Life.*) But a minute of random

---

19, 1991, the day the wind chimes were stolen; on July 8, 1994, the day a store called Noizmakers burned to the ground with all its noisy wares (kazoos and megaphones, sleigh bells and foghorns, cherry bombs and dancing taps — to mention only those named in the article I saw); and on June 20, 1998, the day (about two months before I moved to Forest City) when a man in a gorilla mask charged out of the bushes at the corner of Fourth and Tree and knocked the tiny ice-cream truck on its side, causing its elderly driver a career-ending head injury.

* The only leitmotif that I've been able to identify in Silber's lifelong diary. I subsequently checked for an "assault-and-battery chord," an "arson chord," and an "incarceration chord," but no such luck.

flipping uncovered one more murder chord on December 25, 1997 — a recent murder that hadn't made the news, or had escaped my hurried, bleariied skimming of two decades worth.

Some future musicologist or possibly biographer will no doubt want to read through the entire score of *My Life* — all ten thousand entries — in search of other instances of the murder chord. If my eyes weren't still so tired, I'd do it myself, if only to determine when the chord was introduced as the diarist's standard way of commemorating a kill — that is, at what point we can start assuming, from the failure of that chord to sound on a given date, that Silber *didn't* kill anything that day (if we also assume, as I do, that Silber had a compulsion to confess his murders to his diary). He didn't, for example, play the murder chord the day his sister's canary was strangled; if we could determine that by that point he had in fact started using the chord, we'd be able to exonerate the composer of *that* crime, at any rate.

As for the most recent instance of the chord, it wasn't hard to find: the final entry — dated August 5, 1999, though I hadn't found the manuscript in Silber's trash until August 7 — was a murder chord. Now, the Websters' collie had been killed in the wee hours of August 8 (the day I'm still recounting, the day I overworked my eyes in hot pursuit of the truth), so the final murder chord could hardly refer to *that* dog. I still had the August 6 edition of the *Forest City Ranger* lying around, and was about to take another look at it (though I'd read the edition in question when it was news, and was pretty sure I would remember a dead dog) when — a little before midnight — Billy pounded on my door, for the second time that day, to announce that the police had found a dead body in a clump of bushes just outside of town, off Route 28.

"Dead body. You mean *human* body?"

Billy did.

Now, in a town the size of Forest City, a dead body is exciting even if you *don't* suspect the cause of death to be your employer. I drove to the site — where, by that point, there was nothing left to see but black-and-yellow plastic tape (POLICE LINE — DO NOT CROSS) — and ascertained that, just as I'd suspected, it was on the route of Silber's late-night drive. When I got back home, the death was on the local late-night news. According to our anchorman, the victim was a vagrant, had apparently been strangled, and had already been dead for two or three days when they found him. When the weather news came on, I turned off the TV, made sure my door was locked, got in bed, got up, turned on the ceiling light, made sure the door was locked, got back in bed, and finally fell asleep.

## 4. *Day* 0:24

After closing the books on Silber with a resounding verdict of Guilty, I made no further efforts to contact him. For the next two weeks I told myself I didn't want the friendship of a man who killed dogs when annoyed and who, for all I knew, had started killing vagrants as well. If I'd been sure about the vagrant, I'd have gone to the police, but my evidence was less than circumstantial. As for the dogs, I was appalled, but I wasn't enough of a dog lover myself to violate for their sake the trust invested in me as biographer, any more than a priest would have reported a confession of such acts.

I was looking forward to leaving town forever at the end of the month. The only thing still keeping me in Forest City was an absurd determination to inhabit my rented room till August 31, since I'd paid Helen so much for the privilege, and since she'd said she wouldn't prorate my rent if I moved out early, even though she had another godforsaken bachelor waiting to move in. I spent the days taking walks, watching videos, and reminding myself how much I loathed and pitied Silber.

Now and then I may have walked past his house, but only because I'd grown accustomed to a certain route, and wasn't about to reroute it for *him*. I was sick of humoring a lunatic. I no longer even made a point of passing on the far side of the street, or of muting my steps as I went by. Once I happened to tramp past on garbage night, and at the curb I found a cardboard box that had contained — and still said so on the side — twenty-four single-serving packages of trail mix, but now contained a foot-thick stack of staff paper that with a shock I recognized as *Day*. Silber had once boasted that he never changed a note because he always got it right the first time ("just like Mozart"), but I saw now that he'd been lying: the manuscript was overgrown with second thoughts, insertions and deletions, split seconds and intercalary minutes. Presumably he had made a clean copy and was getting rid of this one to sweep up his paper trail. Or maybe he'd finally sat down and recorded the seventeen hours he'd finished — he always said that his recordings were his real legacy, and the manuscripts no more than byproducts. Or could he be discarding the precious sole copy of his magnum opus *un*recorded, in a snit he'd soon regret? Shrugging, I went on my way: why should *I* save Silber from his tantrums?

The next week I found another carton at his curb. In its day, this one too had contained trail mix (for a while there in the mid-eighties, the roving composer had eaten nothing else), but now contained a dozen scores — including *Helen, Aphorisms, Crows, The Music Room,* and *Ode to the West Wind* — all bearing evidence of revision. I spat in the box and walked on.

And yet I felt a surge of fondness when, at six A.M. on August 21 as I was crossing over to the Bean, I saw my composer coming up the sidewalk in a brown tuxedo, using his thermometer to conduct some piece of music only he could hear. He no longer wore any kind of ear protection, and he wasn't wincing at the noise of passing cars: evidently he was back to normal, or what passed with him for normal. Though his eyes were open and his face was aimed my way, he didn't seem to see me, and I resisted the urge to run up and welcome him back: Silber's early-morning walks were sleepwalks even when his eyes were *open*. (He'd once said that at such times he saw other pedestrians simply as dark shapes to be avoided, as if his normal vision were switched off in favor of a rudimentary heat sensing that required less energy from an already overloaded circuit.)

So I let him flail past — he'd reached a fevered *presto* and was whipping his baton around as if to shake the mercury down. I knew he needed to see me, but that could wait till later, till his eyes reverted to their normal mode of operation. I knew he needed to see me because he'd called that morning while I was in the shower: he had just completed *Day*. After four years squandered on a single minute, he had composed the last seven hours in a matter of weeks. He had the whole thing now, he said, and wanted me to be the first to see it. (I'd replayed the message twice, wondering what he meant by *see it*. Didn't he mean *hear it*?)

That afternoon at two, I drove over to Silber's, as always more interested in the man than in the music; after all, I'm a biographer and not a musicologist. I also looked forward to another peek inside his house, since I assumed he'd want to play selected minutes for me (or more likely the whole thing, though I had no intention of sitting through a twenty-four-hour recital). I parked out front, beneath a paper birch with a LOST DOG notice stapled to its trunk, and walked around to the back door, working up the nerve to knock this time. When I saw that the side door of the garage was open, though, I went over to investigate — just in time to see the composer descending, in an apron, from the carriage house, a wooden spoon in one hand and a saucepan in the other. The garage was now cluttered with objects — machines, maybe thirty in all, big and small — that I'd never seen before and didn't know the names of.

Silber smiled and I saw at once that I'd been wrong: he wasn't back to normal. Farther than ever from that. He no longer looked tormented, but seemed not all there, as if he'd sacrificed something essential in exchange for peace of mind. Perhaps his ears, perhaps his mind itself (or, anyhow, a piece; I looked for a lobotomy scar).

On the bright side, he had shaved and washed his hair — in the past hour, to judge by the odors of shampoo, soap, and shower steam drifting downstairs from the carriage house.

"Do you live out here now?"

"Yep," he said, still beaming with hysterical serenity.

"How come?"

He shrugged. "I felt like it. But let me show you *Day*."

Silber had said over the phone that the work still needed "some minor adjustments, a little fine-tuning." He would have to "loosen some screws and tighten some others," he told me, "maybe change a fuse or two, replace a fan belt, oil a few gears." All summer he'd been favoring mechanical metaphors when he talked about his work, but I was still surprised when he led me over to the largest of the mystery objects, an enigma the size of a washing machine, bristling with vacuum tubes, fuses, gears, and other parts that in most machines are hidden from view. It reminded me (not really, but in retrospect it does) of a body with its skin removed to expose the muscles, veins, and nerves.

Before I could ask what it was, Silber said, "Here goes nothing!" He pushed a big red button on top and I heard a grinding noise — the same faint sound you'll hear on your disc if you turn the volume way up for this track. (Careful, though — the next track is louder.) Silber had always enforced the strictest silence when he performed his works for me, or even played a tape of one, but he now ate noisily (the pan contained macaroni and cheese) while his machine did whatever it was doing. I saw a few gears barely turning, but otherwise (as he'd warned) nothing. After twenty-four seconds, the machine subsided and Silber beamed with pride. "So what do you think?"

"What *is* it?"

"I told you already — it's *Day*."

"You mean that grinding noise is *music*?"

Again he looked puzzled, then embarrassed. "Oh — no, that's just a bad bearing. Like I said, it still needs work. When I'm done it'll be a hundred percent silent, unless you press your ear against the housing maybe."

"Wait — it's supposed to be silent? But then what do you need this thing for? If it doesn't make music."

"It doesn't *make* music, stupid — it *is* music. *Look at it.*"

I took a closer look. The new *Day* was a demented hybrid of low and high technology — massive pistons alongside fragile vacuum tubes, bulky fan belts chafing dainty microchips. A big industrial knife switch — it might've been the circuit breaker for a battleship — was wired to a gleaming emerald green motherboard from a home computer, a board with other wires, sheathed in red and yellow plastic, leading directly to a gasoline engine I recognized as the one from Silber's mower; if he'd thrown the switch, I guess the engine would have kicked in. It must've been the backup power source (or one of them — there was also a cast-iron treadle from an antique sewing machine), assuring that Silber's sonata could function even in a blackout, or on a desert island. Nonetheless, I still assumed that I was looking at a *score* — an insane composer-cum-inventor's three-dimensional score, a motorized reprise of last year's Tinkertoy assemblies. Hadn't Silber said once that two-dimensional notation was inadequate to capture some of his musical ideas?

"Well," I said, "it's very . . . interesting. But can I hear the actual music?"

"No piano ever made could play that for you — don't you get it? *This*" — he waved at the contraption — "is the music."

"Ah." So all that clanking and revving had been the sound of Silber composing — not the sound of the music itself, but of the process by which he now made what he now called music. What he now called music didn't make a sound at all, though the process of its composition made so much that it had driven him insane. He was a sort of martyr to the only cause he'd ever really cared about, the cause of silence. He'd lost what was left of his mind in the desperate pursuit of a silent music, a music that would spare the ears of posterity.

"See, back in June I realized something," said Silber, setting his pan on the concrete floor with a clang, as if to flaunt his new insensitivity to noise. Back in June, the night before destroying that piano, he'd been lying awake in the basement when he had one of his epiphanies: he hated music. Even his own. Especially his own. He hated everything that made a noise, and that was *all* that music did — unlike his car, which made a noise but also served a purpose.

Brutal honesty, of course, is never the best policy, not even with oneself, and by morning Silber had relented (though not enough ever to venture back down to the basement): he no longer admitted to hating music per se, only its audible manifestations (and the instruments — pianos, for example — used to manifest them). He had "understood," he said, that the *essence* of music was silent, and that just because he made music, that didn't mean he had to make noise.

I've been trying to imagine Silber's state of mind right before his big epiphany, which I date to the wee hours of June 27, the day he later called to say he'd added a minute to *Day* (see the note to that minute, 5:00–5:01 P.M.). His desire to get over the five o'clock hump had been so great that on June 21 he had deluded himself into thinking that he'd finally found a way. He must've spent the better part of a week doggedly altering his piano, adding magnets, pulleys, whistles, bells, etc., while fighting back the knowledge — mounting as inexorably as a bout of nausea — that *once again* he had failed to make any headway on his magnum opus, and that he would never, ever finish the work that was supposed to make him famous. At some point on the night of June 26/27, that knowledge had finally forced its way into consciousness. No wonder Silber hadn't been able to sleep; no wonder he had had a big epiphany instead.

"So that's when you moved out here? After your epiphany?"

"Nah — I just moved out the other day." In the meantime he had slept in what had once been Scooter's bed and bedroom.

"So why *did* you move out here?"

"I don't want to talk about it. Let's just say that I have plans for the house. Anyhow, it makes more sense to live out here." He beamed at me again.

I waited for him to elaborate, but waited in vain. As we'll see, Silber did indeed have plans for the house, but those plans are not enough to account for his move (or for his refusal to say more about it). No, my guess is that, one night the week before, he'd had *another* epiphany, realizing something so traumatic as to render the entire house uninhabitable. Or maybe this epiphany had been no worse than many — no worse than the ones that had forced him to seal off the rooms where they'd occurred — but unlike those epiphanies, this one couldn't be confined to just one room because he hadn't had it all at once but bit by bit, in the course of an all-night, all-house pacing session, so that it wasn't the rooms but the hallways — all of them — that had been contaminated. As for *what* he'd realized, we'll never know, but I can think of several possibilities. Did the composer finally understand . . .

— that the house he'd fought so hard to make his own had been a curse?
— that his newfangled method of composing was at least as problematic as the old way?
— that he would never be famous, not even posthumously?
— that he was insane?
— that he'd wasted his life?

"So all these other things are 'music' too?" I asked, indicating with a sweeping gesture the bizarre machines that crowded around us like menacing robots.

"Yep," said Silber proudly. He explained that though at first he'd intended to motorize only *Day*, he had soon decided to convert his whole oeuvre to mechanical form — hence all the other machines, most of them labeled in inch-high black capital letters.

I'm sorry now I didn't spend more time, that afternoon, examining Silber's machines, since I never got another chance; but his insanity spooked me. I was alone with an unstable and unpredictable stranger — a madman — and after a glance at the fruits of his madness, I bolted for the reassuring boredom of the Bean, where the crazy people had all been that way awhile and weren't likely to surprise me. I do recall that ICE CREAM RAG looked like a cross between a steel wastebasket and an old-fashioned hand-cranked ice-cream maker. APHORISMS looked just like a motorized can opener, and in fact I think our composer may have adapted the one in his kitchen. Like that gadget, this one had a chrome-plated lever on top and an electric plug leading to a wall outlet; when Silber pressed the lever, I heard a succession of clicks — maybe a dozen, or one per aphorism. ROUTE 111 was a red metal box about the size of a compact fridge, the kind you find in freshman dorms. To my surprise, MY LIFE was a featherweight object no bigger than a little girl's locking, leatherette-bound diary, though *Silber's* diary was clad in shiny stainless steel that hid its inner workings, if any (a toggle switch suggested that it must "do" something, even if that something wasn't audible, and a heavy-duty cord emerging from the back terminated in a three-pronged plug). As a rule, there seemed to be no correlation between the size of a composition and the size of the machine that — as far as Silber was concerned — had superseded it. Thus, though *Crows* is only four seconds long as performed on your disc, the corresponding machine was the size of a stove.

DAY, on the other hand, *was* appropriately bulky for a twenty-four-hour sonata, but disturbed the sound waves — with a faint grinding noise — for exactly twenty-four seconds, which works out to one second per hour. (It is the commentator's job, I've always held, to do the math, even at the risk of insulting certain readers.) I realize that by including that noise in this set, I am playing a trick on the listener, but the trick is Silber's: I want you to feel some of the incredulity and horror *I* felt, that day in his garage, as it dawned on me that my employer had finally lost his mind altogether. The piece can also serve, perhaps, as a palate cleanser, a welcome change of pace from the rest of Silber's music, which all frankly sounds the same to me.

I last saw Silber on a rainy Wednesday night, August 25, 1999, or actually early the following morning. It had rained all day Wednesday with intermittent thunderstorms, one of them loud enough to set off car alarms, though not loud enough to set off another attack of hypersensitive hearing in our composer, who said that for a week or two *after* an attack, he was not only immune to loud noises but outright enjoyed them. (He'd even celebrated one recovery by firing a gun into the air — not just the BB gun he used for killing crows, but the Smith & Wesson pistol he'd bought in 1981 after Scooter issued his first death threat.) I'd spent the day in bed rereading *Twilight of the Idols,* and maybe that was why I was still awake, a little after one A.M., when a car roared into earshot, slammed on its brakes in front of my building, and started to honk. Though the horn had just one pitch, the hornist seemed to have in mind the "Fate" motif — the first four notes — of Beethoven's Fifth Symphony. As indignant as if I'd been sleeping soundly, I got up and went to the window to see who answered the summons — who among my fellow roomers had a friend so thoughtless as to honk like that at one A.M. A red sports car idled at the curb. As I strained to see the driver, the curbside door swung open and a hand reached out and up, then jerked backed in, out of the rain, in a peremptory beckoning gesture. Wondering what had prompted this unprecedented deviation from the course of Silber's late-night drives, I threw on some clothes — kept on task by Silber's horn — and ran downstairs and out into the rain, which stopped as soon as I got to the car.

"What's up?" I asked, and Silber shrugged.

We took Twelfth Avenue to Main Street, turned right, and headed south, though the KwikStop was due north. Silber seemed depressed and drove more slowly than I'd ever seen him go before; to my cheerful questions (such as, Why that right just now? or Why so slow? or Why so late in getting under way?), he replied with gloomy shrugs or sometimes (when a "yes" or "no" was called for) with an "mmm" or "nnn."

At First Avenue we paused to watch the traffic light make smears of brilliant yellow, red, and green on the wet black asphalt of the ever regulated though deserted intersection. Then we crossed the road, Main Street became Route 28, and it dawned on me that Silber had swung by my rooming house toward the end of a drive and not at the outset. A little later — just as we were turning onto 111 — the rain resumed and Silber started talking about suicide, as he'd often done before. Maybe that was why I didn't take him seriously now, though he knew how he wanted to go now: by putting a bullet through his head — in one ear and out the other, if he could. He even knew *when:* stressing that his announcement was "*not* a cry for help" — and it didn't sound like one — he said he planned to end his life "in the next few days." When I asked him why now and not next year, or last, he patiently explained that the monument he'd custom-ordered for his grave* had just arrived.

But Silber's talk of suicide somehow sounded insincere, though it was clear he'd picked me up specifically to talk — not so much to say farewell to a friend as to brief a reporter. Yes, that was what our final chat reminded me of: a press conference granted by somebody anxious to put the right "spin" on some dubious act he's about to commit. But more likely (I assured myself), all this was just a prank for me to cite in the biography as evidence of the composer's puckish sense of humor. Nonetheless, just in case, I did my best to cheer him up, as I always did (and as I'd done with Gordon, though to no avail), with the consolations — the cold comforts — of philosophy. Life is a gift, I argued (sounding, to my own ears, even less sincere than Silber), and like most gifts it isn't what you would have picked out for yourself, but you still have to act pleased with it.

---

* I'm afraid it was I who gave him the idea for this monument a few weeks before by responding to one of his infantile boasts with an infantile taunt: "What do you want — a medal or a monument?"

We were about halfway to Lumber when Silber stopped the car along a dark and wooded stretch of 111, pulling over onto the needle-strewn shoulder. We sat there for a while with the engine running, Silber with his face averted, gazing off into the pines.

I finally said: "So this is where you had that picnic, right?"

"Huh?" said Silber. "Yeah." As if to prevent any further questions, he put the car in gear again and we continued on to Lumber in a silence punctuated only by the click whenever he adjusted the customized windshield wipers (see *Tinkertoy Fugue*). As always, we came to a halt in the bright but empty parking lot of Erlenmeyer Hall. We stopped where we always did, under a dazzling halogen streetlight by the pay phone from which Silber sometimes called KDOA to request his own works. We sat in silence for so long I finally got impatient and said what you are not supposed to say to the quasi-suicidal: "I don't believe you're really going to kill yourself."

Ignoring or maybe evading my comment, Silber started to hum — a strange, tense hum I'd never heard before. I assumed he was composing and wondered why he wasn't recording.

After a minute, I thought of a dictum, indeed a string of dicta, interspersed with aphorisms, maxims, mottoes, and adages, each igniting the next. I knew I was forbidden, though, to use my own recorder on these rides with Silber; the time I'd tried, he'd shushed me angrily, though he himself had been singing the theme song from an old sitcom. I was resigning myself to losing my latest inspirations when I blinked and envisioned my book, my poor unread book, in the depths of Silber's trash can.

I got out my recorder and spoke aloud into the built-in mike, wanting the composer to try to shut me up so I could finally tell him that, in my opinion, *my* ideas were as good as his, and had as much right to break the silence. *Why is it so much harder to write than to read*, I wondered aloud, *and yet so much easier to talk than to listen?* For several minutes I continued addressing the void, glancing over nervously at my employer now and then, but he didn't seem to hear me until I reached the end of side B and my recorder shut itself off with a click.

"QUIET!"

I opened my mouth to argue but settled for a yawn instead, like a gymnast who at the last moment substitutes a safe maneuver for a tricky one. There was no point in making a fuss: I couldn't dictate any further dicta that night anyhow, not without obliterating others.

As if I'd given him the idea, Silber got out his recorder and resumed his hum, with the air of someone taking it from the top. Soon a chewing noise alerted him to the fact that the gadget was destroying his cassette rather than recording on it. When he tried to eject the cassette, it dropped out and hung in midair, suspended by a tangled ribbon of brown plastic.

"Quick — give me your recorder."

"What?"

"Give me your recorder — I'm revising *Route 111*."

"I thought you said you never revised."

"Just give me the goddamn recorder."

"I can't — there's no more room on the tape."

For a moment he looked hurt — offended that I'd hesitate to let him tape his inspirations over mine. Then he set his jaw and said: "I gave you that recorder and I can take it back. Give it back."

Sighing, I surrendered the recorder, but only after I'd ejected the cassette, which he *hadn't* given me. As mentioned earlier, I had to keep buying cassettes because I filled them faster than I could transcribe them to my notebook. The cassette I'd just ejected was one I still haven't transcribed, and even then I knew I probably never would.* And yet I was unwilling to surrender it.

---

* Sometimes, at my most grandiose, I thought of my backlog of microcassettes as an oeuvre in its own right, or at least as much of one as the shelf of tapes in Silber's studio, the tapes on which he staked his dream of future glory. It

"You never read my book! You think I'd let you tape your stupid music over my ideas when you never even read my book?"

"Oh, shit on your *ideas*!" He made a grab for the cassette and I jerked my arm out of the way, and then — not quite by accident — jerked it back a moment later, elbowing him in the face. And then I got out of the car and slammed the door.

Silber sat with his face in his hands for what felt like a long time; the rain was falling hard. When he finally looked up, he was bleeding — from both nostrils, it appeared. He started the car, then stepped on the gas and slammed on the brakes in such rapid succession that he traveled only a few feet. The purpose of his noisy lurch had evidently been to put him closer to the pay phone, and now he rolled down his window, put a quarter in the slot, and dialed what I recognized as his own number. He drummed the fingers of his free hand on the dashboard, no doubt wishing (as I'd often wished) that his recorded greeting weren't so long. After a minute, he burst into song. It took another minute for me to understand that Silber was dictating his latest inspiration to his answering machine. Silber's message to himself — a sort of fitful, atonal scat — was so prolix that he had to pause and drop another quarter in the slot. The armored phone cord wasn't long enough for him to get the whole receiver into the car, and by the time he hung up, his head was drenched — as I was drenched from head to foot.

Our friendship was dead, but I still had to get back to Forest City somehow. I approached the car and started to open the door, but Silber reached over and grabbed the inside handle. There ensued a tug-of-war that I'm ashamed to say he won. He locked the door and glared at me, with growing satisfaction, through the streaming window, still bleeding from

seemed unlikely that anyone — even the composer — would ever listen to those either.

one nostril. It was clear that we were both where we belonged, as far as Silber was concerned: he inside the nice dry car, I standing in the rain. It all seemed so right to him that at last he had to laugh, more raucously than I had ever heard him laugh before. After about a minute of that, I started to pound on the glass, and Silber, still laughing hilariously, turned to the controls, put the car in gear again, and sped away — not onward into unfamiliar territory, I'm afraid, but back to Forest City.

Since I was already soaked, the rain subsided to a drizzle; the droplets made white ringlets in the parking lot's black puddles. I stood and watched, and felt the satisfaction — an almost audible click — of finally running out of goodwill altogether toward someone I'd squandered a year attempting to please and impress and appease.

By now it must be obvious that whatever else the future may remember Silber for, it will make a big point of forgetting his music. Even so, I'd be shirking my duty if I didn't tack on at least a passing reference to the half-hour composition that is the pretext of this note. One rainy night in April '86, then, as he was driving the usual route and humming an old show tune ("Stormy Weather"), Silber realized that he'd been humming to the tempo of his windshield wipers, as if they were batons conducting in 2/4 time. (Like batons, and unlike normal wipers, Silber's were not strictly intermittent even at their slowest setting; they kept moving back and forth continually, however imperceptibly.) He started adjusting his tempo each time he adjusted the wipers. The upshot was *Rainy Night,* a verbatim transcript of someone else's music that Silber, by recklessly stretching and squeezing, molded into something he was pleased to call his own. Beginning in a drizzle at one beat per minute, the melody doubles its pace after every other bar until it reaches top speed — 128 per minute — then decelerates in the same stepwise fashion as the improbably symmetrical downpour subsides.

When he left me standing in the rain that night, I vowed not to speak to Silber ever again. (I'd still be standing in that parking lot today if I hadn't thought to call Cletus, who came and got me even though I hadn't spoken to *him* since dropping his class back in April.) I told myself I no longer cared what became of our composer, but that wasn't true: I positively wished him ill. The next afternoon when two policemen, short and tall, sought me out at the Bean (whither Billy had directed them, I think), I welcomed the chance to incriminate my ex-employer.

"Do you work for Simon Silber?" demanded the short cop.

"I did." I explained that I'd been his biographer until our latest falling-out.

"Right," said the short cop. "Did you ever see this man?" He showed me a headshot of a dead or sleeping man with long stringy hair and a reddish unkempt beard.

I readily identified the vagrant in the photo as the one that Silber had almost assaulted a month ago in an alley, though in fact all vagrants look the same to me, and I hadn't gotten a good look at the one in the alley. The policemen nodded and I added that my research had established that their suspect had been killing dogs for decades now, but the same cop cut me off before I could explain about the murder chord: "Yeah, yeah, we know about all that. Did he ever to your knowledge kill a human *being*?"

Addressing my reply to the other, taller, younger, nicer cop, who'd been smiling encouragingly, I said, "Well, not to my *knowledge*, but —"

"Did he ever *threaten* to kill a human being?" The short one again.

I was tempted to claim that our composer had vowed to kill the vagrant in the photograph (as he likely *had* vowed, after all, if not out loud), but the cops would ask me why I hadn't come forth sooner. I did tell them that Silber often threatened to murder his brother — but that too, I gathered from the way the short cop rolled his eyes, was no news to the authorities.

This interrogation took place outside the Bean. When the short cop went inside for coffee, the other one, who hadn't spoken once, used the opportunity to introduce himself as Officer Potts ("but my friends call me Chuck") and, suddenly blushing, to tell me that he too was writing a book — the wacky true-life adventures of a small-town policeman. He was plainly thrilled to talk to a real man of letters, and in consequence was so ingratiating that I didn't recognize him as the cop who, back in June, had gruffly ordered me to clean up all that ice cream, not till he apologized for the episode. Though I was leaving town soon, I found myself assessing Potts as a potential friend (or at least a rebound friend, a friend *pro tem*), and by the time the short cop came back with a coffee for himself and a latte for his partner (who, in his aspirations to higher things, briefly reminded me of Gordon), Chuck and I had made plans to go bowling that weekend. After dinner I even drove to Lumber Lanes and, after making sure Chuck wasn't there, bowled a couple of "frames," since I was afraid he'd think I was a weirdo if he found out that I'd never bowled.

I spent the next day, August 27, packing (my lease expired on the thirty-first, at which point I planned to drive to Colorado and stay with my mom while I figured out what to do next), then passed the evening reading at the Bean, too worked up about my fight with Silber and my pending move — and, I was hoping, his pending arrest — to remain in my room. When I finally returned to that room at eleven and checked my voice mail, I found I had a message — left, according to the message lady, at 9:10 P.M. "To listen to your message, press 1," she instructed. I pressed 1.

*"Norm, can you forgive me for what I said the other night? I've been rereading your book and it's amazing. I predict that unlike me, you'll be recognized in your own lifetime as a genius — the only genius I've been fortunate enough to know. I can't begin to tell you how much our friendship meant to me. Anyhow, I would've*

*liked to take another walk with you, but I guess I can't. I can't go on another minute. I'm sorry, I — I'm gonna shoot myself. Right now. Just like I said I would. So long. Take care of my reputation like the hungry orphan it is now. There's no one but you to keep it alive. So long."*

I moved to replay the message, but in my excitement hit 3 — delete — instead of 2, so I've quoted Silber's final words from memory. (I may have polished them a bit, but I haven't changed their gist.) I dialed Silber's number but didn't get even the answering machine. I ran down to my car. I wasn't ruling out a hoax, but Silber really did sound shaken, as he *hadn't* sounded the other night when he announced his plan to kill himself.

I won't pretend the prospect of Silber's bloody death dispelled in a moment a year's worth of resentment, but I can say I felt dread, not just exhilaration, as I sped to the composer's house. There were two traffic lights en route, but both happened to be green when I got to them, so I was unable to express the urgency of my mission the way they do on TV, by running a red. But I did exceed the speed limit (and in a school zone, no less, so maybe that's equivalent). And after parking where I always did, I sprinted back to the garage.

The yard-side door was open wide and all the lights were on. The car was in its customary spot, hood up, but the other machines — the demented contraptions that Silber called music — had vanished. I ran upstairs to look for him in the carriage house, but the door at the top of the stairs was locked, and no one answered when I knocked.

I ran back downstairs and out into the yard. I went to the back door and pounded for at least a minute. (Despite the gravity of my mission, my thumps insisted on grouping themselves into a "shave and a haircut — two bits" rhythmic pattern.) Then I ran back into the garage and back upstairs and knocked again, called Silber's name, and tried the knob again. Still locked.

I had just gone back downstairs, taking my time, and was

wondering what to do next when I spotted the boxy red contraption that had replaced *Route 111*. It sat on a blue plastic milk crate in front of Silber's car. Jumper cables ran from under the vehicle's hood to an opening in the back of the contraption, where a small hinged metal door afforded a glimpse of the demented inner workings: in addition to all sorts of gears and pistons, there was an odometer in there (it had already logged twenty-six miles, or twenty-six of something), and several fat tan rubber bands stretched almost to the breaking point, and what, if you saw it on a trumpet, you would call a spit valve. On top of the machine lay a socket wrench and several screwdrivers — evidently this was what Silber had meant by "revising." Among the tools, my tiny tape recorder — the one the composer had just repossessed — rested like a paperweight on a few sheets of manuscript paper covered with musical notes and smeared with black grease, as if someone had used it to wipe off a dipstick.

Shrugging, I picked up the tape recorder, hit PLAY, and heard myself say "Anyhow, I think I broke my VCR" — not a sentence I remembered dictating to that recorder, or could even picture myself dictating. I ejected the cassette and saw that it was one designed for answering machines, though of the same size as my dictation tapes. Silber must've been too busy to buy a blank tape, and so had made do with a message cassette — he'd never liked to get messages anyhow, only to leave them. I hit REWIND, went back a minute, hit PLAY, and heard what sounded like a mental defective howling in pain; but then I recognized the tune — if tune it was — that I'd heard Silber shout the other night into a pay phone. I could even hear the rain. On a hunch, I picked up the papers, which turned out to be the score of *Route 111* — the old-fashioned, superseded paper version. There were four sheets of manuscript paper covered on one side with black handwritten notes; on the back of the first, Silber had written sixteen bars of music with red ink. Above the red notes was a big red asterisk and a small red title: *Side Trip*. The only other emendation was another red asterisk near the top of the second page. It was another of Silber's musical footnotes, but this one sidetracking his own composition. As far as I could tell, *Side Trip* digressed from *Route 111* at a point corresponding to a desolate and unlit segment of the title route — right around the point, by the abandoned picnic spot, where we'd pulled off the road the other night. Staring at the red interpolation, I recognized the music I'd heard Silber sing into the pay phone at the end of that ill-fated drive, and had just heard again on the cassette. To be accurate, the long recorded blurt had been no more than a sketch, or sheaf of sketches; in the final red-inked version there were chords.* With a gasp I recognized one as the murder chord; it occurred, below the only *fortississimo* I'm aware of in Silber's oeuvre, at the end of the eighth bar, or exactly midway through the side trip. Below the murder chord, in tiny script, he'd written:

R.I.P.

I ran out to my car, taking the score of *Route 111* along as a road map. As I sped away, I saw Helen pulling up, but there was no time to stop and chat. I headed for Route 111, keeping an eye out for Silber. Had he walked to his death? Hitchhiked? Called a cab? And was I too late? It only takes a moment to blow your head off, once you're ready, but wouldn't he want to sit on a stump and brood a bit first?

When I reached the stretch of road where, according to the score and to my recollection of the other night, the picnic spot should be, I drove slowly back and forth a dozen times. I was beginning to think I had the wrong stretch when I glimpsed a little footpath branching off into the forest. I pulled off onto

---

* On your disc, that version is played by the author, since by the time it was composed, Silber no longer made recordings; for him the score of *Side Trip* was only a blueprint, or redprint, for a modification of the machine that had already superseded *Route 111*. One reason I've put the two tracks on different discs is that they were never meant to be heard together; *Side Trip* wasn't meant to be *heard* at all. Even so, I ought to justify the tempo at which I perform it, notably slower than the tempo Silber chose for the passage of *Route 111* from which (on paper) his side trip digresses. Bear in mind that the music is trudging through the woods now and not speeding down the highway.

the shoulder, got a flashlight from my glove compartment, and headed into the pines, along a trail muddy from the recent rain, and pocked — I was surprised to see — with *two* sets of footprints, coming and going, all made by the same pair of shoes. Bigger than mine — were they Silber's? Was it possible his last or latest Murder Chord marked the site of yet another *homicide* and not a suicide? Who now, though, and why here?

My flashlight was an ingenious no-batteries model, its bulb lit by a little generator run by repeatedly squeezing a lever attached to the handle, but the lever broke after a few squeezes — if not for the full moon, I would've had to wait till day to solve the Mystery of the Hidden Footpath. Even with the moon, the forest was so dense that I could barely see; I kept mistaking trees for open space and trying to walk through them. After some hundred yards I barked a shin on something — on a fallen, decomposing picnic table, maybe the same one at which Silber's family had sat laughing thirty years ago, while he sat apart and sulked. I hopped around on one leg for a minute, clutching the other, and then lost my balance and fell — at which instant, as if I'd toppled a lamp, the moon went behind a cloud and I couldn't see a thing. I started groping around on my hands and knees, then jumped up when it occurred to me how little I wanted to reach out in that blackness and touch a corpse, no matter whose. I waited for the cloud to pass so I could search the picnic site with my eyes and not my hands. But the moon stayed hidden. Finally I decided to go home, but couldn't see the trail either. Just as I was starting to think I was stuck there till dawn, I saw headlights through the trees and heard a car drive by on 111. Taking my bearings from that, I was able to find the road after only twenty minutes or so of lurching into trunks and tripping over roots. Bruised and muddy, I drove back to my rooming house and parked out front, behind a car with two dark figures sitting in it. I was looking forward to a shower and a good night's sleep, but as I got out of my car, two uniformed policemen, fat and thin, got out of theirs, and it wasn't even a police car.

"Norman Fayrewether?" asked the fat one.

"Yes?"

"Put your hands on the car," said the thin, who was pointing a gun.

"But I —"

"PUT YOUR HANDS ON THE CAR!"

I put my hands on the car. "What did I do now?"

"You're under arrest for the murder of Simon Silber."

## 7. Afterthoughts                                    19:43

Like *Digression,* this piece is parasitic, attaching itself to another man's music, and unable to survive on its own, apart from its host. In this case, the host is a Beethoven sonata, the *Tempest* (Opus 31, no. 2). *Afterthoughts* — composed in 1993 — is an additional movement, a new, absurdly muted, slow, and pensive ending that for twenty minutes rains on Beethoven's parade, undercutting the triumphant finale with a more dubious mood, the mood in which you might drive home from a party where, despite the noisy joviality with which you left, you did not have a very good time. Silber himself once compared the original finale of Beethoven's sonata — like most finales, the loudest and most animated movement — to the way that people raise their voices on taking their leave. Just as the jollity that marks such partings often rings false, he said, so do most finales. Back in Silber's performing days, he'd often omitted the last movement altogether.

Throughout these notes I have alluded to his hatred of Beethoven, but as a teenager Silber himself went through a Beethoven phase, dashing off a series of grandiose sonatas inspired by that composer at his most meteorological. He'd even given the sonatas nicknames — the *Tornado,* the *Blizzard,* the *Earthquake,* the *Tidal Wave* — just like the more famous Beethoven sonatas (e.g., the *Tempest,* though as regards emotional force, Silber's adolescent imitations probably had more in common with that tempest in a teapot, "The Rage over a Lost Penny"). All these works were destroyed by the composer following a quarrel with his father. *You're no Beethoven,* Mr. Silber made the mistake of observing, after his fifteen-year-old son played the *Volcano* for him; our composer's oeuvre may be heard as one long tantrum provoked by his father's hurtful remark.

And now that tantrum was over. I spent the night of Silber's death in custody. Helen had seen me hurriedly leaving her brother's place and had mentioned that to the police a little later, after she'd persuaded them to break into the carriage house and they'd discovered Silber in the moonlit studio, in a red tuxedo — the one his father had bought him for the Erlenmeyer Competition — with a bullet hole through his head. The gun had been fired point-blank, and just as Silber had promised the last time we spoke, the bullet had entered through his left ear and exited through his right, embedding itself in the bedroom door. Nothing at the crime scene proclaimed the death a murder, but nothing proved it a suicide either.

And so they hauled me in for questioning. In the course of the night it was determined that the gun that had killed him was a Smith & Wesson pistol registered to Silber, and the fingerprints on the gun (found at the scene) his own, but they found my fingerprints on the door to the garage and the door to the carriage house upstairs — and I'd deleted the telephone message that would've explained why I went over to Silber's that night. Luckily, Helen's account of the composer's last words to her corroborated my account of his last to me: he had called her too, around the time that he called me, and had told her too that he was just about to shoot himself, though at first she'd assumed he was lying and had in fact hung up on him; not for a few hours did her second thoughts send her over to Silber's just in time to see me leaving.

As for my whereabouts at the time of the death — no later

than ten, the coroner said* — it's a good thing I was at the Bean that evening, and that I have a habit of laughing out loud at the imbecilities I come across in books (even though that habit had gotten me banned, back in June, from the Quiet Room of the public library), and that I happened to be reading the over-rated ruminations of some pop "philosopher": half a dozen regulars attested to my unrelenting presence between seven and eleven.

I still had to explain my behavior on leaving Silber's garage — explain about the murder chord and the logical or musico-logical deductions that had brought me to the abandoned pic-nic spot. In the morning, I returned to that spot in the back seat of a squad car, with two stolid detectives in front and a sturdy wire grid between us. It was an anxious ride, an anxious hike: if we found another body, they might just lock me up af-ter all. And we did find something just beyond the picnic table — a big mound of recently disturbed earth, just as if someone had dug a hole and buried a corpse. There were footprints leading to and from the mound, and these the detectives fussed over as if we'd found the fossil tracks of some minor dinosaur. Then, though anyone could see that the footprints weren't mine (they turned out to match the clay-spattered dress shoes that Silber had on when he died), my escorts ordered *me* to dig — with my hands, since we hadn't brought a shovel — as if pre-suming me guilty of killing whatever was under that mound. They took over, though, as soon as I uncovered something — what turned out to be a big black plastic bag. The bag did not contain a corpse, however, but only an oeuvre's worth of re-cordings in gray steel canisters, canisters the gloved detectives

---

* The studio was sufficiently soundproof that none of Silber's neighbors seem to have heard the shot above the other noises of a summer evening. Mrs. Tal-bot told police that around 8:30, in the advertising break between successive sitcoms, she'd heard a thud that later, in hindsight (or hindhearing), she recog-nized as a shot, but Silber's final phone calls weren't made till after 9:00, so Mrs. Talbot must've been wrong about either the time (and the sitcoms in question?) or the nature of the noise. Or both.

transferred each to its very own evidence bag. Readers know by now what I think of Silber's music, and they'll understand why, in my overwrought condition, I was unable to suppress a brief, inappropriate laugh at the only-too-appropriate container — a heavy-duty garbage bag — in which Silber had seen fit to abandon his musical ambitions. At the same time — and happy as I was not to have found a body in that bag — the tapes upset me, almost as if I already foresaw, or foreheard, this egregious boxed set. If not for the tenuous chain of events and deductions that had led me to the picnic spot by moonlight, then led me there again with the police, all the strenuous and uninspired noise on your CDs might've been allowed to rest in peace.

That evening Chuck and I went bowling. Though he'd been off-duty the night of Silber's death, he apologized for my night in custody, assuring me that the verbal abuse I'd endured was nothing personal, just a heuristic aid, and that fingerprinting had been a formality — that they'd printed "everybody." Oh? Who else? Well, Helen and Edna. Not Scooter? Scooter's fingerprints had already been on file at the precinct — as had Simon's, for that matter, since his arrest for stealing wind chimes back in '91, so they hadn't needed to re-print the dead composer either (not even identical twins have identical prints).

It gives me pleasure to report that Helen was not only fingerprinted but interrogated — and the icy self-possession with which (according to Chuck) she'd beheld her brother's corpse the night of his death, and identified it as Silber, could almost lead one to wonder if she had a hand in that death (a gloved hand, of course — *she* was far too shrewd to leave a fingerprint at the scene of the crime).

Not surprisingly, though, the principal suspect was Scooter: not only had he been phoning in death threats to Silber for years, but he'd been seen in town the day of the death — at the Warthog, where he'd boasted to a barroom full of bikers that he was about to get "a ton of money" and would soon be buying drinks for everyone. He too spent a night in custody, after the police caught up with him, at two A.M., gazing in the darkened window of a travel agency on Main Street. I didn't get a chance to speak to him that night, but I glimpsed him, from behind, at the station house, in a different leather jacket — this one looked older, and didn't say BADASS.

How much of a "badass" Scooter really is we may never know. I used to assume he was harmless, but since his brother's death he's been so different that I've come to think I never really knew him, and for all I do know he may well have killed the composer, even if he didn't come to town intending to. He told police he'd been "summoned" by Silber, who'd supposedly promised to pay him some unspecified bounty for some unspecified "job." Scooter admitted that he'd come to Forest City assuming that the job would be illegal, but said he'd never found out for sure: when he called on Simon at around nine on the night of his death, no one had answered. Scooter said that he — like me — had gone up and knocked on the carriage-house door, which would explain his fingerprints on the hand-rail. (Evidently he didn't try the doorknob, unless I wiped off his prints when *I* tried it.) Beyond that door, the only recent prints were Silber's, but several surfaces looked freshly wiped.

Nonetheless, Scooter was never arraigned, partly because he still had the letter (though not the envelope) he said had fetched him to Silber's, a handwritten note he claimed he'd received in Missoula the day before his brother's death. According to Chuck, the note said something like: "Scooter, let's bury the hatchet. I've got a job for you, and I'll pay you more than you could ever spend, but you need to get here *fast.* Come to the carriage house after dark, and don't let anyone see you." Forensics established that the handwriting really was Silber's. They'd already known it wasn't Scooter's, since — as his sister confirmed — he'd never learned to write cursive. But of course that doesn't prove he didn't kill his brother, whether in cold blood or hot. (Maybe BADASS vanished because Scooter got blood on the jacket and had to bury or burn it.) Chuck's theory is that Simon, eager to die but afraid to kill himself, planned to *pay* Scooter to kill him. Chuck isn't sure, though, if Scooter complied — tearfully or gleefully — or if Simon got impatient and, emboldened by a few pints of Dutch courage,* did the job himself.

What does seem certain is that our composer wanted to die — and the real reason Scooter "walked" was the overwhelming evidence for suicide. It turns out that Silber had talked *ad nauseum,* for days before his death, of nothing but killing himself, not just to me but to Helen, to Edna, and even — in sorry-for-everything letters that came to light later — to David Altschul and to Myra Handler (the latter still hanging in there at 103, though no longer judging competitions, one assumes). Now, I for one would be tickled if it came out that Silber had only been bluffing with all that gloomy talk, and that Scooter had somehow gotten wind of the bluffs and seen a chance to kill his hated brother with impunity. Readers may recall that in my final talk with Silber, I myself thought he was bluffing (as Helen claims to have thought†) and even told him as much; but since then I've been forced to "eat my hat" and to concede that Silber *wasn't* bluffing, that he really did decide, in the end, to kill himself. How else can we explain the will he drew up just before he died, or his burial of the master tapes, or his ominous custom-ordering of a funerary monument, or any of a dozen other acts that prove he knew the end was near? His very garbage can, on the day of his death, suggested the last-minute housecleaning of someone tidying up for posterity; among other possessions he'd deemed unworthy of a great composer were a small TV set, a large unopened jar of nondairy creamer,

---

* According to the coroner's report, his blood alcohol level at the time of death was .15.

† Helen also claimed, though, that Silber had promised her the house outright the last time they talked, the night of his death; and judging by her fury when that promise wasn't kept, it seems fair to speculate that even if she *hadn't* believed he was bluffing, any sisterly concern she might have felt would've been tempered by the thought of her inheritance.

and a bundle of pornographic magazines dating back to the mid-seventies.*

Why did Silber kill himself? Partly, I suspect, because he'd lost faith in his destiny. The puzzle is how he held out as long as he did — but of course self-love is even blinder than the other kind, and even better at overlooking a mountain of evidence as to the unworthiness of the beloved, while never losing sight of the molehill of evidence to the contrary. For decades Silber honestly believed he was a great composer. Insofar as that belief wasn't just an axiom, as purely *a priori* as a lunatic's conviction of being Jesus or Napoleon, just what was the evidence from which Silber drew his thrilling conclusion? Oh, there were all kinds of hints and intimations: a fan letter from an anonymous admirer in Idaho who called Silber "the greatest composer since Gottschalk"; the inclusion of *Look, Dad — No Hands* on a compilation disc of "Novelty Tunes" still being advertised on late-night TV; a mention (in the company of seven other equally obscure composers) in a footnote to a musicology student's 1991 dissertation, *Mockingbirds and Cagelings: The Crisis in Contemporary Music;* an encouraging word or two from Altschul, before their falling-out; and even KDOA's annual mean-spirited broadcast of *Ode to the West Wind.* In August 1999, Silber finally rechecked his addition and found that the actual sum of these trifles was smaller than he'd been assuming. He killed himself, in other words, not because he went mad but because he went sane.

The more urgent reason, though, was that the law was closing in — the police had paid him several visits in connection with the strangled vagrant. Chuck says they'd been about to arrest him and would've done so sooner if not for the phobia — they knew about that too — that could be counted on to keep the suspect in Forest City. Hobbled by that phobia, unable to

---

* I've had a chance to examine those magazines at my leisure, and I will say for the record that not one of them supports Tom's conjecture as to Silber's "orientation."

skip town as other felons would, our composer had fled in the only direction he could: earthward.

Silber's burial was not well attended. Due to the heavy rain, perhaps, the only mourners were Helen, Scooter (tricked out for the occasion in a brand-new leather jacket), Billy, myself, and Edna. Aside from Edna (the only one who cried), Scooter seemed the most upset, and even seemed indignant that the rest of us weren't more so. At one point he shouted, "He was a great man!" and then scowled at his fellow mourners, as if daring anyone to contradict him. A little later, in a reverential voice: "It should be *taller*," meaning Silber's monument, a fluted marble column twenty-four feet tall — and replaced a few weeks later, over Scooter's loud objections, by a much less ostentatious tablet, after the column was deemed a violation of the cemetery's canons of good taste. That afternoon, though, the gleaming monument dominated the family plot, looming alongside the graves of Silber's parents. Idly gazing at the parents' streaming headstone, my eye was arrested by Mr. Silber's date of death: June 21, 1980. It took me a moment to remember why that date looked so familiar. Oh, right: that was day the composer had spent half his life commemorating (solemnizing? celebrating?) with *Day*.

Scooter's graveside change of heart was all the more remarkable because it preceded the reading of the will our composer drew up the week he died. When that will was finally read a few days later in the office of the family lawyer, the surprise winner was Scooter. Apparently in reparation for their childhood, Silber left his not-so-identical twin ("my beloved brother, fellow musician, and fellow guinea pig") almost a million dollars — his entire fortune, in fact, once he'd set aside enough to subsidize the publication of my mealy-mouthed authorized biography,* due out from Vanitas this summer.

_____

* That money, incidentally, and the sum that subsidized the *writing* of the book — subsidized, in other words, my year as a biographer — had once been earmarked for a charity devoted to a famous internal organ that will remain unnamed here, since I continue to assuage my conscience by telling myself

(Don't bother: though I did manage to sneak a few truths past the censor, these liner notes represent the last word on Silber, incorporating as they do all the best parts of the abandoned tell-all biography.) Scooter also got the red convertible.

The house went to Helen, but only on condition that the rooms be left exactly as Silber had left them — and one of his last acts had been to lug those demented contraptions inside and install each in a room of its own. Silber also stipulated that henceforth the house be listed in tour guides as the Simon Silber Museum, and that visitors be allowed in, free of charge, seven days a week — and till 9:00 P.M. on Tuesdays.

Helen was enraged by these conditions: she maintained that more than once in the days before his death, Silber had promised her the house outright, no strings attached. For a day or two, she spoke of challenging in court the soundness of her brother's mind when he drew up the will, and indeed the twelve preceding wills. A tireless reviser of his compositions, Silber had been in the habit of changing his will constantly — after every intimation of mortality. A chest pain or a near collision on a late-night drive would send him trembling to his study to reread his *last* last will and rewrite it to account for recent changes in his feelings for this or that good cause. He'd written his first will — leaving everything to UNICEF — back in 1980, soon after his father's death. Since then, he had averaged one new will per year, though he wrote three the year I knew him, when the intimations of mortality were coming thick and fast. At the time of his death there were twenty-one last wills in all. Till number twenty-one, he'd never left Scooter a penny, and only once had he ever favored Helen with anything better than a piano or two: on December 17, 1987, in a restaurant where they'd met to discuss their brother's latest death threats — Helen too had gotten one — she used the Heimlich maneuver to expel a chunk of steak from the com-

---

that no doubt the charity in question spends most of its money on itself — its water coolers, conference rooms, receptionists, etc. — and not on the organ in question.

poser's windpipe, and the next day Silber revised his will to leave her the house out of which he had thrown her seven years before. (Up till then his wills had all decreed that it be sold and that the proceeds go to charity.)

Silber's lawyer had kept copies of the superseded wills. After reading through them all, Helen decided that she would've made out best if Simon had died while number eight was in force, between December 18, 1987, and October 23, 1988, at which point Silber, in a suicidal if not misogynistic mood after the Conchita incident (see *Annex to "My House"*), drew up another will. By that point he had thought the better of the grateful gesture toward his sister, as the suicidal must often do with people who saved their lives back when those lives seemed worth saving. The new will, number nine, and every will that followed (except the last, which I've discussed), stipulated that the house be sold and the proceeds endow a foundation for the study of Silber's works.

And so Helen had considered claiming, on no grounds but wishful thinking, that Simon had gone decisively insane at some point between December 19, 1987, and October 22, 1988, which would mean that number eight was the last valid will, and the thirteen that followed just the ravings of a lunatic. She'd even spoken of engaging a celebrated shyster who specialized in proving the sanest of felons psychotic. She'd also planned to enlist *me* in this battle, and on September 7 offered me five thousand dollars to alter my biography in such a way as to make it look like Silber had gone crazy, or gone crazier, in the spring of '88.* And I confess that I agreed to do it — after a year of prostituting my talents, there were few acts so unnatu-

---

* The truth, as far as I can tell, is that Silber didn't go entirely, certifiably insane until a month or two before his death, or if he *had* already been crazy when I met him, he'd been crazy all his adult life — ever since the Erlenmeyer breakdown, probably. Recently I spent two hours poring over the time-lapse film of Silber's face — backward, fast-forward, in slow-mo, in freeze-frame — watching attitudes blossom and wilt like flowers in a nature film, trying to pinpoint the exact moment when Silber had "snapped," and that was the only point where something seemed to break instead of bending.

ral that I was still unwilling to perform them, if the price was right — but the very next day, Helen retracted her offer, having evidently decided in the meantime on what has been her policy ever since: to act as if Silber had in fact kept his promise and left her the house with no strings attached, to disregard his conditions, and to dare anyone to object. By the time his will was read, in any case, it was already too late to honor Silber's wishes to the letter, since Helen had sold his machines for scrap metal the minute the authorities ruled them irrelevant as evidence.*

I too was disgruntled when the will was read. (I'd remained in town for the occasion, sleeping in my car.) Knowing how Silber hated his siblings, I'd been assuming that the childless composer would leave at least some of his money to me. I won't deny I even drew some solace from that prospect the night of his death. As it turned out, he didn't leave me a thing: indeed, at no point in the year I knew him did he even consider "cutting me in on the action" (if I may be forgiven such a vulgarism, in consideration of my hard-earned indignation), to judge by the three wills he drew up that year. But he did have plans for me, and may have shot himself believing that he'd left me well provided for. A museum needs a curator, and the curator of the Simon Silber Museum, the one who'd get to live in the carriage house for free (the garage was to become a gift shop) as long as he pretended, to the throngs of slack-jawed tourists, that our composer had been a great man, his birthplace as worthy of a pilgrimage as Edison's — that lucky peon was me.

Though it wasn't what I'd hoped for, I'm embarrassed to confess that far from rejecting this humiliating offer, I made a

---

* The destruction of those machines made for a legal enigma that wouldn't be easy to resolve even if Helen were a more faithful executor, since Silber's will also ordained that if his sister failed to comply with each and every one of her benefactor's conditions, the house was to be sold and the profits used to endow in perpetuity a smaller, more cluttered museum for Silber's machines, to assure that his music could be seen and not heard by posterity. But of course that too was now impossible.

stink when Helen told me that there was to be no museum. I even threatened to sue her for cheating me out of my legacy, and at length she grudgingly agreed to let me live in the carriage house after all, in exchange for helping her with some home improvements, such as unsealing the five sealed rooms. But she wouldn't let me borrow one of the six pianos that had come with her house, claiming (even though she never plays) to "need" them all, so I'm renting a humble upright model from a shop in Lumber, anxious not to lose my "chops." (Gordon's synthesizer — on which I spilled a bowl of soup — no longer synthesizes.)

I wasn't the only out-of-towner to stay on in Forest City: Scooter stuck around as well, renting a small clapboard house on the edge of town, just outside the city limits, on several acres of virgin woodland, with a gravel driveway leading straight to Route 28. Evidently all it took to reconcile him to his hometown was his brother's death and a huge inheritance. It was the prospect of hanging out with Scooter as much as anything that had induced me to stay in town myself: granted, he had swindled me out of three hundred dollars (one month's rent) and maybe killed his brother too, but even so he was — had been — more fun to "pal around" with than anybody else in town. To my disappointment, though, I found Scooter a changed man. He was so sobered by his brother's drunken suicide that he swore off alcohol completely and broke off all contact with his former drinking buddies (even me, as if even I were a bad influence!). I tried to speak to him the day the will was read, but though he grudgingly repaid me the three hundred dollars (after first refusing on the grounds that he'd turned over a new leaf and could no longer be held accountable for the follies of his former life), he made it clear that he wanted nothing more to do with me. As far as I can tell, he has no friends at all now. According to his nearest neighbor, a Bean regular named Robert, Scooter hardly ever leaves his property, though he spends a lot of time outdoors, walking around in the woods, and a lot of time in the garage. Robert also tells me that as far as he's aware, his new neighbor hasn't left town once, or not for more than an hour or two: evidently Silber's brother has renounced not only alcohol, but his whole nomadic lifestyle, though he does still wear a leather jacket.

While it doesn't look like money has made Scooter any happier — *au contraire* — there's no denying his abiding gratitude toward his dead benefactor, or his touching if misguided efforts to uphold the dying wishes of the man he'd threatened so often to kill. A few weeks after Silber's death, I was repainting Helen's living-room ceiling when Scooter pounded on the back door (he may not have known that we had unsealed the front) and demanded to see the museum. He became so loud and angry when I told him there was no museum that Helen had to come downstairs and handle him herself, sending me back to my task and speaking to Scooter outside. As soon as she had closed the door between us, she said something that shut him up — so effectively that even with my ear pressed to the door, I could hear only her side of the colloquy. Actually, I couldn't hear that much of her side either, but at one point I gathered that Scooter had made yet another of his death threats, since Helen raised her voice to say: "You'd better hope I live a good long time, 'cause when I die the truth comes out — I've made sure of that." Scooter left a little later, and I wondered, as I scurried back to my drop cloth, just what "truth" Helen referred to. But of course siblings must know things about each other that no biographer will ever unearth.

A few days later, in what was patently a compromise between Scooter's vision for the museum and hers, I helped Helen load a truck with such of Silber's odds and ends as she hadn't yet gotten around to throwing away, and we hauled them to a tiny vacant storefont, on a seedy stretch of Main Street, between a liquor store and a topless bar called Doug's. Since that day, the Simon Silber Museum has been open five days a week, eight hours a day, and I've received $4.85 an hour for minding the store. (I understand that Scooter pays my salary, though Helen may donate the space.) Among other specimens of Silberiana, the museum features an ancient Monopoly set, a Little League uniform, a boy's green three-speed bicycle, a BB gun, some canceled checks, an assortment of tools, a pale blue tuxedo, an old purple toothbrush I found behind the toilet in the carriage house (where I still live, though now I'm paying rent), and ROUTE 111, the only contraption to escape Helen's purge.*

The centerpiece of the collection, though, is the larger-than-life white marble statue of himself that Silber commissioned a few weeks before his death to stand atop his column in the cemetery (like another Simon atop another column), but that wasn't finished till after the column was toppled. The sculptor portrayed our composer — presumably at his instructions — with his head cocked back, his eyes shut, and a hand cupped to his ear, as if hearkening to a distant music; the other hand once held a marble pen, but that snapped off at some point, and now the great man appears to be holding a stick of chalk, or maybe a white marble AA battery.

There is also a shelf of souvenirs — T-shirts, coffee mugs, and frisbees, each one enhanced with an image of Silber — and an old cash register I've yet to get the hang of. Though the pay is low, and I have to wear a uniform (black dress shoes, black pants, and white button-down shirt, an ensemble Scooter somehow thought would make me look like a museum guard and not a busboy), I only have to stand if there's a visitor, and I've got lots of time to write. I just put the finishing touches on *By the Way*, and have so many aphorisms left over that I'm planning a third volume I will call *To Say the Least*.

Now and then a wino wanders in off the street, demands to use the rest room, and grows belligerent when told there isn't one (there isn't — I go next door to Doug's), but so far the only bona fide visitor has been Scooter, who comes in every other

---

* Someone at the Bean told me recently that Scooter has been speaking of rebuilding his brother's machines — he claims to have found blueprints — and possibly "publishing" them, in other words persuading some appliance manufacturer to mass-produce the contraptions.

week or so, gazes at the statue for a while — ignoring me completely — and then goes away. Once I could've sworn I saw him taking his temperature (leading me to wonder if the twins inherited that eccentric habit, and one or two others — Robert says that Scooter sometimes wanders through the woods with eyes shut — from their eccentric father). Once he made off with his brother's socket wrenches, either thinking I wasn't watching or pretending I don't exist. Even the time he bought a coffee mug, he didn't say a word.

On the bright side, Cletus and I have rekindled our friendship, though his teaching load is such that he can spare me only one hour a month. We almost always take a walk, and I develop my ideas on life and art, friendship and fame, fathers and sons, while every so often Cletus chips in with a "Yep" or an "Mmm." Sometimes when my mind is racing I can't bear to walk so slowly, and — with his good-natured consent — I circle Cletus as he lumbers along, so that my trajectory must resemble a series of loops, like a telephone cord at half-stretch.

Though the museum has yet to "pack 'em in," there are indications that Silber is gaining a following after all, maybe even an international one: the other day, the KDOA announcer reluctantly played *Crows* after remarking that three different callers, all (he said) with heavy foreign accents, had requested works by Silber. Long before this evidence of a demand for our composer's music, though, his sister had decided to release a grandiose boxed set (the set you're stuck with now, alas — also subsidized, though in this case by Helen). Maybe she imagines that the mere existence of the set will rehabilitate his memory. She claims that even Scooter says their brother would've wanted such a set as better than nothing, now that the definitive motorized versions of his works have been lost.

If I could stop the release of these worthless recordings, I would; as it is, I've had to content myself with exposing the man behind the music, the ugly truth behind the no-less-ugly sounds. The manuscript of my tell-nothing authorized biography persuaded Helen that I could be trusted to write the liner notes, and since I volunteered to do the job for free (desperate to get to Silber's audience before he did), I was able to demand full editorial control. Do I have any qualms about betraying Helen's trust? Not when it's so clearly a product of contempt — like Silber's trust, such as it was. Helen recently conjectured that her brother *wanted* me to find the buried treasure, that he'd made a point of leaving the updated score of *Side Trip* lying out where I would see it. If so, our composer went to his grave without understanding how badly he'd hurt me, how much I'd come to hate him. If only I had gotten to those tapes before the cops, I would have erased every note.